Time Lapse

Jane Ann Tun

avid
press LLC

Brighton, Michigan USA

AVID PRESS, LLC
5470 Red Fox Drive
Brighton, MI 48114-9079
http://www.avidpress.com

Copyright 1999 by Jane Ann Tun

Published by arrangement with the author
ISBN: 1-929613-12-1

All rights reserved, which includes the right to reproduce this book or portions thereof in any form whatsoever except as provided by U.S. Copyright Law.

For information contact Avid Press, LLC.

First Avid Press printing October 1999

*For Tony--
my husband, my lover, my best friend*

Chapter One

He stumbled, fell to his hands and knees and began to retch, dry heaves shaking his large frame. Pain tore at him everywhere, his head pulsing and throbbing with every harsh gasp for breath. Behind him the shimmering green circle faded, then winked out abruptly.

When the dizziness finally passed, he slowly raised his head and gazed around. He was alone, on the flat surface of a large rock, enclosed in a thick circle of trees. He listened. Only the fiddling of crickets and the far-off barking of dogs broke the silence. He looked up in time to see the silhouette of a hawk drop gracefully to the top of a nearby tree. As it folded its wings and cocked its head in his direction, his chest expanded with a sense of wonder and awe. To his knowledge, none of the raptor family of birds had been seen in Ottawa for twenty years or more.

Suddenly, a sense of wrongness exploded in his head. The hawk....The trees . . . . Panic pushed him to his feet. He swayed and took a step to brace himself. Agony shot through him as his leg buckled beneath him. Seconds before his head met the rock, he saw the hawk tense and spread its wings, then sink back upon its perch.

Molly set her cup of tea on the wicker table and sank into the time-battered rocker on the back porch. The drizzle had subsided with the breeze in the early evening. The damp air lay like cool silk on her skin. Mac jumped silently into her lap and melted into a boneless black puddle. Together they listened to the silence, broken only by the sound of crickets and distant farm dogs.

Her gaze traveled over the fields of young trees, grown now to head height. As always, she thought of Duncan at the sight of them—how he had thrilled, even near the end, to wander the mini-forest he had planted. He told her once that the forest sustained him and brought him a kind of peace that helped him accept the knowledge of his disease and the loss of his son. Now Molly was alone to watch his legacy flourish.

Duncan was four months gone now. She still missed him. Pensive, Molly watched the twilight deepen until the world became a thing of shadows and the birds sought their nighttime roosts. She rocked gently and thought about her dead husband.

Then she felt Mac stiffen under her hand. He rose to his feet, his body suddenly expanding as his fur rose. A low growl throbbed in his throat as he jumped from her lap and crouched on the porch, staring into the darkness. Surprised, Molly followed his gaze.

She could see nothing that might have disturbed the cat. The dark forms of the trees had blended into a single dense wall. Only their tips were silhouetted against the rapidly fading light in the sky.

What had Mac sensed? A groundhog? A raccoon? She murmured softly to the cat and reached down to stroke his back. By slow degrees he relaxed and sat back, though he kept his nose and ears pointed alertly ahead.

As the sky darkened overhead, she looked up and watched the stars, tiny points of light winking on in a vast velvet room. She could just make out the mounds of white Shasta daisies edging the porch.

A bright rectangle on the lawn to her left told her she had forgotten to turn off the ceiling light in her upstairs office. The practical side of her nature urged her to go inside and switch it off. She shook her head. It could wait.

Suddenly, a loud crashing came from the forest, as if a large body were forcing its way through the fields that had once grown corn and alfalfa. Mac hissed and crouched low on the porch. Could it be a deer? Molly's heart jumped in anticipation. She and Duncan had hoped the 200-acre forest would eventually attract some of the wildlife seen occasionally in the area.

But no, it couldn't be. No deer moved so clumsily. Her pulse skipped a beat, then accelerated. She rose to her feet, straining to see into the darkness. Beside her, Mac hissed and slunk to the edge of the porch.

Abruptly conscious of the remoteness of her home, Molly felt a bolt of fear slam into her chest. She turned and yanked open the screen door. She looked back over her shoulder just as a large figure burst from the trees and stumbled into the yard.

At her strangled cry, the man stopped and lifted his head. "Please." Pain laced his hoarse voice. He threw up his hands in a gesture of appeal. His body swayed, then he toppled forward to collapse in the rectangle of light.

Molly stood frozen at the open door. Was it a trick? But if he meant to attack her why would he give her time to barricade herself in the house? Uncertain, she waited, ready to run if he so much as twitched. He lay still as stone. Was he dead?

Mac crept toward the man, one wary step at a time. Every muscle in his body was tense, ready to leap away if the shape on the ground stirred. Molly held her breath.

Mac sniffed and cautiously extended a paw to touch the stranger's cheek. When nothing happened, he drew closer. Satisfied, the cat sat on his rear beside the man's head and looked back over his shoulder at Molly. When she didn't move, he lowered his head to lick the man's face.

Molly exhaled in disbelief. Mac had been Duncan's cat, a wild stray that had adopted Duncan for his own. He had resisted Molly's overtures of friendship for a long time and had accepted her fully only after Duncan's death. His behavior now seemed an endorsement of the stranger. Deciding to trust the cat's instincts, she hurried to the body on her back lawn.

She fell to her knees beside him and immediately smelled the coppery tang of blood. A dark streak covered the left leg of his trousers. Gingerly, she laid her palm on the stain. Her hand came away wet and sticky.

Shivering with distaste, she wiped the blood on the grass. Was he dead? Surely a leg wound couldn't have killed him. She hesitated, then lowered her face to his back. His muscles moved beneath her cheek. He was alive.

Beside her, Mac watched intently. Then he meowed and impatiently butted his head against her arm, as if insisting that she do something.

"Yes, Mac, I know. We can't leave him out here. But look at the size of him. How do you expect me to move him?"

She sat back on her heels and contemplated the still figure. Despite his prone position she could see that he must be well over six feet tall. His shoulders were the broadest she'd ever seen, though his waist was narrow and his hips slim—no fat, then, but muscle to spare. The arm not hidden beneath his body reached out toward the house. The long fingers of his hand curled like those of a sleeping child.

He moaned. Her eyes darted to his face. She shifted back a few inches, her heart in her throat. Mac flicked her a scolding look and gently batted at the man's face. Slowly his eyes opened to stare blankly ahead. Mac began to purr. The man blinked, focused, and drew in a deep breath.

"Hello, cat. Where'd you come from?" he mumbled. Without taking his gaze from the cat, he pulled his free arm back and began to stroke the cat's head. His eyes closed again. Mac's purr became a deep rumble of pleasure.

Molly watched in astonishment. Apprehension melted away at the sight of the stranger's gentle handling of the cat. A man who could ignore his pain to please an animal was not a man to fear. In any case, it wasn't in her not to help someone in distress.

His eyes opened again just as she stretched out her hand to touch his shoulder. The movement caught his attention. His startled gaze swung to her face, his indrawn breath loud in the night's quiet. Molly paused, then offered a reassuring smile.

"Hello. I....You're hurt. Do you think you can stand?"

He stared at her, then flicked a quick glance at the dark bulk of the house.

"Can you stand?" she repeated. "You need help. But I can't lift you by myself."

He nodded and laboriously pushed himself to a sitting position. A gasp broke from his lips. One hand went to his leg while the other clutched his head.

"Dizzy. Just a minute." His eyes closed as he panted through his open mouth. When his breathing slowed, Molly moved to his side, knelt on one knee, and lifted his left arm over her shoulder.

"Pull your right leg under you when I lift." She heaved his body up a few inches and strained to hold him. When he was balanced on one foot, he leaned on her shoulder and lifted the other hand from the ground to fold his damaged leg close to his body. They paused again, both breathing heavily. Molly could almost taste the groans he kept trapped in his throat. Compassion and admiration for his courage filled her heart.

"Now, at the count of three, push up with your good leg. I'll stand at the same time. Then put your weight on me, not your bad leg. Ready? One...two...three!"

Molly braced herself and surged to her feet. Somehow, the stranger rose with her. His weight on her shoulder almost toppled her but she moved her legs apart to balance them both and gripped him around the waist. They stood weaving a moment while he gulped huge drafts of air.

Finally he lifted his head.

"You're stronger than you look. I thought I would have to claw my way to the house on my belly." The admiration in his voice disconcerted her.

"I think it was a joint effort." She laughed a little breathlessly. "Do you think you can walk? It's not far and there's a bedroom on the ground floor."

"I'm ready to try."

One slow step at a time they made their way to the porch, Mac leading the way, his tail held straight up like a parade-master's baton. When they reached the foot of the ramp Molly was glad she hadn't yet replaced it with steps. They paused in the doorway to the kitchen while she reached for the light switch.

When her eyes adjusted to the light Molly turned her head for her first clear look at the stranger who had emerged from her woods. Her eyes widened in surprise. Somehow she had expected a handsome face, perhaps because her feminine senses had recognized the beauty of his massive build. Instead his face was rough, angular, almost unfinished looking. But not his mouth. She stared at the clearly defined, sensual fullness of his lips and felt her stomach tighten. Shocked at her reaction, she started to wrench her gaze away just as his lids rose to reveal eyes as dark as chocolate.

Their gazes locked. She saw surprise, admiration, then

a hint of recognition that turned to confusion. His mouth opened then closed. He started to shake his head then stopped abruptly, a small moan escaping his throat. Only then did she see the pallor beneath his skin and feel the tremor that shook his body.

Appalled at her thoughtlessness and disconcerted by her reaction to his masculinity, she half-walked, half-carried him to the table and dragged a chair around behind him. He sat down heavily and dropped his head on his arms. Fresh blood had seeped through the denim covering his left leg.

"Water," he croaked. "Please."

With something specific to do, Molly pulled herself together. As he lifted his head and gulped greedily at the cold well water, she cut through his pant leg with her kitchen shears. She gasped when the denim parted to reveal a bloody gash on the outside of his upper thigh.

A knife wound? She leaned closer. No. A clean stroke would have opened and parted the flesh. There were two wounds here, as if something had punched through his leg. A bullet wound? Should she call the doctor? But it was late and Doc Brown was surely drunk. Even semi-sober, he'd been of little use when Duncan was ill. She decided her knowledge of first aid would suffice for now.

Molly bit back the questions that rose to her lips. She filled a pan with warm water and began to wipe away the blood as gently as she could. Tremors shook his leg but no sound escaped his lips. When the wound was clean, she rose and gripped his shoulder.

"Don't try to move yet. I'm going to apply some antibiotic powder and then bandage it." She felt his shoulder muscles relax slightly under her hand.

The procedure took only few minutes. Molly emptied the bloody water into the sink, rinsed out the pan and washed her hands. Then she filled the kettle and made instant coffee. Finally she sank down at the table opposite him.

Neither spoke for long minutes as they drank the hot beverage. Finally he looked up and placed a large hand over hers. Molly started and looked up. A hint of mischief in his eyes surprised her.

"It's not easy to find words to thank someone whose name you don't know."

"Oh. It's Molly. Molly Barnes."

"Thank you, Molly Barnes. Is that Miss or Ms.?"

"Mrs." Something moved in his eyes. "I'm a widow," she added hastily, then blushed. Why had she been so quick to tell him that?

"I'm sorry." His sympathy was genuine. "Do you have any children? I wouldn't want them to be frightened of me."

"No, no children. But now you have me at a disadvantage."

His eyebrows rose.

Molly smiled. "It's not easy to say you're welcome to someone whose name you don't know."

"Touché." He grinned and Molly wondered how she could have thought him homely. His face had regained some color and his eyes were warm with appreciation. He opened his mouth then closed it and swallowed hard. Molly sensed his whole body tense and reached out to grip his upper arm.

"What's wrong? Is it your stomach? I'll get a bowl."

"No." He shook his head, then winced. "I...need to lie down."

Molly jumped to her feet.

"I wasn't thinking. I'm sorry. There's a bed in there." She waved her hand toward a partially opened door in the side wall of the kitchen.

"The room used to be a pantry. I'm afraid it's very small but it was the most convenient . . . ." Her voice trailed away. "Let me help you up."

She saw his face whiten and his lips thin as he pushed himself up from the chair, but he didn't make a sound.

She again slipped under his left arm and took his weight on her shoulders. Progress was slow but finally they reached the side of the bed. When she would have nudged him around to sit down, he resisted. She glanced up in surprise.

"My clothes. I'll make a mess of the bedclothes."

"No problem." She stripped off the white chenille spread and turned down the sheets. "If you'll hang on to the bedpost, I'll get your clothes off." His chuckle made her blush but she ignored it and added, as matter-of-factly as she could, "You won't be comfortable, otherwise."

Refusing to meet his gaze, she quickly pulled off his jacket and T-shirt, then removed his belt. Despite the care she took to ease his trousers down over his wound, his face was white with strain when he sat on the bed and fell back on the pillow. She lifted his bandaged leg and gently laid it on the bed, then pulled the summer-weight blanket up to his chest.

He sighed deeply and flashed her an engaging grin, though his mouth was ringed with white. "Are you sure your name's not Florence?"

"Florence?"

"Of Nightingale fame. Surely all nurses have heard of the heroine of the Crimean War."

"Oh, the Lady with the Lamp. No, I'm not a nurse. But I think sleep is what you need right now. When you wake, we'll see about a doctor. And then I suppose we'd better notify the police."

"The police? Why?"

"Well, don't you think you should report the person who shot you?"

"*Shot* me?" An incredulous look filled his face. "Nobody shot me! Why would anyone shoot me?"

He struggled up on his elbows, then fell back with a groan. His head rolled toward her, then stopped. When he didn't move again, Molly realized he had passed out.

For a moment she could do no more than stare at him,

her mind caught by his unexpected reaction to her words. How could he not know he'd been shot? Was she wrong about the nature of his wound? Unconsciously, she shook her head. She wasn't a nurse but she knew a bullet hole when she saw one.

A bullet hole. Made by a gun. She really should call Brad and report the stranger. Some part of her mind protested the thought. She didn't want Brad to come to the house. Besides, she rationalized, what could he do when the man in Duncan's bed hadn't even realized he'd been shot? Questioning him would be of no use and could very well delay his recovery. She didn't want that for this man who'd erupted from her woods.

No, she'd wait. If it became necessary to consult a doctor, then she'd have no choice but to reveal the stranger's presence to the police.

Satisfied with her reasoning, she leaned over to pull the blanket higher and noticed a blood-matted area on the right side of his head. She explored the area with gentle fingers and winced at the bump she found.

Setting her speculations aside she moved quickly to cleanse and treat the wound before he awakened. Remembering how her mother had treated her childhood bumps and bruises, she filled a small plastic bag with ice-cubes. Then she sat down on the folding chair in the narrow space between the bed and the freezer. Tucking the bag of ice against his goose egg, she settled back to watch and wonder about the man sleeping in Duncan's last bed.

He became aware first of the numbing cold against his ear. He opened his eyes a crack and stared at the unfamiliar ceiling. Light from the open door at the foot of the bed illuminated the room dimly. Without moving his head he lowered his gaze and looked around. On his left, a row of upright bars rose inches from his face. He realized that the bed must be hospital issue. No more than two feet away, cream-colored cupboards rose from shoulder height to the ceiling. Leaning against the wall beneath the cupboards were a folded wheelchair, two umbrellas and two bicycles. A bedpan balanced on the wheelchair. He remembered the ramp and guessed that someone had been nursed in this room.

Something cool and moist touched his chin. He looked down. A cat, black as midnight, lay curled on his chest. Its head was lifted to stare with unblinking eyes into his. The man grinned and murmured a greeting.

Soft snoring at his cold right ear startled him. He turned his head and saw a mass of tousled hair spread on an outflung arm beside his pillow. What the devil . . . ?

Then he remembered—the strange forest, the pain, the lone woman. She had washed and bandaged his leg. What had she said? A bullet wound? He searched his mind but couldn't remember a shooting.

Cautiously, he raised a hand to his head. His fingers encountered a sizable bump. There was no pain and immediately he recognized that the cold was due to the small bag of ice that had slipped down to his ear.

When the cat began to purr he dropped his hand and began to knead the fur on its head. The urge to sit up lost out to the need to understand what had happened. Had he been in an accident? But why had he been in a forest? And why did the forest seem so . . . alien? Dread budded and grew in his chest. His breath quickened and panic washed over him. Something was terribly wrong!

He must have made a sound because the woman lifted her head and peered sleepily at him. Then her eyes cleared. She sat up quickly and gazed intently into his eyes.

"Are you all right? Are you in pain?" She laid a cool hand on his forehead. "Your fever seems to be gone. Are you thirsty?"

He bit back his panic and tried to smile. "Yes, no, and I'm dry as a desert dune."

"Here, hold this on your goose egg. I'll get you juice."

When she left the room he dragged himself up against the headboard. The cat huffed at the disturbance and moved to the foot of the bed. Ignoring the cold sweat on his face and the painful throbbing of his left leg, he examined the tiny room. A window above the chest freezer indicated twilight. Had he slept around the clock?

When she returned he had unwound the bandages and was staring in disbelief at the holes in his leg. Bullet holes. A small voice in his mind whispered 'Who? Why?' even as he acknowledged his luck. The bullet had passed cleanly through the fleshy part of his thigh, missing the bone and the major artery.

"Here you are, freshly squeezed and cold."

While he gulped the delicious juice, she bent over to examine his wound.

"Not bad, if I do say so myself. Guess I would have made a great doctor. I'll just clean it up again. It's weeping a little but it doesn't seem to be infected."

When she had applied a fresh wrapping of gauze, she straightened and gave him a smile that made his breath catch in his throat.

"You are a lucky man, Mr. Dune, and a fast healer." She took the empty glass from his hand. "You must be hungry."

At the mention of food, his stomach growled in agreement. Molly grinned and turned to leave. His hand shot out to grasp her wrist.

"Wait. How long have I been here?"

"Let me think. Mmm, two days. You've been pretty sick."

He gasped. "Two *days*?" For a moment he couldn't take it in. Then the fatigue in her face told the story.

"You've been taking care of me for two days? Why would you do that for a stranger?"

She smiled, a mischievous gleam in her eyes. "Well, I suppose for the same reason people climb mountains. You were there, you see. I mean here. That's all."

He stared at her in astonishment, then felt a wide grin bisected his face. "I see. I think. Molly Barnes, you are some kind of woman." Molly blushed. "Why did you call me Mr. Dune?"

"Oh, that!" She laughed lightly. "You passed out before you could tell me your name. You said you were as dry as a desert dune. So, well, I had to call you something."

"I did? Well, Molly Barnes, I'm pleased to meet you. My name is . . . is . . . ."

Surprise then horror flooded through him as he struggled in vain to finish the sentence. *My name is*....For the first time he noticed the empty space in his mind. His hands began to shake. "I'm . . . I'm . . ."

Molly quickly set the glass down on the freezer and took his hands in hers.

"You had a nasty bump on your head. Some confusion is natural and the fever didn't help matters. Don't worry, Dune. Just give it some time. I'm sure it'll come back to you. Some food, then another sleep and you'll be right as rain again."

She brushed the hair back from his forehead and tucked a small round pillow behind his head. She hesitated, then dropped a light kiss on his cheek and hurried from the room.

Dune stared after her. His hand rose to touch his cheek. Her lips had been warm and soft and gentle.

Ignoring the sudden longing that swelled in his chest, he closed his eyes and began to search the corners in his memory. Faces floated into his mind, faces he recognized but couldn't identify: a middle-aged couple, a pretty young woman, a small, scowling man, two children splashing in a tot-sized pool. They seemed familiar but he had no idea who they were. A shudder ran through his body.

All right, forget people for now. Where was he from? He relaxed slightly when the answer came. He lived in Ottawa. Immediately he pictured an apartment overlooking the small forest bequeathed to the city. His mind flew to the forest behind Molly's house but, frowning, he shook the image away. Wherever this was, it couldn't be the same area. The trees here were too young.

Then how did he get here? What had he done to earn himself a bullet through the leg? *Who was he?* A policeman, a criminal, a man on the run, what? Could he have accidentally shot himself? But why would he own a gun? No answers surfaced.

Breathing deeply to control his panic, he shut off the questions and tried to focus on the woman moving quietly about the kitchen. Even in slacks and a man's shirt she appeared decidedly feminine. The outfit revealed, rather than hid, her womanly figure. She was tall, at least five foot eight. No makeup masked the flawless, lightly tanned skin. No penciling defined the perfect arch of her eyebrows. Her nose was narrow and straight, her oval face lovely. He smiled.

Heavenly smells of bacon and toast drifted into the pantry. His stomach growled impatiently as he deliberately set about relaxing every set of muscles in his body, starting with his feet and working up. Where had he learned that technique?

Somehow, he knew he was safe here, though why the word safe should come to mind he couldn't say. Molly Barnes seemed willing to nurse him and surely she was correct in saying his memory would return. Almost unconsciously he decided to remain here, wherever *here* was, until his wound healed and he was back on his feet. That is, if Molly Barnes would allow it. He had the feeling she wouldn't object. Not that either of them really had a choice in the matter. His leg wasn't about to take him anywhere very soon.

By the time Molly returned with a tray he felt almost content. The fact that his nurse was beautiful had nothing to do with his decision to stay.

Chapter Two

Molly rolled over, thumped her pillow, then pulled it under her neck with an exasperated sigh. Sheer exhaustion was keeping her awake—that and, of course, relief that Dune had pulled through the fever and seemed to be on the mend—physically at least.

Dune. The name suited him. A force of nature that moved where it pleased, when it pleased, as slowly or quickly as it pleased. She sensed that very few people could shift Dune from whatever path he chose. Yet, like the desert, he could surprise—and impress.

He could joke and tease even when in pain. Nor had he been thrown when he realized he had lost his own identity. Most people would have gone into hysterics, given the same circumstances.

But not Dune.

Incredibly, he had been lounging on the bed looking completely relaxed when she took him dinner. Her face must have revealed her astonishment because he laughed and said an enforced vacation was better than no vacation at all. She shook her head in remembered amusement and marveled at his composure.

Her admiration faded as the questions that had plagued her for two days returned. Who was Dune? Where had he come from? Who had shot him, and why? She knew she should have notified the police. But Dune had no answers for them, and in his lucid moments, had begged her not to. She couldn't bring herself to betray him when he was helpless.

Or was it that she didn't want him taken away? Even feverish, sweaty and white with pain, the man fascinated her. The thought made her recognize, for the first time, just how lonely she'd been since Duncan died.

Still, just because Mac had given him his purr of approval didn't mean the man was a paragon of virtue.

How had Dune come to be in Duncan's forest? The day before, when he dropped into a normal sleep, she had driven around the area but found no sign of an abandoned car. The city boundary was seven miles away, too far to walk with a damaged leg.

Damaged leg or not, he had made his way, with her help, to the downstairs bathroom after eating his fill. She smiled to herself at the memory of the horrified look he'd given her when she gestured at the old fashioned thunder pot sitting on the freezer. Caring for Duncan's needs in the terrible final stages of his disease had overcome her natural embarrassment about body functions.

Her face flamed at the memory of his near-naked body. Granted, his build was magnificent—but that didn't explain the feelings that surged to life, feelings she hadn't expected to surface again. Other men in her past, men whose faces sent thousands of women into raptures every week, had elicited no such breathlessness, no such fluttering in her stomach. She didn't want those feelings. She would have to be careful. The man sleeping in her pantry might prove dangerous after all.

Suddenly impatient with her thoughts, she dismissed him from her mind. She had a problem of her own to consider and a difficult decision to make. Dune's presence changed nothing.

She swung her legs out of bed and sat up. A full moon lit her path to the window. Looking up, she searched the starry sky for an answer.

"How I wish you were here, Duncan," she whispered. "I need your advice."

The stars were silent. She sighed. Duncan was four months gone and she still hadn't decided her future. Should she stay? Should she go back? *Could* she go back?

The old farmhouse was hers, free and clear. With the money Duncan had left her, augmented by the small-but-steady income from her at-home job of reviewing the latest best-selling novels, she could afford to live out her life here—a safe, peaceful life. A solitary life with no daily companionship. A lonely life, perhaps, but a life free of turmoil and dissension.

The neighbors accepted her now. At first they had been suspicious of the young woman the elderly farmer had married. She couldn't blame them. With time, however, her devoted care for the dying man had erased their skepticism. They had long since accepted that the widow Barnes, while not very sociable, was nonetheless agreeable and trustworthy.

If she *could* go back, did she really want to? A part of her missed her former world and the excitement of her work. Were people even aware she'd been away for two years? Could she simply take up where she left off? Only by returning would that question be answered. She had to decide soon.

Her thoughts returned to Dune. He would leave in a week or two, when he had recovered enough to travel. The thought brought a small ache to her chest. She chose to ignore the feeling. When he was gone, she would decide what she wanted for the rest of her life.

She returned to bed and finally fell into an exhausted sleep.

The smell of coffee and the clatter of cutlery awakened her. For just a moment she thought that Duncan had returned to the house after milking Daisy. Then she remembered that both he and the cow were gone. She tensed. Who—?

Alarm filled her as she realized that Dune must be up. The idiot! True, the worst seemed to be over but a complete recovery was some time away. What did he think he was proving by getting up so soon? His wound would probably be bleeding again. Time to play the role of Florence. Stifling a yawn she rolled out of bed, tidied the bedclothes and headed for the shower.

Molly stopped in astonishment at the kitchen doorway. Clad only in trousers and a pink flowered bib apron that had belonged to Duncan's first wife, Dune stood scrambling eggs. His hip rested against the front of the stove, allowing his good leg to take most of his weight. She stared at his muscular shoulders and hair-matted chest, the frilly apron somehow accentuating the virility of his large torso.

This was a man so confident of his masculinity that the feminine apron and the ill-fitting pants didn't faze him. The trousers were Duncan's. Her husband had been a robust man before his heart deteriorated. The over-large pants were bunched around Dune's waist and ended at the middle of his calves.

Dune turned and saw her expression. A wide smile split his face.

"Good morning, Miss Molly. Now don't say a word." He shook the spatula at her. "I'm too sloppy to cook without an apron. But if you ever tell, I'll . . . I'll . . . ."

"You'll what?" Molly grinned when a clump of scrambled eggs flew from the spatula and landed with a plop on the floor.

"I'll . . . I'll reveal your true identity!"

His teasing expression changed to one of surprise, as if he hadn't known what he was going to say.

Molly felt the blood drain from her face. "What do you mean?"

He hesitated, then shrugged and leaned forward and spoke in an exaggerated whisper. His smile was strained. "I'll tell everyone you're Florence Nightingale reincarnated. Guaranteed to hit the front page of the local supermarket rag." His face changed again as he gave Molly a beseeching look. "I don't know why I said that."

Molly walked into the kitchen. To hide her shaking hands she reached for the coffee pot.

"I know why," she said, hoping he hadn't noticed her reaction to his unexpected words. "You're trying to distract me from lecturing you about being on that leg so soon. And it won't work."

She glanced at him over her shoulder and threw him an exaggerated look of disapproval. "Men! They make such terrible patients. All that macho nonsense, I suppose. Such tedious creatures."

Dune wriggled his eyebrows. "But you women think we're adorable anyway, right?"

"Just keep on believing that if it makes you feel good. Who am I to puncture your ego?"

"Now that's what I'd really like to know."

"What?" Molly filled two mugs and carried them to the table. When he didn't answer, she looked up to find him staring at her intently. The humor was gone from his face. Her scalp prickled. "What is it?"

"Who are you, Molly?" His voice had deepened and slowed. "I keep thinking I know you. Maybe if I could remember you, I would remember the rest. Tell me who you are. Who you *really* are."

Apprehension shivered down Molly's spine. Her mouth felt dry. She cleared her throat and shrugged one shoulder.

"Molly Barnes. Just Molly Barnes. I'm certain we've never met before, Dune." *As if she could have forgotten a man like him.* "Perhaps I look like someone you know. They say everyone has a double somewhere in the world."

Dune shook his head. "I don't feel we've actually met

before. But I know you. Are you a celebrity of some kind? Could I have seen your picture somewhere?"

Molly gave a nervous laugh. "Me, a celebrity? I'm a farmer's widow." She inhaled a deep breath and reached for the plates. "And I'm starved. Aren't those eggs done yet? You hobble to the table while I dish up."

Dune's eyes narrowed but he said nothing more. Molly mechanically filled the plates with bacon and eggs, then slipped bread into the toaster. As she bustled about, she avoided his eyes and kept her head averted, aware that he was watching her every move. He couldn't possibly recognize her.... So why was she nervous?

A knock on the front door startled them both. Before either could move the knock sounded again and a masculine voice called through the screen.

"Molly? It's me, Brad. I've brought your glasses with me."

Annoyance accompanied Molly's recognition of her unwanted visitor. The man was nothing if not persistent. Somehow, she had to convince him that she wasn't interested.

The front door opened and footsteps started down the hallway toward the kitchen. Dune released her arm, stood up and leaned against the table, one hand gripping the back of his chair. His eyes were hooded and opaque, and his expression reserved. Beneath his outwardly relaxed posture Molly sensed a taut watchfulness.

"Molly? Ah, here you are."

A tall, thin, policeman stepped into the kitchen. His narrow, attractive face creased in a wide smile when he saw her.

"Hello, Brad." Molly spoke politely but didn't return the smile. "What is so important that you walked right in?"

Faltering, he stopped and held out a package, only then spotting Dune. His face hardened immediately. His gaze swung back to Molly.

"Brad, this is a friend of mine. I'd like you to meet—"

"Dune." Dune shifted his weight to his good leg and held out his hand, a noncommittal expression on his face. "I'm visiting for awhile."

Wearing a strained smile, the uniformed man took Dune's hand for a perfunctory shake.

"Brad Baylor. Pleased to meet you, Mr. Dune." He hesitated then turned back to Molly. "Never knew you to have visitors before. I mean, except for Duncan's friends. I hope this means you're ready to circulate again." He ignored Molly's quick frown and pushed on.

"The Lion's club is putting on a dance next weekend to raise money for the Stewarts." In an aside to Dune, he explained that the Stewart home had been struck by lightning the week before. "I was hoping you might let me escort you, Molly. It's time you got out of the house for a bit. You're welcome, too, Mr. Dune, if you're still here." The last was said with obvious reluctance.

Before Molly could answer, Dune shook his head.

"I doubt we'll be able to make it, though thanks for the invitation." Without looking at Molly he stared into the policeman's eyes, a cool smile on his expressionless face.

Molly's gaze swung from one to the other. Instinctively she knew Dune's remark held an unspoken message. Brad's slow flush indicated he understood.

Ignoring the spark of anger at Dune's possessive tone, she took the package from the policeman. "It was thoughtful of you to bring these out to me. Thank you. I meant to pick them up yesterday but I was . . . busy." She blushed when the policeman's eyes narrowed.

"You know I like to help you out any way I can. Well, uh, I'm on duty, so I guess I'd better shove off."

He nodded briefly to Dune and retraced his steps to the front door. Molly followed him. Leaning forward, he spoke in a low tone.

"Remember, if there's ever anything you need . . . ." His knuckles brushed her cheek, then he turned on his heel to leave. Molly stepped out on the porch behind him.

"Brad, just a moment."

When he paused on the porch step and turned back to face her, she took a deep breath and forced herself to speak calmly. "I don't want to sound ungrateful, but I've told you before that I can run my own errands. I'm perfectly capable of looking after myself. I must also ask that you refrain from walking into my house without invitation. Please call first, or at least wait at the door."

Seeing his wounded expression, she softened her voice. "I'm not ready to resume a social life, Brad. I may never be ready. Please don't waste your time on me. I'm sorry."

Something like anger moved in his eyes, and his lips tightened as he glanced behind her into the house. Avoiding her eyes, he jumped the three steps to the ground and strode to his car.

Molly watched the cruiser disappear down the road in a cloud of dust. She had been aware of Brad's interest from the moment Duncan had introduced her to his friend's son. Brad had kept his distance, but since Duncan's death the policeman had found countless excuses to drop by the farm. He was an attractive man, but Molly knew she would never be interested in him in the way he hoped. Lately, his unwanted attentions had begun to annoy her. Maybe Dune's presence would persuade him to turn his interest to another.

When she returned to the kitchen, Dune was seated at the table with his bad leg propped up on a chair and his arms folded on his chest. She stopped short at the expression on his face.

"What's the matter?"

"What's Brad Baylor to you?"

She stiffened at his terse question, the barely perceptible accusation in his voice triggering memories of similar scenes. She would *not* go through this again.

"He's nothing to me. Not that it's any of your business."

Deciding the best defense was offense, she added, "You had no right to turn down his invitation for me. I can speak for myself. Don't ever do anything like that again."

"You're right, of course. I apologize." The tension in his face dissolved slowly. "It's just that . . . I got the feeling that he could be trouble."

"Trouble? What do you mean?"

Dune lifted his hands in a gesture of helplessness. "I don't know. But my gut is telling me there's something . . . I can't explain it. I feel I should know him. He's looks familiar and yet he doesn't. God, I wish I could remember!"

Molly's anger at Dune's interference drained away. Dropping into the chair beside him, she covered his clenched fist with her hand.

"You'll remember. It's only been two days. Maybe you knew Brad's father, Douglas Baylor. They did look very alike. That might explain it."

Suddenly Dune looked alert. "*Did* look alike?"

"His father died three months ago. Picture an older version of Brad—"

"That's it! Officer Doug Baylor. He swallowed his gun, years ago. I saw his picture somewhere recently. No wonder Brad looked so familiar."

Shocked, Molly shook her head. "No, you're wrong. His death was an accident. He was cleaning his gun. Besides, it happened just a few months ago. You must be thinking of someone else."

"Months? But . . . ." The animation fled from Dune's eyes, to be replaced by confusion. Then he shook his head. His face cleared. The corners of his lips rose in a wry grimace.

"Guess that wasn't a memory breakthrough after all. Whoever it was that almost came to mind died years ago." He shrugged carelessly. "I think."

His gaze lowered to the table and only then did Molly realize that her hand still covered his. He seized her wrist before she could snatch it away. His voice dropped to a low, seductive rumble.

"Why didn't you tell him I've been shot?"

"I don't know."

Their gazes met and held. Suddenly her lungs locked. She couldn't breathe or move. Currents of heat raced from her wrist to engulf her body. Her small gasp drew his gaze to her lips. His face drew closer to hers, until she could feel his breath ruffling her lashes.

Panic erupted in her chest. No! She didn't want this! Jerking her wrist from his grasp she pushed herself to her feet and stared down at him. His look of astonishment told her she had overreacted. Deliberately, she blanked her face and forced a light note into her voice.

"Florence thinks the patient has been up long enough. It's time you return to bed and elevate that leg. Hop to it, mister."

He stared at her intently for a moment then his face relaxed into a satisfied grin.

"Yes, ma'am, I'm hopping." He snapped a saucy salute and pushed himself up from the table.

Grateful that he didn't question her, she watched him maneuver awkwardly back to the pantry. She should help him, she knew, but the thought of his arm around her shoulders daunted her. She refused to wonder why.

He paused in the doorway to catch his breath, his large hands gripping the frame. Molly stared, mesmerized, at the flexing of the muscles in the broad expanse of his back. Her fingers curled and uncurled, yearning to touch. His mop of curls bounced with every hop and she wondered if it was as silky as she imagined.

Then she shook her head. She, of all people, knew what flaws could be hidden in attractive packages. Just because her long dormant sensuality was stirring was no reason to indulge her imagination now. She knew literally nothing about the man, not even his name. Dune would leave soon, and, in any case, brief flings weren't her style—despite David's accusations.

But she didn't want to think about David. He had no part in her life now. As her customary calm settled over her, she hurried into the pantry to lift Dune's wounded leg onto the bed.

Guilt struck her when she saw the sweat-beaded pallor of his face. How could she have let him struggle alone? She hurried from the room and returned a moment later with a painkiller and a glass of water.

Slipping her arm beneath his neck she lifted his head. His eyes opened, pain making them glow with a heavy sheen. He smiled. Molly felt her heart stop, then accelerate. Training enabled her to keep the impersonal mask securely on her face but she couldn't control the blush that pinked her cheeks.

"Hello, Florence. Have you come to minister to me?" Beneath his hoarse whisper Molly heard both pain and a sly teasing.

She ignored the double meaning of his words and ordered firmly, "Put this pill in your mouth and swallow it."

"Yes, Florence."

She frowned to conceal her amusement at his pretended meekness. "It's your own fault. You shouldn't have put weight on your leg so soon. Men have no common sense at all!"

"Yes, Florence. You're absolutely right, Florence. No sense at all. Will you forgive me?" His voice was docile. His dancing eyes were not.

She tutted at his nonsense but a smile curled her lips as she set the empty glass on the freezer and lowered his head to the pillow.

"Only if you promise to stay put for awhile. And that you won't try to get up again without help."

"I promise."

"Good." Molly pulled the lightweight blanket up to his waist, then picked up the empty glass and headed for the kitchen. She paused in the doorway and looked back.

Dune's eyes were closed. For a moment she allowed her gaze to travel the length of his body. Even lying down, his massive size seemed to fill the small room. She swallowed and forced herself to leave.

Nursing Dune had put her behind schedule. With a pad and pencil beside her she curled up on the couch and began to read the first of the three novels that had arrived in the mail the week before.

Dune woke with a start. The pain in his leg had diminished to a dull ache. He ignored it and searched for the last trailing tendrils of a dream. Computers, he remembered that, a room filled with computers. A dark street, a dilapidated building, a feeble cone of light illuminating an outside wall. Shadows, shouts, noise. Then pain. Then nothing.

That was all. What did it mean? The images had to come from somewhere. Was it real life or a movie long forgotten? None of it made sense. He growled in frustration.

He thought of Molly Barnes. Even in slacks and a checked shirt, even without makeup, she projected an air of elegance, of sophistication — an arresting contrast with the rural setting. She might be a farmer's widow but she was much more than that.

If he was sure of anything, it was that they had never met. No mere bump on the head could make him forget a woman so natural, so warm, so unconsciously sensual. No, they hadn't met before. And yet—he knew her.

Dune frowned at the memory of the man who had entered the house without waiting for an invitation. Did he and Molly have a history together? Or was he one of those policemen who used the authority of his uniform to assume privileges beyond the established limits?

His gut told him that Molly had not been pleased to see Brad Baylor, though she had been polite. What had they said to each other on the front porch? From his position in the kitchen he had been able to hear their voices but not their words.

Still, Molly hadn't accepted Brad's invitation. Dune grinned to himself, remembering her indignation that he had answered for her. His amusement faded. Why had he done that? It was no business of his. Why should he care if Molly Barnes chose to date Brad Baylor?

But he did care. He sensed a mystery lurking behind those huge, gray eyes. A mystery he meant to solve—but first, he had to solve the mystery of his own identity.

Dune watched from the front porch until the old car disappeared in a cloud of dust. Bemused, he wondered how Molly's husband had kept it in such perfect shape, almost like new, for so many years. He pushed the thought away. Molly would be back in an hour or less. If he were to take advantage of her absence, he had to move.

Halfway up the stairs to the second floor, he paused to rest his protesting leg. The respite proved a tactical error. Guilt crept into his mind. How could he repay Molly's care and kindness by snooping in her home?

His conscience berated him. Just because he sensed a mystery in her life, there was no excuse for trespassing on her privacy. Still, the conviction that her secret was important had been growing for days. His mind swung endlessly between the puzzle of his own identity and the riddle named Molly Barnes.

Dune shook his head and with one hand gripping the worn banister, continued up the stairs. The need to know overcame the nagging of his conscience. He wondered what this surrender of his scruples said about his character.

The upstairs hall stretched the length of the house. Four doors, two on each side, were all closed. A fifth door at the far end of the hall stood ajar, revealing the end of a large, claw-footed tub.

Dune opened the first door on the right and stepped over the threshold. Immediately in front of him and flanked by two narrow sash windows, stood a dilapidated pedestal desk of the kind favored by the teachers of his childhood. A manual typewriter, a dictionary and an old-fashioned gooseneck lamp rested on the desk. A chair matching those in the kitchen was the only other furniture in the room.

An examination of the desk drawers revealed a cache of business envelopes, a ream of letter-sized paper and three novels. He recognized two of them as bestsellers in their day. What did Molly do in this room? Or had it been Duncan's domain, a place to work on his farm records?

He closed the door behind him and veered across the hall to open a door on the left. Sports trophies lined two shelves suspended on the wall above a narrow bed. Model airplanes hung from the ceiling, and a Beatles poster occupied the place of honor on a narrow door set in the far corner. Dune didn't need to see the young man's clothing in the closet to realize that the room belonged to a teenager. Why hadn't Molly mentioned a son? And where was the boy now?

Surely Molly wasn't old enough to have a child of an age to build these elaborate models. Maybe the boy was her stepson. Or had she been a teenage bride? The arrow of pain that skewered his heart surprised Dune. Absently, he rubbed his chest as if to massage away the ache. Although the room had been dusted recently, it held an air of melancholy, as if waiting for an occupant who would never arrive. It struck him forcibly that he had entered a shrine.

Abruptly he turned and left, snorting in self-derision. His imagination was running amuck. The boy was probably at summer camp or visiting relatives.

Angling across the hall he opened the second door on the right. A double bed with a masculine black and brown spread and one pillow caught his eye first. Mismatched dark furniture filled every wall space. Every flat surface was littered with framed pictures. Curiosity drew him into the room. As he examined the photographs, he knew a lifetime of memories had been captured by the camera.

Most of the pictures portrayed a boy, from babyhood to young adulthood. Was the boy the owner of the bedroom across the hall? The woman in the pictures with the young boy was short, round and pretty.

Some pictures, alone and with the boy, were of a medium-height, husky man with a kind face and proud eyes. Duncan Barnes?

Dune turned to the bedside table, his attention caught by the single, ornate frame, which was angled to face the bed. It contained a wedding picture. The groom had his arm around the waist of the pretty woman. They both appeared radiant with happiness.

Frowning, Dune realized the couple's clothing was decades out of date. If this man was Duncan, Molly must be his second wife. Just how old a man was he when he and Molly married? A swift perusal of the room uncovered no pictures of Molly and Duncan together. Had Molly slept here with Duncan, surrounded by pictures of his first wife? Somehow, Dune couldn't imagine a second wife that accommodating.

Quickly, he opened bureau drawers and checked the crowded closet. Every piece of clothing was masculine. Evidently Molly had a separate bedroom. He didn't question the relief that flooded through him.

Dune hesitated at the last door, knowing it must be Molly's. Mindful of the minutes ticking by, he cursed softly under his breath, pushed aside his qualms and forced his hand to turn the doorknob. The door swung open.

That it was a woman's room was immediately obvious. Rose, Wedgewood blue and cream colors predominated. Floral curtains matched the bedspread. A rocking chair stood by the window. Suddenly, Dune felt like a voyeur.

Quickly, before he lost his determination, he opened

the dresser drawers. The items of clothing were few, almost as if Molly were only a visitor. The near-empty closet reinforced the idea of temporary occupancy.

Puzzled and even more curious than before, Dune limped to the window and stared down at the front yard. How could a woman like Molly not leave her imprint on the house, not even in her own room? It was almost as if she wished to remain invisible, unnoticed.

Sunlight reflecting from a car window distracted him. He leaned forward and peered at the vehicle intermittently visible between the trees lining the gravel road. When it slowed he realized someone meant to turn into Molly's lane. Jerking away from the window, he hurried as fast as he could from the room, closed the door behind him and descended the stairs.

Panting from the exertion, he dropped into the chair in the front parlor, just as the car drew up at the front door. When the driver turned off the motor he heard Molly's voice. Resentment tightened his mouth when Brad Baylor answered. What was he doing here again? Where was Molly's car?

When two sets of footsteps climbed the porch steps, Dune lifted both feet to the leather footrest and picked up the book from the end table, hoping he gave the appearance of a man long-settled in place.

Molly smiled tightly at the policeman and repeated her thanks for the lift home, hoping her voice didn't reveal her insincerity. It *would* have to be Brad who found her on the side of the road with a flat tire. She ignored the appeal in his eyes and didn't invite him in. Her mother would have been appalled at her lack of manners, but she didn't care. She was angry.

"I won't keep you from your work any longer. Thanks for calling the garage for me. Joe is very good, he'll have my car returned shortly." She reached for the door handle. "Now I'd better get this food inside. Bye."

"You're sure you'll be all right here?"

Molly sighed inwardly at the stubborn note in his voice. But she could be stubborn, too. "I'm positive. Just drop it, Brad. You're worrying for nothing." She drew in a deep breath. "And in any case, it really isn't any of your business."

Before he could protest, she shook her head. "I don't mean to be rude, but I wish you'd understand that you have nothing to say about the way I live my life. My friends are no concern of yours. You had no business doing what you did. Now I really must go in."

The officer wheeled and stamped down the steps, climbed into his car and drove away with a screech of tires. Grimacing unhappily, Molly entered the house and started down the hall for the kitchen, not noticing Dune as she passed the entrance to the parlor.

When she finished putting the last of the groceries away, she straightened and stopped short at the sight of her house guest lounging in the doorway.

"Your leg must be better. I didn't hear you come in." Against her will, her gaze settled on his broad shoulders and the muscular forearms matted with fur. His own trousers, now washed and mended, fit him like a second skin. Her heart began to thump in response to his blatant masculinity.

"Just what did Brad do that he had no business doing?"

Startled by the edge in his voice she looked up and saw hot anger in his eyes. "You were eavesdropping?"

"I was in the parlor, reading. I couldn't help hearing. Did he make a pass at you?"

Molly blinked and saw that his relaxed pose was just that, a pose. His hands were curled in white-knuckled fists. Was he jealous? Despite herself, a thread of excitement curled in her stomach. She ignored it.

"No. He investigated you."

Dune's surprised look gave way to a frown.

"Why would he do that?"

"He's suspicious of you. I've never been known to have a visitor that wasn't a friend of Duncan's. Still, he had no right."

A medley of expressions flickered over Dune's face too quickly for Molly to identify. Damn, she shouldn't have admitted she had no friends of her own. Hoping to distract him she molded her face into a gleeful grin.

"He thinks you're a con man."

"What!"

Nodding emphatically, Molly reached for the kettle and began to fill it. Striving for a light, careless voice, she continued.

"He couldn't find any information about you, you see. It seems no one by the name of Dune lives in Ottawa. The man is frustrated. It didn't help that I refused to tell him anything about you. Not that I would have, even if I could. Now he seems to think that you're some kind of con man and I'm a gullible fool."

Dune limped to the table and sat down heavily. His mouth twisted in a wry smile. "Maybe Baylor's right. Maybe I tried to con the wrong people and got a bullet for my trouble."

"Nonsense!"

"Maybe not. There has to be a reason why someone shot me. How can you be sure my amnesia isn't faked?"

Molly didn't respond until she finished making coffee and joined Dune at the table.

"That's utter nonsense," she repeated. I don't know who you are, but I do know you're not a con man."

"And just how can you know that? I may be the world's best actor."

"I know," she said firmly, "because if you're a con man, that would make me a gullible fool. And I'm *not* a gullible fool!"

Dune's sudden grin was contagious. Molly smiled back into his warm, amused eyes. Together they burst into whoops of laughter. A full five minutes passed before they could catch their breaths. Finally subsiding, Molly wondered how long it had been since she'd laughed aloud.

As she wiped the moisture from her eyes Molly glanced at Dune. The glowing admiration she saw in his face disconcerted her. Hastily, she jumped up and went to the counter to fill their cups. Stalling, she filled a plate with cookies. When she returned to the table she was again in control.

To her relief, Dune didn't refer to the episode again, nor to her declaration of faith in him. Oh, she didn't believe she was gullible—David had demolished any naiveté she had once had—but she couldn't explain, even to herself, her absolute certainty that the man seated at her table couldn't possibly be a criminal. Brad's not-very-subtle hints that Dune might be dangerous were ludicrous.

The confrontation with the policeman had upset her. She only hoped her very real anger convinced him to leave her alone.

They sat sipping their drinks in companionable silence. Molly relished the comfort of Dune's presence and silently acknowledged the loneliness she'd felt since her husband's death. Duncan had been wonderful company.

When she reached for a second cookie, Dune's hand shot out to cover hers. Startled, she jerked in surprise and would have risen but his grip tightened. Not daring to meet his eyes, she stared at his hand. Heat crept up her arm and spread over her skin.

"You are a very special lady, Molly Barnes." His voice was low and husky. Her stomach clenched.

"Not special," she whispered.

"Yes, special. No woman has ever believed in me before with so little reason."

Molly looked up and forced herself to meet his eyes.

"How can you know that? Hasn't it occurred to you

that you may be married? Somewhere a special woman, your wife, may be waiting for you."

Dune's look of dismay was almost comical. His grip on her hand loosened. Molly drew her hand back and wrapped it around the warm mug.

"Damn!" Dune thrust his hands through his hair. "That never even crossed my mind. God, what a mess!"

Gritting his teeth in despair, Dune threw her an anguished look. "What am I going to do? I still haven't remembered anything about myself or my life."

Molly wanted to take him in her arms and comfort him. She could scarcely imagine the frustration and agony he must be experiencing, but it would be foolish to do anything that might draw them closer. Once his memory returned, he would leave to take up his life again, with or without a wife.

And she would leave, too. Dune's presence had shown her just how lonely she was here, now that Duncan was gone. Even if she couldn't go home, she couldn't stay in this house and live the rest of her life in solitude.

"Maybe you're trying too hard to remember. Why don't you prop that leg up again and nap, or finish the book you're reading. I'm going to put together a stew for supper."

She grinned. "If all else fails, I could take the frying pan to your head. A second blow might knock the memories into place again."

To her relief, Dune laughed and the tension was broken.

"If all else fails, I may just let you do that. Though I doubt Florence would approve." Chuckling, he stood up and started for the front room.

Molly watched him leave, unaware of the soft smile on her lips and the tenderness in her gray eyes. The smile disappeared abruptly when he called back cheerfully from the hallway.

"Great story, isn't it? It's years since I read it, but I'm enjoying it now just as much as I did the first time."

She remembered the book he'd been reading when she entered the house. Years since he read it? That wasn't possible. She shook her head. He must be confusing the book with another. Yes, that must be it. Of course.

Deliberately blanking her mind, she rose to prepare the stew.

Chapter Three

"Tell me about your husband."

Though he was watching the changing colors in the sky as the sun offered its parting salute, Dune heard Molly's small gasp and felt her sudden tension. He glanced at her and, even in the receding light, saw her facial muscles tighten.

"Molly, I'm sorry." His tongue stumbled over the apology. "I should have realized it's too soon for you to talk about Duncan. Forget I asked."

"Duncan?" She covered her mouth with a trembling hand. After a moment, she straightened, clasped her hands together in her lap, and smiled up at the sunset.

"I'd like to tell you about my husband. Duncan gave me a home when I had none. Many times we sat here together like this to watch the sun go down. He was a quiet, intelligent, peaceful man. I felt safe here with him. We were content in each other's company."

Dune's stomach clenched at the wistful note in Molly's

voice. Had she loved him so much then? Fighting back the jealousy that burst into life, he reminded himself that Duncan was gone. He swallowed hard and hoped his voice didn't sound as strangled to Molly's ears as it did to his own.

"It's nice when a husband and wife are in love." Nice! He winced at his use of such a trite word.

Molly looked squarely at him for the first time since they'd sat down on the porch. A soft dreamy expression shimmered in her eyes but her voice was matter-of-fact.

"It wasn't like that. I wasn't in love with Duncan, nor he with me. I did love him though. He was a good man, a kind man, and in some ways I think he saved my life."

Molly turned her face to the sky again.

"Saved your life? What do you mean?"

"I was alone when Duncan took me in. He was alone, too. His first wife died many years ago. They had only one child, a boy. Duncan and Tom were very close. More than most fathers and sons, perhaps because Grace died when Tom was only fourteen. Tom loved farming, too, but he never returned from Vietnam."

Molly sighed.

"Duncan had no other family. I think he turned the fields into woods because he'd lost heart. There was no one to carry on the farm after him." She smiled at Dune. "When I arrived the trees were only waist height. They've grown quickly." She gestured at the woods in front of them. "One day this will be known as the Thomas Barnes Memorial Woods."

Dune froze as a memory surfaced of a wooded area just inside the city limits, close to his apartment—or what he thought was his apartment. Lighted nature trails wove through the trees and were used for hiking in summer and cross-country skiing in winter. He tried to remember the little he knew about the area whose upkeep was the responsibility of the city. Tom's Woods! The popular name jumped into his mind.

His heart thumping, he stared at the trees. No. No, it couldn't be the same small forest. These trees were too short, too young—and anyway, this region was still rural. True, the city was growing rapidly but it would be years before it spread to encompass this area.

As his heartbeat slowed, Dune glanced at Molly and for the first time noticed the cat sprawled on her lap. Her head was bent over the softly purring animal. She hadn't noticed his shocked reaction to the sudden memory. He sent a silent thank you to Mac for distracting her.

"When I had been here about six months, Duncan discovered his heart was weak and his time short. He insisted we marry so that I would have a home when he was gone. Three months after the wedding, he suffered a stroke and was partially paralyzed—though his mind was unaffected. A second stroke four months ago killed him. He was a wonderful friend. I still miss him."

She paused and blinked the tears from her eyes. Without thinking, Dune reached across and took her hand in his. She didn't pull away. Her fingers curled up like a small animal in its lair. Tenderness filled his heart. When she spoke again, Dune heard the shyness in her voice.

"We weren't lovers. But we were husband and wife in every other way. I cared for him very much and I know his life was less lonely after I came."

"How could it be anything else? Duncan Barnes was a very lucky man to have you with him for the last years of his life." Dune spoke from the heart and was gratified to see Molly's pleased smile.

As they watched the last rim of the fiery sun sink below the treetops, Dune gnawed at his thoughts. Why had she reacted so strangely when he first asked about her husband? She relaxed and spoke readily enough after he mentioned Duncan's name. Whom had she thought he meant? Had Duncan been her *second* husband? His jealousy, which had faded when she explained that she and Duncan had never been lovers, flared again.

When Molly gasped softly he realized his grip on her hand had unconsciously tightened. He loosened his hold and threw her an apologetic smile. To his delight, she left her hand in his.

"How did you and Duncan meet?"

Her reaction to his innocent question startled him. She stilled, her body suddenly as rigid as concrete. Her hand slipped from his and rested, trembling, on Mac's back. The ebony cat seemed to sense the change in the atmosphere between them. He lifted his head and focused his golden gaze on Dune.

Confused, Dune could only stare up at her as she rose unsteadily from the chair and set Mac on the porch. Avoiding his eyes, she murmured something about being tired and was gone before he could speak. He listened to her footsteps climb the stairs and knew he wouldn't see her again that evening.

Dune lifted the cat to his lap.

"What was that all about, Mac? Why did such a simple question drive her away? I don't get it."

The cat didn't enlighten him. Dune sighed and began to stroke the silky animal. The mystery deepens, he mused. He still knew nothing about Molly herself; where she came from, what her life was like before she met Duncan, why she seemed so familiar—and why she used such odd phraseology—Duncan 'took her in' and 'gave her a home'. Strange.

Very strange.

By the time he headed for his own bed in the pantry, Dune was more determined than ever to uncover his hostess' story. A light breeze rustled the curtains and carried the tangy scent of the evergreen trees through his window. Mac stretched out on his chest and presented his head for scratching. Hours passed before Dune slept.

Molly watched from behind the curtains of her office window as her house guest criss-crossed the front yard with the lawn mower. Dune had overridden her protest, insisting he needed the exercise. It seemed he knew what was best. His limp had almost disappeared. Surprisingly, his step was almost jaunty. Over the clatter of the mower he whistled the same tune over and over. She smiled as she recognized his slightly off-key rendition of The Yellow Submarine.

Considering the stress he must feel, not knowing who he was, how could he behave with such irrepressible cheerfulness? He must have inherited his good nature from both sides of his family. *His family*. Molly's smile faded.

Somewhere, people must be searching for him—parents, a wife, friends, co-workers. She knew without a doubt that there were people who must be worried sick over his disappearance, people who loved him.

With one exception. One person wanted him dead. Or had the shooting been an accident? Maybe Dune had been an innocent bystander, in the wrong place at the wrong time. Until he remembered exactly what happened, he could still be in danger.

Molly dropped the curtain and retreated to her desk. She fed another sheet into the typewriter, determined to clear her mind of everything but the review that had to be in the mail the next day. The small income from her reviews supplemented the meager cash legacy from Duncan. Those earnings, plus the savings accrued by the cultivation of a large vegetable garden, enabled her to live comfortably—though in a style quite unlike the luxury she had once known—and didn't miss.

An hour later, satisfied with her work, she folded the review, put it into the already addressed and stamped envelope, and carried it down to the small table in the hall. Later, she would walk down the lane to the mailbox and leave it for tomorrow's pickup.

She reached the kitchen doorway just as Dune flung

open the door to the back porch. He had removed his shirt, and the sight of his broad shoulders, his skin glowing with sweat, stopped her cold. Droplets of perspiration trickled down through the dark curls that matted his magnificent chest and narrowed into a vee to disappear beneath his trousers. A bolt of heat stabbed her belly and radiated outward to scorch every inch of skin on her body. Her heart stopped then leaped into double-time, even as her lungs constricted in her chest. Damn! She didn't want this.

Gratefully, she realized that Dune hadn't seen her, his eyes having not yet adjusted to the relative dimness of the house after the bright sunlight outside. She eased back silently, willing her traitorous body to calm. As she watched, Dune swiveled to his left and reached for the tap. The rush of cold well water drummed loudly in the metal sink. Dune cupped his hands under the spray and splashed his chest and underarms. Then he leaned forward to thrust his head directly under the gushing water. The movement tightened his trousers over rounded muscular buttocks.

Molly sucked in a deep breath and forced herself to turn away. It made no sense to torture herself with tantalizing images. Dune's leg was healing rapidly. She knew in her heart he would leave, whether or not his memory returned—and she would be alone again. Which was exactly what she wanted, she assured herself.

"There you are, Miss Molly. Come for a walk with me."

Gulping back the fear that Dune had seen something of her reaction to his near-nakedness, Molly slowly pivoted to face him. Her knees softened in relief when he threw her a bright, open smile. He hadn't seen.

"A walk?" Molly cleared her throat. "Don't you think you've punished your leg enough for one day?"

"My leg is fine," he declared confidently. "Exercise is just what it needs. Come on, sweetheart. You haven't been out in the fresh air all day. Walk with me in the woods."

Molly couldn't resist the appeal in his voice.

"All right, but put your shirt on first." At his suddenly intense look she turned her head away and tried to stem the hot blush rising from her shoulders to her face. "I . . . the branches will scratch you to pieces."

When he didn't answer, she glanced at him from the corner of her eye and watched him shrug into his shirt. Nothing in his face indicated he had noticed her agitation. She swung past him and stepped through the door to the porch, every inch of her body aware of him at her back. Maybe it would be best, after all, if he left soon. The strain of her ever-growing sensual attraction to him was undermining her sanity as well as her celebrated poise.

Dune tucked her arm through his as they strolled across the yard to the tree line. Molly would have tugged her arm free to walk single file, but Dune pressed her closer to his body and swept branches out of their way with his free arm. Molly walked stiffly, trying futilely to keep a little space between them. She finally gave up and relaxed against him, perversely regretting and enjoying the brush of their hips and thighs and the warmth of his shoulder against hers. When had she become a masochist?

Sunshine, hot but not oppressive, warmed their faces. Her shoulder length, black hair bounced lightly in the ponytail she usually wore. The style did little for her, but she had decided that an attractive hairdo and makeup might give Dune the wrong idea and embarrass them both.

Annoyed with her thoughts, she mentally shook herself. Dune gave no indication her nearness disturbed him. The attraction was obviously one-sided and she would do well to remember that. If he felt any affection for her, it was due to gratitude.

"Look," Dune whispered. They stopped and stood still, watching in delight as three chipmunks enjoyed a noisy game of tag among the trees.

A harsh caw lifted their faces to the sky. Above them,

Time Lapse

a huge crow circled and squawked his displeasure at their presence. Dune laughed and imitated the bird's call. The crow flew off, telegraphing its indignation in every line of its feathered body.

Molly felt a surge of pleasure, a feeling of rightness with the company and the place. If only time would stop right here and now, she would be content to remain on this spot—with Dune.

Through the trees, she caught a glimpse of the vast rock that had been left behind and scoured almost flat eons before, when the ice had retreated north. Like the giant icebergs, the greater part of the rock was invisible beneath the earth and impossible to remove. Duncan had told her of the many times he and Grace and their son had picnicked on the rock face.

Something moved on the rock. Molly pulled Dune back when he would have stepped out into the clearing.

"Shhh," she hissed. "Don't move."

Dune threw her a quizzical look. Slowly, Molly reached out and carefully swept back a large branch, revealing the animal lolling on the rock in the sunshine. Dune inhaled sharply. His face split into an appreciative grin at the sight of the black and white spill of fur.

"A skunk!" He swallowed a laugh and pulled Molly closer to his side. "Sammy and Susie should see this!"

Delighted by his pleasure, Molly smiled up at him. Then the sense of what he'd said burst into her mind like a rocket.

"Who?" A froggy croak escaped her tight throat.

Dune peered at the skunk, a grin hovering on his lips. "Sammy and Susie. They're my sister's twins. They'd really get a kick—" Dune's body locked, nearly crushing Molly's arm. Open-mouthed, he looked down into her wide-eyed face. His throat worked uselessly for a moment, then he continued, his voice growing in volume and speed until he was almost shouting.

"My sister Gwen. Married to Don Adams. An insurance

salesman. They live near my parents. Beth and Michael Anderson. And—my name is Jake Anderson." He lifted one arm and roared at the sky. "You hear that, world? I remember! Jacob Michael Anderson, that's me!"

He stilled suddenly and looked down at the woman locked against his side. His triumphant grin faded. A light suddenly blazed hot and hard in his eyes. Then he lowered his head and before Molly realized his intention, his arms crushed her to his chest and his mouth descended to hers.

Surprise evaporated in the heat of her instant response. Her mouth opened under his. A low growl rumbled in his throat as his tongue plunged inside. Molly felt her breasts swell against his hard chest. An ache started low in her stomach. Her arms crept up to circle his neck. Her fingers caressed the silky curls at the nape of his neck. His earthy, male scent intoxicated her senses and set her heart pounding relentlessly in her chest. She felt her knees weaken and pressed closer to his large body. When his large hands smoothed down her sides and cupped her to his lower body, she gasped and moaned her pleasure at the feel of the hard column of flesh pressing against her stomach.

The sound penetrated the haze of desire that cocooned her. Aghast at her uninhibited reaction, Molly wrenched her mouth from his and dropped her head against his chest. Two sets of lungs, starved for oxygen, gulped noisy draughts of air. Trembling violently, her legs ignored her mind's order to move away. Against her cheek, Dune's heart pulsed in double time. Shudders ran the length of his body, revealing the desire that matched her own. What had she done?

Finally her heartbeat slowed to match the lingering throbbing in her abdomen. Her hands slid to his shoulders to push herself away. There was a moment's hesitation, then Dune dropped his arms. She heard his rough, indrawn breath and despised herself for reacting so wantonly to what he surely meant to be a simple, celebratory kiss. She opened her eyes and turned to stone.

"Are you okay?" A thread of anxiety edged Dune's ragged voice.

"Dune—Jake—we've got trouble." Molly hiccuped as hysteria bubbled up in her throat. "Look over your left shoulder. *Slowly.*"

His gasp told her he had spotted the skunk. Five feet away the animal stood watching them, his gleaming black eyes curious and a little wary. As if undecided whether or not the intruders needed his special brand of discouragement, his upright tail swayed in white-striped warning.

The two humans didn't move, didn't twitch, didn't breathe. Finally, the skunk lost interest. He dropped his tail, turned around and waddled in royal unconcern back to his rocky throne.

Molly turned her head and met Jake's gaze. Their grins flowered at the same moment. He grabbed her hand and plunged ahead to sweep the branches from their path. Whooping with laughter they retraced their steps, blundering and stumbling through the trees.

When they broke through to the back lawn they stopped to catch their breath. Molly wiped tears of laughter from her cheeks and turned to Jake. The expression in his dark eyes caught at her throat.

Warmth, admiration, wanting shone from his eyes. She wondered if he knew what his gaze revealed. She wondered if her own feelings were as visible to him.

Her hand slipped easily from his. "I'll put on the kettle." It was all she could think to say, an excuse to put some distance between them. She needed to escape the powerful pull he seemed able to exert without effort, or she would embarrass them both by flinging herself into his arms—because now that his memory had returned, Jake would be leaving. It was for the best.

Wasn't it?

Molly crossed the yard to the house without looking

back. As she filled the kettle at the tap, she watched him through the kitchen window. He moved slowly toward the house, as if deep in thought and unaware of his surroundings. His face was closed. She felt certain he'd forgotten their kiss. Was he remembering a wife?

When she joined him on the porch, his long legs were stretched before him, his chin resting on his chest. About to retreat into the house, she halted when he stirred and looked up. His face was unreadable.

She hesitated then offered him a mug. Taking it with a smile of thanks, he patted the empty chair beside him. Loath to break the silence, though she was fairly bursting with questions, Molly sat down and prepared to wait. It was silly, but somehow Jake suddenly seemed a stranger she had just met, not the same man who had shared her home for the last week. She knew a little about Dune. She didn't know Jake Anderson at all.

His first words were the last she would have expected.

"Molly, would you mind very much if I stayed a few days longer?"

"Not at all." Her spirits soared. He didn't want to leave. Was it because of her?

"It's just that there's something I have to work out. And there may be some information I need . . . " He stared toward the trees and fell silent.

Molly's heart sank. His wanting to stay had nothing to do with her. She struggled to keep her voice steady.

"You haven't remembered everything?"

"Almost everything. I'm thirty-four, single, though just barely, and I'm a reporter for The Ottawa Chronicle."

Unable to stop herself, Molly interrupted.

"Just barely single? You're engaged?"

"No. My divorce came through six months ago. My fault. Sherri was too young. I think I knew that from the beginning, but I was bowled over by her looks and she thought my job was glamorous. She changed her mind when she discovered the weird hours I keep, chasing stories."

He cocked one eyebrow. "Her idea of married life consisted of parties, social events, a husband who's home every night at five. I don't blame her. For a man in my line of work, marriage isn't a viable option. I seldom have time for even casual relationships."

Jake sighed and crossed his feet at the ankles.

"We might have made it work but one day I found her birth control pills on the dresser." He grimaced. "She knew I wanted children., but it turned out she had no intention of spoiling her figure. We parted fairly amicably and she went on to a modeling career."

When he finally raised his face, Molly was relieved to see neither hurt nor bitterness in his eyes. "You may know of her." The indulgent tone in his voice might have been for a precocious child. "She calls herself Sherri-Lee. About two years ago she graduated from the covers of Sassy and Teen Life to Vogue and Cosmopolitan. Not bad for a hometown girl."

Molly nodded. The image of a blonde, blue-eyed Bardot look-alike floated into her mind. The girl's pouty face combined innocence and sexuality in a potent mix.

The young model had auditioned for the role of Dr. Whitfield's unsuspected illegitimate daughter, come to town to blackmail the father she believed abandoned her pregnant mother years before. The perfect face for the role, but to the director's disappointment she hadn't an ounce of acting ability in her perfect body. To think they might have worked on the same set . . . . .

Sherri-Lee! But that meant that Jake . . . . The mug of coffee fell into her lap from her suddenly nerveless fingers.

Dazed, she came back to her surroundings when Jake's frantic voice pierced the roaring in her head. Her head bobbled loosely on her neck as he shook her roughly by the shoulders.

"Molly! What is it? Speak to me. Molly!"

She grabbed his forearms.

"Stop. I'm all right. The coffee was only lukewarm." She looked into his anxious eyes then down to her dripping lap.

"Are you sure?" At her nod, Jake withdrew his hands and straightened. "I'll make more coffee while you change. Or maybe you should lie down for awhile."

Molly seized the chance to escape to the privacy of her room. She needed time to think. How was she going to tell him? "I think I *will* lie down."

Refusing his help, she climbed the stairs and closed the bedroom door behind her. Her wet clothes fell in a heap at her feet. She kicked them into a corner and collapsed full-length on the bed. Only then did she allow herself to consider the revelation that had literally knocked her for a loop.

No matter how she looked at the facts, there was only one plausible conclusion. The coincidence was astounding, but then, if the impossible could happen once, why not twice? The difference was that she had been aware, not knocked witless by a blow to the head. Even so, it had taken several days and Duncan's kind support, before belief, and then acceptance, had sunk into her bones.

She hadn't minded, not really. She'd just run further than she'd imagined possible. So much misery had happened in that last year, she'd been desperate to get away.

But Jake would be appalled when he realized how far he was from his home. Should she tell him today? No, coming on top of the return of his memory, it would be too much. Tomorrow would be soon enough.

What would he do if it proved impossible to go back? He was smart, experienced. She had no doubt he could find a job. Either way, she'd be alone again.

She wouldn't cry. She *wouldn't*. Emotionally exhausted, Molly pulled the spread up to her chin and escaped into sleep.

* * *

Jake glanced at the clock and wondered if he should wake Molly. She'd had nothing but juice and coffee for breakfast. If she didn't eat soon she might get sick.

Making up his mind, he pulled bacon from the refrigerator and set it cooking in the frying pan. Then he climbed the stairs and knocked on Molly's door. When she mumbled something he couldn't catch, he opened the door and stuck his head inside the room.

"Rise and shine, pretty lady. Lunch will be served in ten minutes. Or would you rather I brought it up here?"

When Molly rolled over to face the door, Jake gulped. The creamy white skin of one shoulder showed above the spread. Her face was soft from sleep, framed by glossy black hair spread in disarray over her pillow. The line of her hip jutting beneath the coverlet brought his every male cell to instant awareness. His fingers curled tighter around the doorknob as his pulse began to race. This was a mistake.

"What?" Sleep made her voice a husky whisper that sent shivers of desire down his spine.

"Lunch. Ten minutes. Downstairs." He pulled the door closed then opened it a crack. "You awake?"

"Mmmm? Yes. I'll be right there."

One hand sliding against the wall for support, Jake lurched clumsily down the stairs. What would it be like to wake up beside Molly Barnes every morning? Better yet, what would it be like to lie down beside her each night?

Shaking his head in a futile attempt to dispel the image his mind had conjured, Jake quickly cracked four eggs into the pan, shoved bread into the toaster, and set the table. When Molly entered the room he wore a wide smile and a dishtowel hanging from his belt to hide his throbbing arousal. He bowed and gestured at the table.

"Please be seated, fair lady, your lunch is ready."

He pulled out her chair then captured her hand and brought it briefly to his lips. Whirling around, he grabbed a plate from the counter and deposited it with a flourish before her. "*Regardez!* Ze food, it is served!" A moment later he sat down with his own meal.

Molly laughed, inhaled deeply, and admitted she was starved. Mac came running from the front parlor, leaped to the empty chair, sat on his haunches, and placed his front paws on the table. The humans took turns feeding him bits of bacon.

When their plates were empty, Jake remained seated at Molly's insistence. He watched as she cleared away the dishes and made coffee.

He lifted his mug in salute when Molly thanked him for preparing lunch. Then he braced both elbows on the table.

"Were you able to figure everything out?" she asked.

"Not everything. At least I know now that I'm not a criminal. The last thing I remember is getting a call from J.J."

"J.J.?"

Jake nodded. "He's unemployed, by choice. One of the invisible people. It's amazing how much information he picks up. We have an arrangement. When he hears anything on the street that might interest me, he passes it on. I pay him, of course. It works well for both of us."

Molly nodded in understanding.

"Anyway," Jake picked up his story. "That evening J.J. called me at work and said to get down to the old warehouse on Brewer Lane, a few blocks from my home. He'd heard that something was going down. I did. And the next thing I remember is waking up here with a hole in my leg. And in my memory."

Molly frowned. "So you don't know who shot you. Or why."

"That's it. And I can't figure out how I got out here in the country. It doesn't make sense."

Frustrated and angry because of it, Jake ran his fingers through his already disheveled hair. He looked up and caught Molly's guarded expression. A jolt of apprehension lifted his chin.

"You know something, don't you? What is it?"

Sympathy, indecision, regret, and finally resignation passed swiftly over her face. She nodded slowly and began to nibble at her lower lip. Then she straightened and met his eyes.

"How long have you worked at The Chronicle?"

Jake's jaw dropped. "Eleven years. What's that got to do with anything?"

"Please Jake, let me do this my own way."

The pleading in her eyes melted his impatience. "Okay, sure."

Molly took a deep breath. "Who's your boss and how long has he been at The Chronicle?"

Baffled by the unlikely questions, Jake bit back an oath. What in the world was she getting at? He would never have expected this kind of run-around from her.

"I report directly to Reg Colfax. He joined the paper as senior editor, oh, about seven years ago. Before that, he worked for the Edmonton Chronicle."

"Call him," Molly whispered.

"How do you know I didn't call while you were sleeping?"

"I know." Molly wrapped both her hands around his. "Please, Jake. If I simply tell you what I know, you'll think I'm crazy. Call Reg Colfax first. Then I have some things to show you."

"He'll want to know what's been happening and I won't be able to tell him."

"No, he won't. Please, trust me. Call him."

From nowhere, dread crept stealthily down his spine. Trust her? He did—but he had the feeling he should hold on tight to something solid. Something solid, heavy and immovable.

"Right," he said gruffly.

He reached for the old-fashioned wall phone. Molly got up and left the room. Jake dialed the familiar number and waited. And waited. He'd probably caught his boss with a mouthful of donut. Reg usually snatched up the phone before the first ring died away.

When Molly returned with a handful of papers, the receiver was dangling on the end of its cord and Jake was standing at the window, his hands closed whitely on the edge of the sink. A fine tremor shivered down his length. The wall clock ticked loudly in the silent room.

She set the papers on the table and hung up the phone. Then she walked up behind Jake and wrapped her arms tightly around his chest. A deep shudder passed through him. He turned around and gathered her close, burying his face in her hair.

Finally he spoke past her ear, more to himself than to her.

"The Ottawa Chronicle has never heard of Reg Colfax. Or of me. Am I crazy? That blow to my head—"

"No. You're not crazy. You're not."

"But . . . where's Reg?"

Molly took a deep breath. "I would guess he's still in Edmonton. He hasn't gone—come—moved—to Ottawa yet."

At her words, the chaos in his mind shifted and cleared, like clouds parting in fast forward, revealing the blue truth that had been there all along. He drew back his head and gaped at her, disbelief churning in his stomach.

"My God. Are you saying I'm . . . in the past?"

Chapter Four

"Yes," she said simply.

"Come on, Molly. You know that's not possible." When she didn't answer, he dropped his arms to his sides and stepped back until the counter blocked his retreat. "This is a joke, right?"

"No joke. I wouldn't do that to you." Knowing exactly the kind of intellectual and emotional turmoil he was experiencing, Molly's heart ached for him. She reached for his hand and drew him, unprotesting, back to the table.

He thudded into the chair, as if his legs had buckled. Silently, Molly pushed the clearly dated evidence in front of him; the envelopes carrying twelve cent stamps, the newspaper dated that day, her marriage certificate, a copy of Duncan's death certificate and the newest edition of the Ottawa phone book. Evidence that proved he had traveled twenty years into the past.

She left him alone in the room. His head was bent over the opened phone book when she returned. He looked up and Molly saw his disbelief had been displaced by reluctant acceptance and a kind of excitement.

"My parents are listed here." His voice shook. "The

address printed here is for the house where we lived when Gwen and I were children."

His eyes lost focus. He pinched the bridge of his nose and spoke in a bemused tone. "There was a huge maple tree in the back yard. Dad and I spent hours building a tree house with walls and a roof and a rope ladder hanging to the ground. When I wanted to be alone, I pulled the ladder up after me. You know, I haven't thought of that tree house in years." Wonder and helpless amazement echoed in his voice.

Molly wet the dishcloth and began to wipe the already-clean counters. She didn't speak. Jake had to think and feel this through for himself.

When his chair scraped back and bumped the wall she didn't turn around. With her body so attuned to his every move, she didn't need to see him rise and walk to the back door. She sensed rather than heard his halting gait. The limp, lately discernible only by the tired end of the day, had returned, as if his feet moved in step with his disjointed thoughts.

He spread his palms against the door frame. "Tom's Woods. It is, isn't it?" He didn't wait for an answer. "No wonder I sensed something wrong about them. Déjà vu with a twist." He paused. "I've actually traveled back in time. That's . . . incredible!"

He looked over his shoulder and stared at Molly, as if even now he expected her to grin and cry 'Gotcha!' Then his eyes narrowed.

"You knew I was from the future, didn't you? For God's sakes, why didn't you tell me?"

Molly drew a deep breath. "Would you have believed me? You would have thought that my husband's death and the solitude had driven me over the edge. Besides," she murmured, "until now you've had enough to cope with, not knowing who you were."

"But how did you know?" he persisted. "It's not as though one meets a time traveler every day."

"I didn't know at first. The book....But even then, I wasn't really sure until you told me about Sherri. She'd be only a toddler right now."

He ignored the reference to his ex-wife. "What book?"

Molly explained that the book he'd read years before was, in fact, just now being published. "It's not in the bookstores yet. I was writing a review based on an advance, pre-publication edition. The only way you could have read it before—"

"—was if I read it in the future," he finished. Raking long fingers through his hair, he sucked in a deep breath then exhaled noisily. Finally, he pushed open the door and stepped out on the porch.

Molly watched through the window as Mac leaped the three steps and rubbed himself against Jake's ankles. Jake looked down. Then he picked up the cat and lifted it to his shoulder.

Mac seemed startled, but soon decided he liked the view from his new perspective. He draped the front half of his body over Jake's shoulder and peered around alertly. Man and cat began a slow trudge around the yard.

Molly watched until she remembered that the crucial question had yet to be asked. Hoping that her house guest would leave the topic alone, for a few hours at least, she dug in the closet for the vacuum cleaner and poured her energies into a thorough cleaning of the ground floor rooms. Jake had to sort out his thoughts. So did she.

As she worked she reviewed the preceding half-hour. Her admiration for Jake Anderson grew. He had been stunned at first, as anyone would be. But few would have accepted the facts, the devastating facts, so quickly and with such an open mind. Most would have retreated into denial, unwilling or unable to accept the obvious conclusion.

Not Jake. He was, she realized, the most intellectually honest person she'd ever met. In a world where people routinely deceived themselves—about the saintliness of their children, the superiority of their chosen brand of car, the rightness of their opinions over all others—Jake stood apart. He was a man who preferred hard truth to soft fiction, a self-disciplined man, a brave man.

A man opposite in every respect to David. Molly shivered with distaste at the thought of her ex-husband. David was a man who believed what he wanted to believe, regardless of any evidence to the contrary. David was an earth-bound gnat and Jake a magnificent, soaring eagle.

The tenor of her thoughts stopped her dead. Dismayed, she inadvertently jerked the cord of the vacuum from the outlet. The sudden silence deafened her to all but the thunder of her heartbeat. Her knees wobbled as she sank into a chair and covered her face with her hands.

Was she falling in love with Jake Anderson? No, it couldn't be, it mustn't be. She was *not* that stupid. It was only the solitude and her body's awakening hunger. The body, after all, was a mindless thing, an entity composed of flesh and bone, a being ruled by needs with no thought of consequences. But *she* was in charge. She had only to remember that Jake believed marriage and his job were incompatible. Besides, she could leash her emotional as well as her physical longings.

She could. She would. She must.

Doubt niggled at her. She turned her back on it. Doubt grew and sidled round to face her. With a muttered expletive, she mentally thrust it into the dungeon of her mind, slammed the trap door and dumped a ton of rocks on top. *There!* She brushed her palms together, stored the cleaning materials away and sat down at the kitchen table to compile a shopping list.

Worn out from the conflicting emotions, Jake was relieved when Molly called to say supper was ready. He'd walked for hours around the property, talking sporadically to Mac who soon stopped listening and drifted into a contented sleep. He envied the cat its simple, sense-dominated life.

His life as a crime reporter had its share of ups and downs, thrills and disappointments, challenges and drudgery. But never, never had he experienced anything as overwhelming, as intoxicating as the knowledge that he had traveled back in time. It was a high to beat all others.

But neither had he ever felt quite so desperate. Everyone he knew was lost to him. His world had turned upside down and inside out.

But as his raging mind tired, he became conscious of a galling sense of frustration. Some slime had tried to kill him and he could do nothing about it. His would-be killer was safely out of his reach, twenty years in the future.

They ate supper in near silence. Jake had a million questions, but couldn't seem to find the words he needed. He watched Molly. How could she be so impassive in such a situation? A man from the future shared her house and table and she hadn't so much as blinked.

Nor, he suddenly thought, had she asked any questions about the world he'd left. Only the dullest of minds could fail to be curious about the future—and Molly was far from dull.

Perplexed, he forgot the fork hovering in front of his mouth and frowned. His earlier impression came back to him—the lady had a secret. But what could it be? He searched her face and again felt the visceral certainty that he knew her. But he had to be wrong. They belonged to two different times.

Then it hit him. He inhaled sharply. She looked up. Their gazes fused and he knew by the color flooding her face that she read the knowledge in his eyes.

"Molly—"

"Jake—"

Slowly, he lowered his fork to the plate. "You, too?"

Reluctantly, she nodded and pushed her half-eaten meal away. "Two years ago. I've been here ever since." She swallowed. "That's why it was easy for me to figure out what had happened to you. I've had plenty of time to get comfortable with the idea of time travel."

"Yeah, I can see that." He leaned back in the chair and folded his arms over his chest. "To quote the inestimable Lewis Carroll, *'The time has come, the walrus said, to speak of many things'*." He paused. "Tell me how you got here."

His brows rose in surprise when Molly paled and responded instantly, "That sounds like an order."

Stunned by her hostile tone, Jake gaped at her. Before he could gather his wits together, Molly looked away, two bright spots of color illuminating her cheeks. "I'm sorry."

She looked so vulnerable, Jake fought the urge to take her in his arms and comfort her. He hadn't meant to hurt her. But her reaction told him he'd struck a nerve. Who had been giving her orders? Not Duncan, he was certain. Brad Baylor? No, she handled the policeman with ease.

He waited. Molly would explain in her own good time. He tamped down the anxiety churning in his gut and began to clear the table. By the time he'd poured them each a cup of coffee, Molly had recovered her composure. Her first words told him she wasn't going to explain her reaction.

"I don't know how either of us got here. But I think we arrived via the same route." Her voice was casual, almost complacent, as if she were describing a Sunday afternoon outing. "I was just walking in Tom's Woods. When I came to Skunk Rock," her lips lifted at the corners, "I thought I'd sit for a bit. Between one step and the next, everything changed. The traffic sounds disappeared, the voices of other walkers just ceased, even the air seemed to change. A green circle, like a doorway, opened up in front of me. I couldn't avoid it."

"You must have been terrified."

"No, not that I recall. I had too much on my mind to be upset by shrinking trees." Her face lighted mischievously. "Like Alice, I just thought 'curiouser and curiouser.' I didn't feel much of anything, actually. Unlike you, I wasn't hurt when I came through. I knew who I was and where I was. So," she shrugged, "I just walked out of the woods and found Duncan. You know the rest."

"But when you realized you were in the past, what did... how did you...?" Jake threw his arms out helplessly.

"You mean, how did I feel about it?" At Jake's nod, Molly said, "Flabbergasted. Awed. Bewildered. Relieved. A little nervous. About what you'd expect."

"Relieved?" Jake seized on the one cryptic word. "An odd reaction, that. Why relieved?"

Molly flushed but hurried past the question. "My purse was left behind. I had no money, no identification. Duncan gave me sanctuary. We married. And here I am." She stopped speaking abruptly and gazed down at her cup.

Jake's eyes narrowed. His reporter's instinct told him there was much more to the story than she was willing to share. Why did she use a word like sanctuary? It almost seemed as if she had been running away when she ended up here. And where better to hide than in the past?

Inside, he smiled. It seemed the enigma named Molly Barnes was even more complicated than he first assumed. His pulse quickened. Puzzles, mysteries, conspiracies—they were his business. The unwelcome thought that Molly might resent his invasion of her privacy made him pause only briefly. He had no choice. She was a challenge his investigative mind couldn't ignore. He didn't admit the possibility of another, more personal reason for discovering all he could about her.

Feeling more buoyant than he had since the incredible revelation, Jake returned to his meal and polished off the cold food with relish. He was pleased to see Molly gradually relax. Tomorrow, when her guard was down, he would return to the subject.

That night he lay on his back, his fingers threaded together on his chest. He listened to the rustle and scratching of Tom's trees, their branches scrabbling in the midnight breeze. He smelled the clean country air and felt regret for the day the city would extend its boundaries to enclose the small woods. And he tasted again the sweet potency of Molly's lips. Sleep finally came with the sunrise.

Molly awoke to the jangle of the phone. A quick glance at the clock showed she'd overslept. Grabbing for the dressing gown at the foot of her bed, she hurried out of the room, hoping the intrusive ringing wouldn't waken Jake. She doubted he'd slept much the night before.

Breathless from her headlong flight down the stairs, she snatched up the receiver.

"Hello. Molly Barnes here."

"Molly, it's Karen McLeod. You know what happened to the Stewart family, don't you?" Typically, Karen didn't wait for an answer. "Smithson's Trailer Travels have donated a mobile home for their use until the house can be repaired. A number of the neighborhood men are working today to hitch up water and power supplies to the trailer and to sift through the ruins for salvageable items."

"That's very kind of them," was all Molly had time to say before Karen plowed on.

"The thing is, I heard about your house guest and I wondered if he'd be willing to lend a hand. I know this is cheeky of me—after all, why should he care about strangers—but every bit of help would be appreciated. Poor Alice is devastated. What do you think?"

"I'll certainly mention it to him. I can't speak for him—wait a minute, he's just come in." She put her hand over the receiver and quickly explained the nature of the call. Jake's ready agreement didn't surprise her. "Yes, he'd be happy to help. We'll be there in half an hour. Wait, I just thought—I suppose they lost their clothes in the fire. I'll bring Duncan's things. They should fit George fairly well." She paused when Karen interrupted. "No, I want to. And I'm sure Duncan would be pleased. I'll pack them up right now. We'll be there as soon as possible. Yes, bye."

She hung up and smiled at Jake, then lifted a cautionary finger.

"As chief of medical matters in this house, I must insist you take extra care not to further damage your leg. Don't take any foolish risks."

Jake clicked his heels and bowed. "I hear and obey, Florence. I promise I'll be the perfect wuss."

Molly grinned at the thought of this huge, muscled man pretending to be a wimp. Even with the talent of a Lawrence Olivier, Jake could never carry off such a role. He was just too masculine, too . . . . She cut off the thought. "We'd better think up a story to explain your limp, in case someone notices. Let's say—"

"—I was so stunned by your beauty I fell off the porch and banged my knee," Jake offered, casting a soulful look to the ceiling.

Molly blushed. "Sure you did," she intoned dryly. "Let's get real here. You tripped over Mac and fell off the porch. Agreed?" Did Jake *really* think she was beautiful?

"Okay, okay." He shook his head in mock sorrow. "Though I never would have guessed you were the kind to blame an innocent animal. Tsk, tsk."

Laughing at his foolishness and hoping he hadn't noticed her pink cheeks, Molly shooed him toward the kitchen.

"For that, you get to make breakfast while I dress and pack up Duncan's things. We'd better eat a big meal. It's going to be a long day."

Chuckling, Jake headed for the kitchen. As she turned to the stairs she heard him say something that sounded like 'me and my big mouth'.

As she dressed in jeans and a cotton shirt, Molly blessed the rural grapevine that had led to Karen's call. She felt sorry for the Stewarts but their predicament insured that, for today at least, Jake would have no chance to quiz her about her former life. Hopefully, he would be too tired by evening for serious conversation.

He would worm the miserable tale from her eventually, of course. She felt certain that Jake the reporter rarely failed to get any story he went after. That didn't bother her. What did was the idea that Jake the man would know how big a mistake she'd made. It hurt to think of his inevitable scorn for her poor judgment. There was no use telling herself that his opinion didn't matter. It mattered more than she cared to admit.

Throwing off her momentary dejection, she pulled her hair back and secured it with a ribbon at her neck, then went into Duncan's room and began to empty the drawers and closets.

"Out, out, out, ladies. Break time."

Molly continued to scrub at the blackened pot until Angie Wilkens elbowed her and giggled. She looked over her shoulder and grinned at the blocky, black-streaked figure standing in the door of the trailer.

"It's the bogeywoman," she stage-whispered to the young woman sharing the double sink. "Ignore her and maybe she'll go away."

"I heard that, Molly Barnes. Talk about stones and glass houses. Have you looked in a mirror lately?" The speaker cocked her head on one side and propped a grimy fist on her ample hip. Marge Thomas had volunteered to work with the men in the ruined interior of the gutted house. Marge was big, strong, and unembarrassed by the frame that nature and a lifetime of heavy farm work had fashioned. Now she beckoned imperiously to the two women elbow-deep in ash-black suds.

"Nora and Alice have lunch all set out. You wanna eat, you'd better come now. There's a bunch of hungry men gettin' ready to chow down. Not to mention me." She turned to leave then swiveled back, her generous bust just clearing the doorframe.

"Say Molly, where'd you find that man of yours? Now there's a body made for a woman like me." She turned away with a wide smile of appreciation. "As my momma used to say—Mmm, mmm, good!" Laughing good-naturedly, she descended the step and disappeared in the direction of the picnic table.

"Let's go," Angie said, "or there won't be a bite left. Nora brought her peach pie. If I don't get a piece of that, I'll die."

The two women dabbed at each other's smudged faces, then discarded their aprons and joined the line-up for the luncheon supplied by the neighborhood wives. Embarrassed that she hadn't thought to bring any food, Molly had worked unceasingly all morning and was more than ready for a break.

She filled her plate and joined two women sitting in the circle of lawn chairs donated for the day by the Home and Garden Emporium. They exchanged brief greetings, more interested in eating than talking.

The circle soon filled up with sweat-streaked men in ash-coated coveralls and women only slightly less blackened. Some were strangers. Others Molly had met when Duncan was alive. She marveled at their generous donation of time and labor to a distressed neighbor, particularly since this was a busy season for farmers.

The farmers' ranks were augmented by others, she noticed for the first time. A dry-cleaner's van, a tow truck and a Department of Roads and Highways pickup lined the driveway, as well as Doc Harrison's battered old jeep and Tory Smithson's motorbike. The Stewart family had been in the area for generations and was well-liked. Molly felt a warm glow of contentment to be part of a community that looked after its own. She would miss them when she left.

The thought brought her up short. Sometime within

the last week and almost without her notice, she had decided to leave. Back to her own time if possible, otherwise far away from here. Perhaps the west coast would be a good place to begin again.

A burst of male laughter caught her attention. She looked up and saw Jake and several hugely grinning men heaping their plates with an astonishing amount of food. Two of the men slapped the newcomer on the back in friendly camaraderie. Molly shook her head. It had taken only one morning for her unknown house guest to be accepted by his fellow laborers. As she watched the noisy male interaction, she realized that Jake seemed energized by the company. He called every man by name and had something to say to each. Even Sam Benoit, the local doomsayer, was smiling.

Jake was a hit, and not only with the men. The women, young and old, seemed captivated by the laughing giant in their midst. Many a sidelong glance was thrown his way. A few, like Marge, were openly admiring. Molly couldn't blame them. She was having difficulty herself, trying not to stare. Jake's shirt was open. The grime smearing his chest did nothing to hide his awesome muscular torso. Against her will, her skin began to tingle. The awestruck voice at her ear made her start.

"Wow, that one's sure a keeper."

Molly looked around. Sophie Baylor leaned over her shoulder, her cornflower blue eyes riveted on Jake. Sophie was young but very pretty, with the same type of looks as Sherrie-Lee. Molly felt a stab of alarm.

"Brad told me about him being at your place, but he sure didn't say he was such a hunk. You know any more like that?"

Molly shook her head and summoned a smile. Would Jake be interested in Sophie? Or had his taste in women changed since he'd divorced his wife?

Without taking her eyes off Jake, Sophie wheedled, "How 'bout I take Jake and you can have Brad? My brother's crazy about you, you know. I'll even throw in half ownership of my ceramic business."

Molly forced a laugh. "No deal. Find your own."

Sophie heaved a gusty sigh. "Oh well, he's too old for me anyway." Then she winked. "How's that for sour grapes?" Laughing, she wandered away.

When Molly turned back she saw Jake heading in her direction. The woman seated beside her nudged her shoulder, grinned in approval and vacated her seat. Jake dropped down beside her.

"What a mess," he commented, gesturing at the damaged house. "Still, quite a bit is salvageable, with some work and elbow grease. Needs a new roof and some window glass, but most of the load-bearing walls seem to have survived. Hope they had insurance. One of the men said George has an appointment with Jason McBride tomorrow. He's the local banker."

Before Molly could reply, she heard her name called and looked over her shoulder. Brad, wearing oversized dungarees, was striding toward her, a delighted smile on his face. A short, paunchy man followed.

Brad's step faltered when he noticed Jake. His smile turned plastic. He nodded at Molly but directed his words to Jake. "Didn't expect to see you here."

"Why not? Extra hands make light work." Jake's voice was friendly but cool. "Who's your friend?"

Brad introduced Harvey Streeter, the area's chief of police. Jake stood and shook the offered hand. Streeter's eyes widened in disbelief and his other hand rose to brush his head, as if he realized the much taller man must have a perfect view of his bald spot.

Molly nibbled at her lunch as the three men discussed the lightning strike and subsequent fire, the state of the economy and the likelihood of the Toronto Blue Jays making the play-offs. A part of her wondered about the tension she sensed in Jake, though his posture and manner were deceptively casual.

Finally, the two officers wandered over to the picnic table. She noticed several women lift their eyebrows and exchange rueful grimaces. After a puzzled moment she caught on. Brad was dressed for work like the other men, but Harvey Streeter wore his uniform. Obviously, the police chief wasn't here to help. She guessed it wasn't the first time he'd cadged a meal he hadn't earned.

A few minutes later the group dispersed to continue their work. Molly helped Nora pack up the leftover food and store it in the trailer for the Stewarts. Shooing Nora back to the women who were hand-washing salvaged curtains and bedclothes in old-fashioned galvanized tubs, she carried the lunch dishes into the trailer and began to wash them.

To her surprise, Marge Thomas appeared in the doorway. The woman's sun-roughened face was somber and a little worried. She glanced quickly over her shoulder then moved inside. "You got a minute?"

"Sure, Marge. What is it?"

"Well . . . " The heavyset woman seemed at a loss for words. Then she spoke in a rush. "Guess first I should tell you that Brad and Sophie are my cousins. Their father, Doug Baylor, was my uncle, my mother's youngest brother. Doug's wife died giving birth to Sophie, so I was kinda big sister to them when they were kids. We were always close. Still are."

She rubbed the back of her hand across her mouth and leaned against the counter. "The thing is, when I was working in the house earlier, I overheard Jake asking questions about Doug. He talked to more than one."

Molly nodded but said nothing. What was Jake up to?

"Now, if he'd been askin' about Brad, I could understand it." She gave Molly a knowing look. "Sussin' out a possible rival, you know?" Molly felt hot color rise to her face.

"But he wanted to know about Doug and how he died. Everyone around here figures he accidentally shot himself cleaning his gun. A terrible accident." She drew a deep breath. "But I don't believe that, and I don't think Brad does either."

"What do you think happened?" Molly remembered Jake's vague notion that the man had taken his own life.

"I don't know." Marge's expression was troubled. "I think Brad suspects suicide, though he's never said it outright. But he's changed in the three months since it happened. Shrunk somehow. As for me, all I know is that Uncle Doug grew up with guns. He respected them. He was never, *never* careless with them. I just can't accept the idea that...."

"Accidents do happen, Marge," Molly said softly.

"Yeah, I know. But not to Doug. Some other kind of accident maybe, but not with a gun. Trouble is, I don't believe he'd commit suicide either. He had no reason. Never showed any of the signs. Even if he wanted to, he'd never do that to Brad, and especially not to Sophie."

"Then that means it was an accident."

"Maybe. Oh, I just don't know," frustration filled Marge's voice. "But what I wanted to say was, I'd like for you to ask Jake not to mention Doug again. I'm afraid Sophie might overhear. She was crazy about her daddy and it'd half kill her to think people were saying he committed suicide. It was bad enough that the casket had to be closed."

"I'll speak to Jake," Molly promised. "But Marge, it must have been an accident. A suicide would have been reported as that."

The older woman shook her head. "It wasn't though. Still, maybe you're right. The cops might have covered it up, to save his kids extra pain. Doug was a topnotch cop and well-liked."

She smiled weakly at Molly, her eyes bright with unshed tears. "Don't mind me. I'm just a fat, middle-aged spinster. What do I know?" She cleared her throat roughly. "Anyway, thanks for listening, Molly. You won't forget to speak to Jake?"

"The first chance I get. I'm sorry for your loss, Marge. I didn't know your uncle well but Duncan thought very highly of him." Impulsively, Molly threw her arms around the anxious woman and gave her a brief hug. She walked her to the door in time to see Harvey Streeter and Brad angling away from the trailer. The two women exchanged glances but neither commented.

By five o'clock many of the farmers had taken their leave. Certain chores couldn't be neglected. Molly and Jake joined the exodus, waved away with the Stewarts' fervent thanks. Too tired for conversation, they drove home in silence, took turns with the shower and met again, comfortable in clean clothes, at the kitchen table.

After a quick supper of soup, salad and sandwiches, they settled on the back porch to watch the sunset. Molly broke into Jake's rambling remarks about the day's labors.

"Why were you asking about Doug Baylor?"

"What?" Jake looked startled. "I don't know." Then he corrected himself. "Yes, I do know. There's something fishy about his death. But how did you know I was—"

"Marge Thomas told me." Molly repeated what she'd learned. "She's still very upset about his death."

Jake rubbed the back of his neck and stretched out his long legs. "Did she say what she thought happened? I mean, if it wasn't an accident and it wasn't suicide, there's only one other possibility."

"Oh!" Molly gulped. "That didn't occur to me." She thought back over her conversation with Marge. "She didn't mention murder." She shuddered. "But what made you curious about it?"

"I'm not sure. But someone said something about him—before I came here—and I just wondered why the event was mentioned, so many years later. I mean, it's not unheard of for a cop to take his own life. And something else happened, something connected to the case or maybe to the family, but I can't remember what it was."

He grinned suddenly. "If I'd known I was going to visit the time of the event I would have taken notes—but of course I didn't. It probably wasn't important anyway."

Tapping his nose with his forefinger, he added, "It's the legendary Anderson schnozzle. Never happy unless it's sniffing around a mystery."

To Molly's amusement and Jake's chagrin, Mac chose that moment to leap up on Jake's lap, lick his nose, then curl up with a loud purr. When the stars made their appearance, the two humans said good-night and went wearily to their beds.

Chapter Five

Jake spent the next three days at the Stewarts' farm, scrubbing down walls and helping to raise a new roof. Molly stripped her kitchen cupboards and linen closet to the bare essentials, keeping just enough for two and offered the rest to Alice. When Jake noticed the packed boxes and the almost empty shelves, he wondered.

But when he overheard her promise to give Duncan's and Tom's beds to the beleaguered Stewarts when repairs to their house were completed, he was certain. Molly was planning to leave. The old farmhouse was beginning to take on the melancholy air of coming abandonment. The thought of her departure bothered him more than he liked.

He kept his thoughts to himself until the evening that marked the two week anniversary of his arrival. After a leisurely meal, they were once again seated on the back porch, talking in a desultory fashion about nothing important while they waited for the nightly celestial display.

Taking advantage of a break in the conversation, Jake inserted quietly, "Where do you plan to go?"

She threw him a swift glance then looked back to the trees. "Back home, I guess, if it's possible. If not, perhaps to the west coast. I'm not sure." Her voice sounded diffident, almost ashamed.

The implication of what she'd said struck Jake like a blow to the heart. He sat up straight and whirled in his chair to face her. For a moment, he was speechless.

"Are you saying . . . it might be possible to go back to our own time?" Hope and disbelief warred in his mind. Why had she stayed here, in the past, if there was a way home? "You mean, in two years you've never tried to get back? *Why not?*"

"I've been happy here," Molly said, after a pause.

Jake stared at her. She looked defensive and vulnerable, like a child expecting a reprimand. He wanted to let it go, but he couldn't. He reached for patience.

"Molly, I've been assuming I was stuck here. Mainly because you've been here for two years. I thought you would have returned if it were possible—at least after Duncan died. I can't believe you didn't tell me something so important." He stopped to gain control of his rising anger. Why hadn't she told him there was a chance? "How *could* you keep that from me?"

Her gaze avoided his. "It may be that we can't return to our own time. I didn't want to get your hopes up," she said to her feet. "And your leg needed to heal."

At Jake's disgusted growl, she finally faced him.

"I planned to tell you. You can't really think I would have just walked out without saying something. How could you think that of me?" Hurt threaded her subdued voice.

Jake immediately felt ashamed of his outburst. His anger dissipated. He looked away, then forced himself to meet her wounded expression.

"I'm sorry. I should have known better. It's just that

it's been hard to come to terms with all this—you know, being trapped in the past with everyone I care about out of reach. It never occurred to me that you might have *chosen* to stay here." He took her hands in his and raised her knuckles to his lips. "I can be an awful jerk sometimes. Will you forgive me?"

To his relief, Molly's face cleared.

"Of course. It's my fault, too. I'm sorry. I should have realized the assumption you'd make. I guess I'm a coward, because as long as I didn't try I could tell myself that the decision to return or not was mine to make. And anyway," she looked down at their clasped hands, "I hate good-byes."

"Good-byes? Are you saying you intend to stay here? In this time, I mean?" He leaned closer. "Come back with me."

Molly looked up and gently pulled her hands free. Her great gray eyes were sad.

"Think about it, Jake." She spoke in a low tone. "If we can return to our own time—and that's a big if—who's to say we'll end up in Ottawa in the same time period. We arrived here one at a time. Maybe we can only return one at a time."

Jake's heart sank. "You don't know that."

"No, but we have to consider the possibility. I mean, we could stand on the same corner, but not at the same time. With two years separating us, we wouldn't be able to communicate or see one another. We wouldn't even know we were standing on the same spot." She shook her head. "Who knows how it might work out."

Jake slumped in his chair. The thought of never seeing Molly again made his heart clench. But he wanted to go back to his own time. If her conjectures were correct, he couldn't win for losing.

A sense of bleak despair enveloped him. Time traveling no longer seemed such a glorious adventure. He had found a wonderful woman, only to be faced with losing her. The thought startled him. How had he come to care so much in such a short time?

Time. Time traveling. What were the rules, anyway? He stared at the fiery underside of the clouds and tried to think intelligently.

"There's another way to look at it." He spoke slowly, trying to reason his way. "We began from the same starting point. That is, we were both in the city, let's say, the day before you came here. What date was that, exactly?"

When she told him, he nodded, his hope rising.

"And I left two years later. Don't you see, the same amount of time, two years, went by for both of us. We just spent the time in different places. I mean in different years. Three weeks have passed since I arrived here. So three weeks have passed there. If we hang on to each other, we'd arrive back at the same moment."

"You really think so?" Molly's voice was laced with cautious optimism.

"Yeah. I mean, it's possible. Maybe. It makes as much sense as anything else, doesn't it?"

His excitement cooled when Molly reminded him that it was by no means certain that there was a way back at all.

"Maybe not, but we have to try. At least, I do. What about you? What do you want to do?" He held his breath.

"I want to go with you. I mean, I'm ready to go back to my own time."

Jake exhaled silently. He wasn't sure what he would have done if she'd decided to stay in the past. Something uniquely special connected them and he didn't want to lose it. He told himself it was because they'd shared such an incredible experience.

Liar, liar, pants on fire! The childhood rhyme echoed in his head and drew a wide smile to his lips. Suddenly his heart felt as buoyant as a freed balloon. They would make it back, he felt sure—and they would make it back together.

"What are you thinking?"

"Nothing," he said gruffly. When Molly raised a disbelieving eyebrow, he added, "I'm glad you want to return. I'd miss you if you stayed behind."

He reached out and clasped her hand. Their gazes met and held. He saw his feelings reflected in her eyes. Like him, Molly didn't want them to part. He yearned, suddenly, to hold her close.

Never taking his gaze from hers, he stood, pulling her to her feet with him. Releasing her hand, he opened his arms and instantly she was there, her breasts crushed against his chest, her arms wrapped around his neck. He dropped his head and buried his face in her hair. The womanly scent of her invaded his senses. Almost unconsciously, he began to caress her back with long sweeping strokes. She pressed closer.

When she burrowed her head in the curve of his neck and placed her lips on the pulse below his ear, desire streaked through him. Shocked at the depth of his instant hunger and the sensual longing he'd never felt so intensely before, he stiffened.

Immediately sensing the rigidity in his body, Molly tried to pull away. What was she doing? How could she have kissed him that way? What must he think of her? When Jake's arms tightened around her, she lifted her head, an apology trembling on her lips. The expression on his face closed her throat.

"You have the most beautiful mouth I've ever seen."

She clung to his shoulders, weak-kneed with her passionate reaction to the desire glowing bright as sunshine in his eyes. Something twisted deep in her abdomen.

"Jake?" She heard the yearning and uncertainty in her whisper.

Jake heard it, too. He told himself to let her go. Neither of them was ready for the passion that had erupted so unexpectedly. But his arms remained locked around her.

One kiss, he thought. One kiss.

Molly must have shared his thought. He slowly lowered his face to hers, granting her time to turn her head aside. She didn't.

Their mouths met. Meaning only to discover if her lips were as soft and warm as they appeared, he tasted her lightly, gently. They were softer, warmer than he had expected. He moistened her lower lip with the tip of his tongue, then slanted his mouth over hers until they were perfectly aligned.

Stop now, he thought. That's enough.

But it wasn't enough. One large hand rose to cup her head. The kiss deepened. When Molly moaned, he slid his tongue between her lips to explore the sweet depths of her mouth. When her fingers tunneled into his hair, his other hand slipped under her shirt to caress the satin skin of her back.

Almost desperate with desire now, he pulled her closer and rejoiced in the erratic thudding of her heart against his chest. He sensed she was as aroused as he. The knowledge threatened his sanity and his control.

Neither heard the rustle of the evergreens or the small cries of nocturnal animals. Neither saw Mac approach the porch and stop on the bottom step to peer up at the abstracted humans. The cat waited for attention. When neither acknowledged his presence, he leaped to Jake's back and scrambled to his now-favorite perch.

"Aah!" Jake jerked and stumbled forward, almost knocking Molly off her feet. "What the—"

When Molly caught her balance, she began to giggle at the sight of Mac draped across Jake's shoulders, his tail hanging down and swishing slowly in feline contentment. The cat rubbed its head against the human's jaw and began to purr loudly. Scowling, Jake reached behind and rubbed his backside.

"It's not funny, woman! This demon cat has left a trail of punctures from my butt to my shoulder blades."

Molly clapped a hand over her mouth and laughed harder. Jake's lips twitched and a moment later, he was shaking with whoops of laughter. Mac favored both humans with a disdainful look, then closed his eyes and dropped his head, clearly distancing himself from their boisterous behavior.

When they caught their breath, Jake reached for Molly's hand. She leaned against him as they stood watching the last of the light fade from the sky. The nearest stars appeared before Molly straightened and slipped her hand free.

Jake didn't object. Their embrace had produced sensations that still vibrated through his body. He couldn't remember when a simple kiss had generated such an instant, almost overwhelming, response. The depth of his physical need astounded him, but that alone didn't particularly disturb him. After all, Molly was beautiful, and it had been some time since he'd been with a woman.

What shook him was the sense of homecoming that filled his heart, as if he'd been unknowingly lost all his life and had finally found his way. As if home were wherever—or whenever—Molly was. As if she were his.

But she wasn't his. She would return to her own life or make a new one in another place. Either would be difficult, and she didn't need a man who led his kind of erratic lifestyle. She deserved better—much better.

Mac still draped over his shoulders, Jake followed her into the house. She paused at the foot of the stairs and looked back at him.

"Good night, Jake." A wistful resignation colored her voice.

"'Night." He listened to her footsteps until he heard her door closed. Sighing, his heart like a lead lump in his chest, he retrieved his book from the front room and settled at the kitchen table to try to distract himself from the memory of what had happened on the back porch.

The novel, destined to be a bestseller, couldn't hold his

attention. After twenty fruitless minutes of reading the same page over and over, he tumbled Mac from his shoulders, filled the cat's bowl with fresh water, and went to his narrow cot in the pantry. Two hours passed before the sensual ache in his body subsided and he slept.

The shrill noise shattered the silence of the dark farmhouse. Molly sat up, unsure what had startled her awake. Then the sound came again and she recognized the peal of the telephone. She peered at the window. The angle of moonlight told her it was past midnight. Who could be calling at this hour? Suddenly anxious, she pulled on her dressing gown and padded barefoot downstairs, hoping the ringing wouldn't waken Jake.

She flipped on the kitchen light and, eyes narrowed against the glare, snatched up the phone. Almost before she put the receiver to her ear, an urgent voice began to rattle on, too low for her to make out the words.

"Wait, I can't hear you. Who is this?"

There was a pause, punctuated only by the sound of deep, quavering breaths. Behind her, Molly heard Jake shuffle into the room. She turned to find him standing in the doorway, his expression mirroring her own feelings of concern. The caller resumed speaking, this time slower, a little louder and more urgently.

"It's Marge Thomas. Please, can you and Jake come over?" The older woman's voice quivered with strain and tension.

Molly squinted at the wall clock. One twenty in the morning!

"You mean *now*? Marge, what's wrong?"

When Jake heard the name of the caller, he stepped close to Molly, put his arm around her waist and leaned toward the receiver. Molly pulled it away from her head a little to enable them both to hear.

"I know it's late. I'm sorry. But I have to talk to you.

Someone's been watching me, following me for the past three days. My house has been searched. I'm frightened and—" She broke off with a sob. "Please come."

"Hang on, Marge. We're on our way." Jake spoke calmly. "Do you want us to call the police?"

"No, don't. I . . . there's a package . . . Doug's package. Please, just come."

"Right away. Make sure your doors are locked."

Molly hung up the phone and lifted her face to Jake. They exchanged worried glances, then turned as one and left the kitchen to dress. A few minutes later the car roared down the lane.

"This is my fault," Jake said through gritted teeth. "If I hadn't been asking about Doug . . . "

"You can't know that. Maybe Marge is upset over nothing."

"I doubt that. She doesn't strike me as a woman who indulges in hysterics."

Molly had to agree. What was this package Doug left with Marge? Did it have anything to do with his death? Instantly disconcerted, she realized that at some point since Marge's call, her subconscious had accepted the woman's certainty that her uncle had not been the victim of an accident, nor had he committed suicide.

Doug Baylor had been murdered. Somehow, she knew it. Chilled, she inched closer to Jake.

They turned off the county road and were forced to slow down to navigate the rutted lane to the Thomas farm. Cattails stood tall and thick in the drainage ditches on both sides of the lane. Queen Anne's lace and purple loosestrife displayed their patchwork beauty in three-foot strips between the ditches and the fields. Beyond the reach of the headlights, darkness held sway.

The land sloped upward in a gentle rise. Suddenly the house loomed before them. Jake stopped the car beside the concrete steps and turned off the motor. The house was dark and still. Only the ticking of the cooling engine broke the silence. Molly shivered.

As her eyes adjusted, she saw a movement at the window. To reassure the watcher of their identity she reached up and turned on the interior light, then waved at the house.

Almost immediately, lights illuminated the front room. A brilliant yard light burst into life and the front door opened. Marge beckoned from the doorway, then immediately backed away from the entrance.

Molly didn't wait for Jake. She hurried into the house and found Marge standing in the hallway. The generously proportioned woman seemed somehow shrunken. She stood huddled in a shapeless robe, her hands clutching her elbows. When Jake entered, she quickly locked the door and walked ahead of them down the hall. In the middle of the kitchen, she stopped and turned around.

Suddenly her face crumpled. Tears spurted from her eyes. Jake stepped past Molly and gathered the shaking woman into his arms. She clung to his shirt and sobbed against his chest.

Molly headed for the sink. She filled the kettle, plugged it into the outlet on the stove and began to open cupboard doors. On the top shelf above the mugs and the jar of instant coffee she spotted a dust-coated bottle of brandy. A few minutes later, she set the steaming mugs, one liberally laced with brandy, on the table and sat down to wait.

Finally running out of tears, Marge drew back from Jake, and began to brush fretfully at his shirt.

"I've about drowned you. I'm sorry, I just—"

"It's not important, Marge. Have some brandy and coffee. It'll do you good. We're not in a hurry, so take your time." He put his arm around her waist and led her to the table. "Just try to relax. You're not alone now."

Molly watched, appreciating Jake's instinctively kind actions. His warm embrace was exactly what Marge needed. Although her full-time worker occupied a small cottage attached to the barn, the middle-aged spinster lived alone. Molly wondered when the frightened woman had last been held.

It seemed strange though—that she had called on a neighbor who was not much more than an acquaintance and a man she'd met only a few days before. Why hadn't she called her hired man or her policeman cousin?

When Marge had blown her nose vigorously, tightened the tie of her dressing gown, and swallowed a few sips of coffee, she sighed heavily and straightened her bulky body in the chair.

"I must be a sight." She tried to smile then gave up. "I hardly know where to begin." She took a deep breath. "Doug was murdered. I can't prove it, but I know."

"This is more than intuition, isn't it," Molly stated rather than asked.

"Yeah. You see, about a week before he died, Doug brought a package to me and asked me to hide it somewhere safe. He didn't say what was in it. I could tell he was worried and angry, but he wouldn't explain. Said it was better that I didn't know."

"This package?" Jake gestured to a heavily-taped bundle in the middle of the table. Dirt clung to the plastic bag enclosing it, but the package itself was unopened.

Marge nodded. For an instant fear glinted in her red-rimmed eyes.

"I put it under the mattress in the spare room. A week later Doug was dead. I didn't remember the package until after the funeral. Somehow, I don't know why, I knew it was important, but Doug had warned me not to open it. I couldn't bring myself to destroy it. So," she shook her head, "I buried it in my vegetable garden."

"What made you decide to dig it up?" Jake leaned forward, his gaze intent on the big woman. It occurred to Molly that he had slipped into his reporter mode.

Marge downed a huge gulp of the potent coffee. She gasped, sputtered and thumped her chest, but her color was back to normal.

She described the sensation of being watched, starting the evening of the first day the neighbors had gathered to help the Stewarts.

"At first I figured I was crazy, or suffering from hormones. But the feeling just got worse. Then last night someone called five times."

"You didn't recognize the voice?"

Marge shook her head. "Whoever it was didn't say a word. I don't know if it was a man or woman." She scrubbed at her face with her hands and when she spoke again her voice was tired. "The calls started in again tonight. Same thing. I decided it was time to look in the package. So right after the third call I went outside and dug it up. But I just can't bring myself to go against Doug's wishes."

"No one saw you dig it up?"

For a moment Marge looked disconcerted by Jake's question. Then she shook her head. "No, I'm sure not. I didn't need any lights and anyway, whoever is calling me couldn't have been outside watching when he'd just been on the phone."

Molly thought of cellular phones. The caller could have been outside the house. But no, cellular phones weren't widely available in this time. Had they even been invented? She couldn't remember. Fortunately for her peace of mind, Marge Thomas seemed to know nothing about them.

"Whatever's in that package must be the reason Doug was killed, but I don't know what to do with it. I thought maybe…. You're both new around here, so I figure you can't be involved in whatever's going on." Marge wrung her hands, a helpless expression twisting her features.

"What do you want us to do?"

"Take the package," she said instantly. "Find out what's going on. Find out who killed Doug. Please."

Jake hesitated. "Shouldn't you bring the police in on this? If Doug was working on a case and his death is connected—"

"No. If Brad knew about this, he might be in danger too. And Streeter believes it was an accident. He said there was no sign of another person's presence the night Doug died. I don't think he'd investigate too hard—and anyway, he'd be sure to tell Brad about it."

The distraught woman threw out her hands in appeal. "Please. Read what's in the package. I can't be objective, but you could. If you decide that Doug's death might be connected to the contents, then I'll talk to the police."

Molly met Jake's eyes and nodded. Whether they could help or not, they couldn't deny Marge. Jake's face reflected the same understanding.

Molly and Jake left a little later, Marge's thanks ringing in their ears. The older woman refused Molly's invitation to stay in her home for a few days, claiming she'd probably overreacted and wasn't in any danger herself since she had no idea what the package contained.

They didn't speak on the way home. Molly stepped into the kitchen and switched on the light. She felt exhausted but too keyed up to sleep.

"Hot chocolate?"

Jake nodded. Rubbing his injured thigh, he tossed Doug Baylor's package on the table and eased into a chair. Mac promptly jumped into his lap. Absently stroking the purring cat, Jake stared at the package. The more he thought about Marge's conviction that her cousin had been murdered, the more he felt the woman must be mistaken.

Possibly more than any other group, the police looked after their own. The slightest indication that Baylor had been murdered would have sparked a massive investigation. The hunt for a cop killer would have been discovered by the media long before now. No, Baylor's death was an accident. Or suicide. Marge, he felt sure, suspected the latter and simply couldn't accept it.

When Molly placed a cup in front of him and sat down, he told her his conclusions. She didn't look convinced.

"What about the phone calls?"

Jake shrugged. "Nuts and lowlifes have used the phone to harass others ever since Bell invented it. Presumably they get some kind of kick frightening people, especially women. The calls are probably just coincidence."

Molly sighed. "I hope you're right." She poked at the package. "If this just contains personal material, we're going to regret opening it. Still, that might set Marge's mind at rest."

"Right. And I think she should tell Brad about the phone calls. He might be able to trace them and catch the jerk. If not, she can always get her number changed, or get an unlisted number."

They stared at the package for a long moment, then Molly suddenly yawned. Jake grinned at her embarrassed flush.

"Off to bed, my lady. Tomorrow's soon enough to look in the package. We can't do anything tonight. I mean this morning."

Molly glanced at the kitchen clock and gasped. It was almost four a.m. She pushed herself from the chair. At the movement, Mac jumped from Jake's lap and began to twine himself around her ankles, perhaps hoping for an early breakfast. She sidestepped to avoid him, lost her balance and landed on her rear. Almost before she realized what had happened she felt herself lifted into the air.

"Are you all right?" Anxiety roughened Jake's voice.

"Y . . . yes. I'm fine." She gave a small laugh. "The demon cat's becoming lethal. But I'm more startled than hurt." When Jake started for the doorway, she became aware that he was holding her against his chest, one arm under her knees and the other around her back.

"Your leg, Jake. Put me down. I can walk."

He ignored her command. Flicking the light switch off with his elbow, he carried her down the hall and started up the stairs.

"Jake! This is crazy. I'm okay."

"Hush, my lady." He shook his head, his expression

mournful as he slowly but steadily climbed the stairs. "I guess it's true what they say—doctors and nurses make the worst patients. Shame on you, Miss Nightingale." He grinned suddenly. "Just think of this as well-deserved revenge for that blasted bedpan."

"Huh!" Molly slapped lightly at his shoulder and relaxed against him. No man had ever carried her before. Though she would have eaten a live beetle before admitting it, she found it an exhilarating experience. Or was it just the heavenly sensation of Jake's arms surrounding her that made her so breathless?

Jake's heart contracted when he stepped into her room. A small lamp on the bedside table illuminated the room. The fringed silk shade cast a soft pink glow that seemed feminine and welcoming. He swallowed hard as his body reacted to the room and the woman cuddling in his arms. This was a mistake; he should have said goodnight in the kitchen.

God, how he wanted to join her on the bed! Hoping she couldn't feel his heart thumping against his ribs, he lowered her to the bed. Afraid his voice would betray him, he smiled in her direction, stepped back and immediately turned to leave.

"Jake?"

He stopped but didn't look around.

"Do you really think Marge will be all right alone there? I'm frightened for her."

The uncertainty and worry in her voice tugged at him. He turned around. Her expression pleaded for reassurance. It was more than he could stand. Quickly, he sat on the edge of the bed and dragged her into his arms.

Her body trembled against him. Sensing that she was almost as upset as Marge had been earlier, he whispered meaningless words of comfort in her ear. When the tremors finally abated, he leaned back and smiled.

"Orders from the doctor to the nurse. I want you to get undressed, get under the covers and then the doctor will tuck you in for the night. For what's left of the night."

Not giving her time to protest, he let her go, swiveled to place his back to the bed and crossed his arms over his chest. "I'm waiting, Miss Nightingale."

Silence. Then a fist thumped him lightly on the back and he heard a muttered "Doctors! Dictators all!" The bed creaked as she shifted to undress. Behind him, he could hear the soft sounds of her clothing sliding off her body and hitting the floor.

Jake stared at the door and tried to blank out the picture of Molly shedding her clothing. But his imagination was too strong. He cursed himself for his foolishness as sweat beaded on his forehead and the ache in his groin intensified.

"I'm ready, Doctor. Tuck me in, please."

With a silent groan, he plastered a light smile on his face and turned around. The smile slipped at the sight of her, her lovely face framed by the shining hair spread over the pillow, the frilly neck of a white flannel gown buttoned high. How could white flannel be so sensual? Then he saw that her gray eyes were huge and still troubled.

Impulsively, he tucked the covers up to her chin, stripped off his shirt and shoes and stretched out beside her, on top of the covers. A look of relief spread over her face when he slid an arm under her neck and pulled her head to his shoulder.

"Go to sleep, Florence."

"Yes, Doctor. Whatever you say." She snuggled against him and closed her eyes. Minutes later she was asleep. Jake lay awake for another hour, wishing he had the self-control to join her under the covers—but a man can take only so much.

A heavy knocking startled Jake awake. He sat up abruptly, for an instant disconcerted by the unfamiliar surroundings. Sunlight streamed into the room, the sheer white curtains being little barrier. The mattress moved beneath him and a warm hand touched his bare back. Memory returned. He looked down and felt his heart lurch in his chest. Her eyes closed, her face sensuous with sleep, Molly looked wanton and utterly desirable. Breathing became suddenly difficult.

The banging began again and he heard low toned voices. A quick glance at the bedside clock told him morning was almost gone. He shook Molly awake and warned her of company. Much as he wanted to holler through the window for the intruders to go away, he didn't think she wanted her neighbors to know that her house guest hadn't slept on the ground floor.

As she swung out of the bed she gave him a questioning look. Jake shrugged. He watched as she approached the window and bent over to look out.

"Who is it?" she called.

Beside the bed, Jake stood spellbound. Daylight streamed through the window, turning the thin flannel almost transparent. He could see the shadowy outline of her hips and long, lovely legs. His manhood stirred and he fought to prevent himself from reaching for her rounded backside.

"Hi, Sophie, Brad. I'll be down in a minute." She backed away from the window and straightened to face Jake. Whatever she was going to say was forgotten when her gaze fell on his bare chest. Jake felt a surge of pure male satisfaction when she blushed furiously, then looked around frantically for her clothes.

Suddenly he remembered the package he'd left on the kitchen table. "Let me go down first. I'll hide those papers and slip out the back door," he whispered. "After a few minutes I'll come back in the house. They'll think I've been outside for the morning."

Molly nodded. "Hurry," she hissed.

Barefoot, he eased down the stairs, keeping to the side nearest the wall. Thank goodness the front door was closed and had no window. He could hear shuffling noises as the visitors waited on the porch.

In the kitchen he swept up the package of papers, dashed into the pantry, and thrust them under the rumpled sheets. Then he quietly opened the back door and settled into Duncan's wicker chair. Mac trotted from the tree line with a small rodent swinging from his jaws. He proudly deposited his gift at Jake's feet, then leaped lightly into his lap, circled around once and collapsed into a contented heap. Jake relaxed and tried to look as though he and Mac had been chair-bound for hours.

A moment later the front door creaked open. From his place on the porch, Jake heard Molly's greeting and invitation to enter.

"No, thanks. We just wondered if you've seen Marge this morning. Jasper, her hired hand, called me when she didn't go out to the barn as usual or answer his knock." Sophie Baylor's voice was thin with worry.

Brad broke in. "He called Sophie because it's unlike Marge not to tell him if she's leaving the farm for the day. We've been in the house and there's no sign of her. Her bed's turned down but there's no sign she slept in it. Have you heard from her?"

Uneasiness crept down Jake's spine. He lifted a protesting Mac from his lap and entered the house. Molly glanced at him, apprehension flickering in her eyes. She opened her mouth, but Jake forestalled her explanation.

"I heard. Have you called all her friends?"

Brad's eyes widened as he took in Jake's bare feet and chest. He shot a swift glance at Molly, but swallowed whatever comment he might have made.

"We came here first because Molly's her closest neighbor and I got the impression at the Stewarts' that they're friends."

"I consider Marge a friend," Molly agreed, "but she hasn't been here." That much was true. When she raised her eyebrows at Jake he gave a slight shake of his head.

Until they had studied the papers Marge had entrusted to them, it was probably wisest to keep silent about her phone call and their middle of the night visit. Now that he thought about it, it again struck him as strange that she hadn't confided in her cousin, given the fact that Brad was a policeman. Was that omission merely to save him heartache, as she'd said, or had she cause to be suspicious of him? Could Brad be responsible for his father's death?

Jake didn't much care for the man but his innate honesty forced him to admit that his aversion was based solely on the man's attentions to Molly. He really couldn't blame Brad for that—but he didn't have to like it either.

He tried to tell himself Marge had likely gone shopping or visiting or something equally innocuous and had simply forgotten to inform Jasper. But his reporter's instinct told him there was more to it than mere forgetfulness. By the older woman's own account, someone was following her and harassing her by phone.

It had all started after his own questions about Doug Baylor that first day at the Stewarts. Jake struggled to hide his sudden sense of guilt. If something had happened to Marge, he might be to blame. Why had he dismissed her fears so readily?

"Is there anything we can do?" Molly asked anxiously. Jake marveled that neither her expression nor her body posture gave any indication of secret knowledge.

"No, thanks anyway," Brad answered. "But if you see her or hear anything, would you call the station? They'll relay the message to me."

Molly and Jake both gave their assurances and the brother and sister left, Sophie clinging to Brad's arm and obviously fighting tears.

Molly closed the door behind them and turned to meet Jake's gaze. Her face now held the same dread and worry that churned in his gut.

"Shouldn't we have told them about last night, and the papers Doug left with her? What if her disappearance has something to do with all that?"

"No, I don't think so. Not yet, anyway. Remember, she could have told Brad about the phone calls herself. For whatever reason, she chose not to." Jake reached to knead the back of his neck. "If she's just off for a time and is all right, we don't want to betray her trust."

Molly's face cleared a little.

"You're right. But I think we'd better examine those papers right away. I'm going to shower. Would you put the coffee on?"

In answer, Jake reached for her hand and pulled her close. "Good morning, dear nurse."

"Good morning to you, too." Molly smiled shyly. "And thank you, Jake, for staying with me last night."

"Any time, my lady, any time." He meant it and that startled him. What was he thinking of? Despite the bedclothes separating them, lying beside Molly had been sweet agony. He found himself wanting to share a bed with her every night, wanting to wake every morning to her sleepy face. Was he falling in love with her?

No, of course not. Love and happily-ever-after weren't for him, not with the kind of life a reporter led. His ill-conceived marriage to Sherri had proved that. It was just the whole incredible situation.

Molly was a link to home. Naturally his impulse was to cling to her. They would part once they were back where they belonged. After all, he knew nothing about this woman. A sudden, unwelcome thought chilled him. For all he knew, a husband and children could be waiting for her. He dropped her hand abruptly and stepped back.

Molly seemed to sense his emotional withdrawal. Avoiding his eyes, she started up the stairs. Jake watched the rigid line of her back until she turned at the top of the stairs and vanished from sight. She didn't look back. Jake knew he'd hurt her but there was nothing he could do about it. Guilt tasted sour in his mouth.

He made the coffee and took his turn in the shower. When he entered the kitchen again Molly had prepared an omelet and toast. They ate quickly, neither referring again to the night they'd spent together. Jake ignored his sense of loss and wondered what Molly was thinking.

After the table was cleared and the dishes washed, he ripped through the binding tape and upended the package on the table. Most of the contents consisted of clippings from various small weekly newspapers. Among them was a piece of an official map, cut into a strip about four inches wide and twelve inches long. Several sheets of dated notepaper were covered with crabbed handwriting. The heading on all but one indicated the information came from interviews with assorted individuals. The lone exception listed nine names, none familiar to Jake. A quick perusal unearthed no obvious connection between the names and the clippings.

"Can you make any sense of this?" Molly stared in bewilderment at the papers littering the table. She picked up the fragment of map and examined it more closely.

"Jake, this has been torn from a map of southeastern Ontario. Look, here's Ottawa," she pointed near the top, "and at the bottom is Highway 401 and the town of Morrisburg. The map shows the towns and villages between. Of course there's no sign of the six-lane highway or the new bridge to the States that was built a few years ago. In our time, I mean. Why would anyone—" She broke off and slid her finger down the back of the partial map.

"What is it?" Jake looked up from the clipping he was reading.

"This is strange." Molly turned and lifted the map toward the window. "Look, there's a line of pinholes the length of the map. You can just see the light through them."

"How many pinholes?"

Molly counted them. "Nine."

"Nine," Jake repeated. He handed her the cryptic sheet of nine names. "Do you recognize any of these names?"

Molly scanned the list and nodded. "Mailer. He was a

farmer about ten miles south of here. He was a distant cousin of Duncan's first wife, Grace."

"Was?"

"Yes. I seem to remember Duncan telling me that he lost all his cows to some disease. The family sold the farm and moved away. I think they went west, Saskatchewan maybe. Mrs. Mailer's family lives out there, I think."

"Any other familiar names?"

"Ye-sss. I'm not sure. Van Dort rings a bell." Molly pursed her lips. "Oh, I remember. Last year, he was killed when his tractor rolled over and crushed him. The authorities were puzzled because the field was absolutely flat where he died. The tractor tracks showed that he made a sudden, very sharp turn, but no one knows why."

Jake rummaged among the clippings and found one that described the tragedy. Molly flinched at the expression on his face. "What is it?"

"Did you ever hear if the widow sold the farm?"

"Yes, I remember Nora talking about it once. She knew the wife from high school. Mrs. Van Dort was left with three children, the oldest only in grade school. I believe she moved back with her parents in Ottawa so she could get a job. She was a hairdresser before she married."

Jake nodded. He divided the pile of clippings in two and handed Molly one stack. An hour later they had matched each clipping to one of the nine names. Each concerned some kind of tragedy: three deaths, including one suicide, failed crops or dead animals, two farmhouses and two barns burned to the ground, and the unexplained death of a newly purchased and very valuable bull. In every case the farmer or his heirs had informed the reporter that he would be forced to sell his farm, many of which had been in the hands of the same families for generations.

"How terrible for those families," Molly said. "But why would Doug have saved these reports of disasters? These sorts of things happen all the time, all over. Do you think he knew all the families?" She shook her head before Jake could answer. "Even if he did, I can't see why...."

Her voice trailed off. Sudden comprehension filled her eyes. "He was a policeman. If he suspected these particular incidents to be more than natural disasters, he would have looked into them. Do you think this package contains the results of his investigation?"

Jake nodded. "That's exactly what I think. You're some smart lady, Molly Barnes. That's what it looks like to me and my job is ferreting out crimes. I'll bet my last dollar that Doug was on to something. What we don't know is if he considered them unrelated crimes or the work of one person."

Her face warm from Jake's praise, Molly added, "If the crimes were committed by one person, there must be something that connects the nine families, something they have in common. I mean, something in addition to the fact that all the properties were farms. But different catastrophes happened to them. And according to the dates on the clippings, the incidents happened over a period of about seventeen months."

"They have one thing in common," Jake said grimly. "All the farms were lost."

Molly suddenly paled. "Jake, if these were all deliberate crimes designed to drive the families from their land, and the criminal discovered Doug was secretly investigating them, that means—that means—"

"It means that Doug was murdered to keep him quiet."

Chapter Six

Molly shivered as a cold blanket of fear enveloped her. The sudden appalling certainty that Marge Thomas was dead ripped through her mind. She stared at Jake and saw the same apprehension in his bleak eyes.

"What are we going to do?" she whispered.

A loud knocking at the front door made them both jump. Instantly, Jake scooped up the papers and shoved them in the plastic wrapped envelope. Four long strides brought him to the cot in the pantry. He shoved the package under the tousled bedclothes again and returned to the kitchen. Giving Molly's hand an encouraging squeeze, he followed her down the hall to the front of the house.

Wearing identical frowns, Brad Baylor and Harvey Streeter stood on the doorstep. Molly took one look at the younger man and her heart sank.

"Is Marge all right?"

The police chief answered. "We haven't found a sign of her. May we come in?" His tone was just short of rude.

"Of course." Molly stepped back to let the two men pass. She and Jake exchanged an anxious look. "Come into the kitchen. I just made coffee."

While they waited for Molly to pour more coffee, Brad told them of the places he'd visited searching for his cousin. Harvey Streeter said nothing until they were all seated, then he signaled his junior officer for silence.

"What were you two doing at Marge's in the middle of the night?" Challenge rang in the chief's voice.

Molly gasped and knew by the satisfied look in Streeter's eyes that he'd seen her shock. Beside her, Jake stiffened. Inwardly cursing her lapse, she called on all her talent to compose her face and voice. It took only an instant to decide that denial would be foolish.

"How in the world did you know we were there?" Her voice held just the right mix of chagrin and curiosity.

"Never mind that, just answer the question."

"Of course." She deliberately edged her tone with a rebuke for his rudeness and felt a wave of approval from Jake roll over her. It gave her a needed dose of confidence.

"Marge called me and asked us to come over. She was very upset. It seems someone's been waking her with threatening phone calls during the last few nights. I live the closest so I suppose—"

Brad looked hurt. "Why would she call you? That doesn't make sense. She should have called me. Not only am I a relative, I'm a cop."

"I don't know, Brad. Maybe she felt she needed to confide in a woman. I'm sure she'll tell you about the calls if they continue."

"They were obscene calls then?" Some of the tension left the police chief.

"Probably, though she didn't say that, exactly. Jake and I stayed about a half-hour, until she calmed down. I invited her to come here for the rest of the night but she refused."

"Does she know who it was?"

"No. She said the caller never spoke."

"Did you see anyone around the farm? Another car?"

"No."

"Was there a call while you were there?"

"No."

"Why didn't you tell Brad about this when he came by this morning?"

Jake spoke for the first time. "Why would we, Chief? Marge called us, not Brad. We figured it's her business, her choice to confide in whom she pleases. In any case, what has our visit last night to do with her disappearance today?"

Streeter glared at him but answered coolly. "Maybe nothing, but you and Mrs. Barnes were the last people to see her. And it's not like Marge to go off without telling anyone. You're sure she didn't mention anything about a trip today?"

"Positive." Jake was equally cool. "Now how about answering Molly's question. How did you know we were there?"

Streeter suddenly looked uncomfortable. "I received an anonymous phone call, about noon, saying that you two were at the missing woman's home in the middle of the night. We had to check it out."

Jake's eyebrows went up. "You're calling Marge a missing woman? She's been out of touch less than a day. And how did this mysterious caller know we were there? More to the point, if this caller saw us at Marge's then he must have been there, too."

Streeter nodded agreement reluctantly. Brad's apprehensive expression deepened.

Jake didn't give either man time to interrupt. "We didn't pass another vehicle on the road, coming or going. Sounds to me as if your caller was on foot and outside the house. Maybe you've got a Peeping Tom on your hands. I take it your informant didn't claim that Marge left with us? Or are you accusing us of kidnapping?"

Molly winced inside at Jake's sarcastic tone, but Chief Streeter's questions had been decidedly unfriendly. She glanced at Brad. His angry expression disturbed her. There was no point in making an enemy of Streeter.

"No, the caller didn't say that. You didn't go back this morning, or call her?"

"No, we didn't."

Streeter took a last gulp of coffee and stood up. Brad rose with him but lingered at the front door to take Molly's hands in his.

"I'm sorry, Molly. The chief sometimes comes on pretty strong. I know you don't have anything to do with this."

Molly wrapped her fingers around his in sympathy. "I understand, Brad. But I'll bet Marge shows up safe and sound this afternoon. She's probably shopping in Ottawa. She'll be mortified by all this fuss."

Brad didn't look convinced.

"Maybe you're right. It's not like her though." He released her hands and followed Streeter to the patrol car.

When she returned to the kitchen Jake enclosed her in his arms. Molly leaned gratefully into his warmth. The effort to appear collected and unconcerned in front of the two policemen had drained her strength. It was a relief to lower her guard and allow her face to reflect her true feelings.

"I'm really worried about Marge now. What if this anonymous caller really is connected to Doug's investigation? It would mean he suspects she knows something."

"Why would the anonymous caller go to Marge's in the middle of the night, though?" Jake asked. "He called five times the night before and only three times last night. Unless he called twice more after we left."

Molly jerked her head back and looked up at him. "I think I know. Marge said she dug up the package immediately following the third call. Then she called us. If he tried to call her again and found the line busy—"

"—he'd want to know who she was calling in the middle of the night and what she was saying—"

"—so he went to Marge's to find out. And saw us. Or at least, saw my car." Molly frowned. "Can you remember if the kitchen curtains were closed? If not, he may have seen her give us the package."

She shuddered. "Jake, maybe he broke into the house after we left to find out what she knows and what the package contains. Maybe he...." Molly covered her mouth with her hands and gazed at Jake, her eyes begging him to tell her she was wrong.

He didn't. They both knew he couldn't deny the possibility. He kissed her forehead and led her to a chair instead. He sat down on the other side of the table and fixed her with a somber look. Molly felt dread creep into her soul.

"We're talking a lot of 'ifs' here," he said. "She's only been missing a few hours. But . . . I think we should assume something really has happened to her. I hope to God I'm wrong! It'll be partly my fault if she's been hurt." He raised his hand to stop Molly's protest. "There's no time to think of that now. We may be in very serious trouble ourselves."

"What kind of trouble?" But she knew what he was going to say.

"We know about Doug's investigation. We know about the threats to Marge. And almost certainly, the guilty person knows we know. That makes us a danger to him—and there's more."

"What more?"

"If Marge is never found, or if her body is found, we could be arrested and accused of kidnapping or murder."

Molly shook her head.

"Nobody would think that. They know me. Anyway, we have no motive, and we both have alibis. We've been together since we left her house."

The words were scarcely out of her mouth, when Molly realized her mistake.

"Oh, no." She took a deep breath. "If someone wanted to set us up to take the blame, they've already got a good start, haven't they?"

Jake nodded. He wasn't surprised that Molly had seen the truth so quickly. He listened while she worked it out.

"We've admitted we went to Marge's in the middle of the night. We haven't any proof that *she* called *us*. As for our alibis, we could be lying to protect each other. We can't prove one or both of us didn't return later, before dawn."

"We did fall asleep." Jake's voice was soft. Molly flashed on the memory of snuggling in his arms. His next words wiped the memory from her mind.

"If she's dead and we're being set up, the weapon is likely to be something stolen from your house or barn, like a crowbar or a kitchen knife. Anyone could have come here when we were at the Stewarts."

"But what about fingerprints?"

"Gloves." Jake said succinctly. "And there's still more."

"No, Jake, please."

"We have to consider the possibilities." He paused, then continued in a gentle voice. "If the worst happens and her body is found, they're going to investigate us. They'll find out that there's no such person as Jake Dune registered anywhere. And your maiden name, if they locate it at all, will be registered to a small child. You know what they'll think about two people using false names."

Molly shuddered. "They'll arrest us."

Molly sat on the back porch and stared at nothing. From the front parlor she could hear the drone of the radio. She and Jake had helped the search party comb every inch of

Marge's property. Nothing was found. Two slow days had passed and Marge was still missing.

When she wasn't answering the calls of neighbors and friends, all eager for any news of the missing woman, she was calling them for the same purpose. No one seemed to know anything. Nor did anyone seem to know she and Jake were suspects.

But another visit from Chief Streeter made it clear they were. He was accompanied by a different officer on his second visit. Molly suspected he hadn't brought Brad because he knew of the officer's fondness for her. Streeter made them repeat in detail everything they'd said before. This time he made no effort to hide his suspicions.

He ignored her when she asked what possible motive either one of them could have to harm Marge, a woman Molly barely knew and Jake had scarcely met. Instead, he used her very words to cast doubt that Marge would have called two near-strangers in the middle of the night. When he finally left, he warned them not to go anywhere without his knowledge. The warning, although expected, sent an arctic chill through Molly's body.

Jake had brushed aside her hopeful assertion that a lack of motive would protect them.

"They might not be able to convict us," he agreed, "but they may eventually decide they've got enough to arrest us and hold us in jail pending trial. I hate to admit it, but we made a mistake not telling Brad and Sophie about our visit to Marge. We played right into the anonymous caller's hands."

What else could they have done? Marge had trusted them. But as the days passed with no word, Molly felt her hope for Marge's safety dribble away. Sophie phoned to say that no hospital within a fifty-mile radius had reported an accident victim matching Marge's description. No one had reported seeing her, and Marge made no attempt to contact anyone she knew. As Brad had said, such worrying behavior was out of character for his cousin. Fear for her friend weighed heavy in Molly's heart.

She heard Jake's footsteps as he entered the kitchen. They had both downed gallons of coffee as they waited for news. A few minutes later he joined her on the back porch, fresh cups in his hands. He eased down beside her, his long legs stretching to the top of the steps.

"Tell me how you got here," Jake said, breaking the late evening silence.

Molly nodded, glad of the distraction. "I was walking in Tom's Woods. It's close to my condo in Ottawa. It was twilight, about like now. I stepped onto the big flat rock—the one where we saw the skunk—intending to sit for a few minutes. In the middle of a step I saw a . . . a circle of winking green light in front of me. It grew to the size of a garage door, but I couldn't stop in time. When I finished the step, the light vanished. I didn't feel anything."

She smiled. "At first everything seemed as always. I thought I'd imagined the green circle. Then I noticed the trees. They had shrunk to less than half their height."

"What did you do?"

Molly grimaced. "Once I decided I wasn't asleep and dreaming, I headed for the only light I could see and found Duncan. I suppose I looked pretty wasted. He took me in. Amazingly, he didn't question what a stranger was doing on his property. I ended up staying."

Molly smiled, remembering how the old farmer had insisted she didn't owe him any explanations. Not that she could have explained. The truth had crept on reluctant feet into her mind over the first few days. The age of the trees, the dates on the newspaper, things Duncan said; it all added up to one inescapable conclusion. The impossible had happened. She had traveled into the past.

"Do you think he figured it out?" Jake's eyes were alight with curiosity.

"I think so," she responded. "We never actually discussed it. He was terribly lonely and grateful for company. He didn't care how I came to be there. He wanted us to marry so I would inherit his farm in case I could never go home again. Those were his words - 'in case you can never go home again.' Yes, I think he knew."

Jake nodded in agreement and returned to his original question.

"We might be in luck. As far as I can remember, I took the same path. I'm certain Skunk Rock is the one that attacked my head. I suppose my leg gave out and I fell. When I came to, the only light I could see was yours. But I still can't remember who shot me. Or why. I need to find J.J. again."

Molly threw him a quick glance.

"You're going to try to go back then?"

"*We're* going, Molly. If we can. I have a feeling we won't have any choice. Not if we want to stay out of jail."

Molly shivered. Chief Streeter's attitude made it clear they were suspects in Marge's disappearance. If the missing woman didn't return, he'd look for someone to blame. Who better than two relative strangers?

The idea of running away disturbed her, but Jake was right. They couldn't help Marge or themselves from a jail cell.

Jake stood and stretched. "We're out of coffee cream. Let's drive into town and do a little shopping."

Molly went into the house to get a sweater. The temperature would drop with the sun's departure and she liked to ride with the windows open. Jake headed for the garage to start the car.

She returned to the kitchen just as a grim-faced Jake plunged into the house, grabbed her hand and all but dragged her back up the stairs.

"Jake, what are you doing?"

"Where's Mac?"

"Sleeping on my bed. Why? What is it?"

"Grab your purse and whatever you want to take with you. You've got one minute. I'll put Mac in a carry-all bag."

"Take where?" Molly skidded to a halt and yanked her

hand from his grip. *Another man giving orders.* "I'm not going anywhere unless you tell me what's wrong."

She stepped back when Jake glared at her. His face softened at her movement. He took a deep breath and exhaled slowly.

"We're going home. If we can."

"*Now*? But why?"

"Because we're likely to be arrested at any moment." His voice was harsh.

"What!"

"Molly, please, we've got to get out of here!"

When she didn't move, Jake muttered a heartfelt curse and put his hands on her shoulders. "The car has a flat tire. When I opened the trunk of the car to look for . . . ." He sighed. "There's no easy way to say this. Marge's body is in the trunk of your car. Our anonymous friend will want to be sure they discover the body as soon as possible. So the police will likely be here any minute. If we don't get away now, we never will."

"Marge is dead?" Molly heard her own words as if from a great distance. Blackness roared in her head. She sagged against his strong hands. "Marge is dead?" she repeated.

Jake yanked her to his chest and wrapped his arms around her shaking body.

"Yeah," he murmured gruffly. "She's been dead for some time. We can't do anything for her." He stood silently holding her for a few moments then slid his hands up to cup her head. He gazed intently into her shocked eyes. "Molly, sweetheart, we've got to go. Someone has framed us good. The only way we're going keep out of prison is to go back to our own time."

Molly choked back the sobs that threatened to overwhelm her. Jake was right. She inhaled deeply and called on all her self-control.

"I'll get my purse."

Following at her heels, Jake scooped Mac up from her

bed, placed him in the carry-all bag and zipped it almost closed, ignoring the cat's indignant yowls. Molly looked around the room. There was nothing she really wanted, except the wedding photograph of herself and Duncan. She tossed it in her bag and followed Jake down the stairs.

"God, they're here." Jake jumped away from the parlor window. He grabbed Molly's hand. They raced to the back of the house, stopping only long enough for Jake to grab Doug's notes. As he eased the door closed behind them, loud knocking reverberated through the house.

"Come on. We've got about half a minute before they discover we're gone. Run!"

They ran. They had just crossed the back lawn and entered the woods when a shout sounded behind them. Molly looked over her shoulder and saw a young officer come around the side of the house and break into a run. The back door banged open and Streeter joined the chase. Desperation fueled her feet.

Branches slapped at their faces and clutched at their clothing. Jake's long legs scissored slightly ahead of her as he used the carry-all bag to push aside the largest branches. Mac's cries had ceased.

Gasping for breath, she forced her legs to keep moving. What if they couldn't . . . . No, she wouldn't think of that. They had to find the way home. A quick glance over her shoulder revealed a welcome sight. The young policeman had dropped behind, with Streeter considerably further back. She realized they had no reason to fear their suspects would get away. The woods were small and their prey was on foot.

When they burst into the small clearing the light was almost gone. Molly led Jake around the edge of the rock until they were facing the direction from which she had arrived two years before. The scene looked normal, ordinary. Nothing at all hinted at the presence of some weird passageway through time. She lifted her face to Jake's.

"Ready?" he whispered. Behind them the sounds of

cursing and stumbling feet drew closer.

"Yes." Her grip tightened on Jake's hand.

He leaned forward and pressed a quick, hard kiss on her mouth. Then, hand in hand, they walked across the flat boulder to the other side.

Chapter Seven

Molly's fingers tightened in his. Jake felt his pulse banging wildly in his neck. The seconds seemed to stretch and slow. His breath solidified in his lungs as the sounds of pursuit drew closer. The thought of Molly in a prison cell almost paralyzed him. Only a step remained before the end of the rock. *Where was that green passageway?*

And then he saw it. A shimmering circle of emerald fire popped into existence at their feet. It grew swiftly, expanding into a perfect sphere. He glanced down at Molly and saw his own relief reflected in her eyes. Together, they took the last step.

Behind them, the shimmering green circle flared, then faded and abruptly winked out. As one, they stopped. As one, they inhaled deeply, starved lungs at last free to move.

"Jake, look!" Molly pointed at the trees surrounding them.

His gaze slowly climbed upwards to treetops high above their heads. It had worked! He whooped in delight and pulled Molly into his arms, crushing her to his chest. Molly clung tightly in return, relief mixed with her anguish over Marge's death.

"We made it! We're home!" He began to chortle. "I wish I could see Streeter's face right now. He must be going crazy trying to figure out how we got away."

"No, he isn't," Molly said as she gazed up into his face. "He gave up the search twenty years ago."

Comprehension hit him like a blow to the head.

"God, you're right." Jake frowned. "If he's still alive, he's probably forgotten all about—"

"—poor Marge." Molly's eyes filled. "I wonder if they ever found her killer."

Jake's heart clenched in compassion at the pain edging Molly's voice. For them, Marge's death was brand new, and Molly had known and liked the woman for two years. Thank God he, and not Molly, had been the one to find Marge's body. His heart ached for her pain.

He gathered her close and stroked her hair in silent sympathy as she released the tears she'd been holding back since his terrible discovery. Although his own acquaintance with the unfortunate woman was slight, a lump blocked his own throat. Marge Thomas had been a good, hardworking, generous woman who hadn't deserved her fate. As he recalled her distress the night she'd called, he felt anger wash through him.

It was unlikely that her killer had ever been brought to justice. Streeter seemed certain he and Molly were the culprits, and with good reason. The fact of their disappearance probably clinched it in Streeter's mind. He wouldn't have looked any further for the guilty party.

A sudden thought jolted him. Though the case would have been shelved long ago, somewhere in the police files almost surely existed outstanding warrants for the apprehension and arrest of Jake Dune and Molly Barnes. Maybe they weren't as safe as they supposed. Then he relaxed. Molly's birth certificate and his own were proof that they could not have been adults at the time of Marge's death.

Molly's sobs gradually diminished. A sudden, forlorn cry made them jump and draw apart. When the cry was repeated Jake remembered Mac, still trapped in the carry-all bag. He hefted the bag and drew back the zipper a few inches. Immediately, a black furry head popped out and Mac began to scold the humans who had so unexpectedly abused his dignity.

Molly sniffed and wiped her face with the backs of her hands.

"Poor Mac. We've mistreated you shamefully, haven't we?" She stroked the head now lifting to examine the trees around them. "But we couldn't leave you behind, all alone." She looked at Jake.

"Just think," he said, "Mac is probably the oldest cat in Canada. Too bad we can't tell anyone about him."

To his relief, Molly chuckled. "I bet he'd appreciate a litter box about now. I sure would." She clapped her hand over her mouth. Jake laughed and took her arm.

"I know what you mean. Come on, we'll go to my place. I have an apartment one block over on the north side of the woods."

Jake led her along the lighted path toward his street. Beyond the wall of trees hummed the early evening traffic. A few feet from the exit, Molly suddenly stopped.

"Wait! What if the person who shot you is watching your apartment? Maybe we should find a hotel."

"I didn't think of that," Jake mumbled. He pinched the bridge of his nose and considered the situation. The present might be as dangerous as the past. Still, three weeks had passed since the shooting. His assailant must be feeling pretty secure.

He looked down at Molly's anxious face. A part of him rejoiced that she was so concerned for his safety. He tried to reassure her.

"Whoever shot me must think I either crawled away and died, or left town because I was afraid. At any rate, he'll assume I didn't recognize him or get a good look at him. If I had, he'd have been picked up by the police before now. It should be safe."

Molly didn't look convinced.

Jake wasn't completely convinced himself. Whatever he'd seen, his assailant had tried to kill him to prevent his talking. Would the three weeks that had passed satisfy the person that he had nothing to fear from Jake?

At Molly's urging, he scouted the area around his home. There was no sign of a watcher.

More relieved than he wanted to admit, he led the way up the outside staircase to his apartment on the top floor of an old brick house. He unlocked the door and ushered Molly inside. Since they had first heard that Marge was missing, he'd kept the key with him at all times. It felt surprisingly good to be home again.

He closed and locked the door behind them and switched on the lights. Finally released from his canvas prison, Mac scorned their attempts to apologize for his incarceration and immediately began to explore his new surroundings. Molly trailed after Mac from room to room.

Jake wondered what she thought of his eclectic tastes. Old and comfortable sat side by side with new and modern. After a year of living with boxes and minimal furniture, he had come home one day to find that his mother and sister had braved his wrath and turned the four-room apartment into a home. Since they hadn't made the mistake of adding strictly feminine touches, he'd been well pleased.

Now he tried to see the room through Molly's eyes. What did she think of the charcoal leather sofa, gray and green plaid recliner, deep gray carpeting and hand-loomed hangings on the cream walls? And why did the answer to that question suddenly seem so important?

"I like your home, Jake." Molly re-entered the living room and stopped a few feet away. She looked uncertain, as if she didn't know quite what to do with herself. "Do you suppose I might have a cup of coffee?"

"Of course. Sit down and be comfortable." Jake headed for the kitchen, suddenly self-conscious himself. The enormity of their trip from past to present was overshadowed by his renewed need to know who Molly Barnes really was. Already, for him, the sojourn in the past was taking on the aspect of a vacation—interesting, incredible even, but now over. He was happy to be home again. But then, he had been away for less than three weeks. Little would have changed in his world in that space of time.

It was different for Molly. He thought of the people she had left behind. Family, friends, co-workers. Husband? A doorknob-sized lump lodged in his throat. Refusing to question his reaction to the thought, he forced himself to consider Molly's situation.

She had disappeared without a trace, unable to communicate with those she knew. After two years of silence, those who cared about her must think she was dead. Now, suddenly, she was back in her own time. No wonder she seemed uncertain. He turned back to her and spread open his arms, offering the only comfort he could at that moment.

She burst into tears and flung herself forward. Her body trembled against his.

"That's right," he murmured into her ear. "Things will look better soon. We'll sort it all out together."

Mac inserted himself between them, twining his urgent body around their ankles and demanding attention.

"I'm sorry," Molly whispered as she stepped back and gave him a watery smile. "I seem to be turning into a watering pot." She stooped and caught Mac up in her arms. "Our elderly friend here wants to see the menu. I suppose some people find time traveling stimulates their appetite."

"Not only feline persons," Jake admitted. "I think I could eat a horse. Come to think of it, anything in the refrigerator must be moldy by now."

He put an arm around Molly's waist and led her to the kitchen. "Why don't you put on the coffee percolator while I go out for milk and food? Blossom Park shopping center should still be open. I'll pick up some kitty litter and a tray while I'm at it." He gestured to the cupboard beside the stove. "There's some tinned salmon there, I think, for our furry friend. I won't be gone long."

Molly nodded, then stopped him with a hand on his arm. She looked embarrassed.

"I feel like a poor relation, Jake. When I went walking that evening, I left my suitcase and purse locked in my car at the entrance to the woods. The car was probably stolen and stripped before dawn. I've no money or identification. Would you pick me up a toothbrush? I'll pay you back later."

Half angry and half amused at her words, Jake stroked her tear-streaked cheek.

"What's this nonsense? You and I don't need to talk about payback, my dear Miss Nightingale. Just feed the black monster. I won't be long."

He dropped a light kiss on her mouth and left before she could say another word.

Molly curled her legs up on the sofa and tried not to yawn. The simple but filling omelet Jake had cooked and a long soak in the tub had left her soothed and sleepy. Mac lay purring on her lap, as appreciative as she was of the cotton nightgown and soft fleecy dressing gown Jake had bought for her, along with a toothbrush and other toiletries.

She watched her host as he skimmed several weeks worth of newspapers, occasionally reading aloud items of interest. He had showered after eating and now wore an ankle-length, maroon velour dressing gown that brought out the auburn lights in his hair.

He looked sexy. Too sexy. In the privacy of her mind, Molly undid the belt and pushed the robe from his shoulders to reveal his broad chest, his flat stomach, and . . . . Molly sighed and forced the vision away. When had she become a masochist?

Deliberately, she looked around the room and imagined the scene through the eyes of a camera. *If this were a movie set, we would resemble a longtime married couple.* When she found herself wishing that the illusion was real, she shook the thought away. Jake had made it clear that he'd be horrified at the very idea.

At her urging, he had called his parents and sister. From the one-sided conversation she gathered that they had been irritated by his silence but not worried. It seemed it was not uncommon for him to be out of touch when he was pursuing a story. He put off their questions with a vague reference about following a lead out of town. She was glad they hadn't suffered over his absence.

His friend J.J. *had* worried about him. The answering machine held numerous calls, each more frantic than the last. Since he was the only person who knew of Jake's intended destination the evening he tumbled back in time, the man was alarmed by Jake's subsequent disappearance.

J.J. didn't answer his phone. Several calls to friends revealed that the man had not been seen in his usual haunts for some time. Though he said nothing, Molly sensed that Jake was worried.

Three of the messages, the last recorded only an hour before they reached the apartment, were loud, brief, sarcastic demands for Jake to call in. His sheepish grin had piqued her curiosity. Shaking his head, Jake had identified the owner of the dictatorial voice as his boss, Reg Colfax, senior editor and pussycat—all spit but no claws.

"We conduct a running war, a friendly one, though you'd never know to hear him. He insists I keep him informed of every move I make and every detail of the story I'm working on."

"But you don't." It was an easy guess.

"Nope. Well, not very often." Jake cocked his head and grinned like a schoolboy. Then the grin faded. "With hindsight, though, I wish Reg could tell me what story I was chasing the night I was shot. Of course, I can't be sure the story and the bullet were connected. Maybe I walked into a mugging." The shooting incident was his memory's only remaining holdout.

Molly's drowsiness vanished abruptly when Jake began to read aloud from one of the older newspapers.

"Listen to this. 'Ex-husband of soap star Celia Chambers found shot to death.' Hmmm," he murmured absently, "the coroner announced that David Ackers, once an actor himself, was found in the parking lot of an abandoned warehouse."

Molly stiffened as horror swamped her. Jake, his gaze on the newspaper, continued to read the article aloud.

"The police suspect the death was drug-related. It was believed, but never proven, that the dead man supplied drugs to users in the entertainment field, until his own erratic behavior ended his career in television. It says here that the police are unable to locate his ex-wife, who took a leave of absence from *Tangled Lives* two years ago. Her former friends and co-workers deny any knowledge of her whereabouts. Huh, that's odd. Why would a talented, successful woman—"

A guttural sound broke from Molly's throat. Instantly, Mac sat up, then bounded from her lap to the floor. He wrapped his tail around his paws, mewed plaintively, and fixed his gaze on Molly.

Jake looked up from the paper. He took one look at her face and rushed to her side. Taking her icy hands in his, he peered into her eyes.

"What's wrong? Are you sick? Sweetheart, speak to me! Molly!"

Mute with shock, Molly stared at the scattered newspaper. Jake turned his head to follow her line of sight. He turned back to her, and Molly saw comprehension dawn in his eyes. His hands tightened around hers. The pain made Molly gasp, but it served to jolt her from her stupor. She met Jake's stunned eyes and saw the knowledge in them.

"My God," he breathed. "You're Celia Chambers."

"Yes. No. I mean, I was," she inhaled a ragged breath, "once upon a long time ago." She closed her eyes and dropped her head on his shoulder.

Jake pulled her closer to his side, tucked her cold hands inside his dressing gown, wrapped his arms around her, and lowered his chin to the top of her head. Mac leaped silently to the couch and, in instant approval of the new arrangement, draped himself across both laps. For some minutes, the only sound in the room was the feline's throaty purr.

The only thought in Jake's mind was the overwhelming evidence that Molly seemed totally shaken by the death of her husband. No, her ex-husband. Was she still in love with David Ackers? Despair at that idea fought with his compassion for her.

At first, Molly's brain drowned in a deluge of memories. Images of David surfaced in foaming confusion. David accusing. David whispering words of love. David sneering. David shrugging in cold rejection. David begging for forgiveness. David shouting and pushing. David blustering, denying, raging in unwarranted jealousy. David naked in their bed, his arms around the equally naked script writer. David—dead. Her body shook with the emotional pounding.

As Jake's body heat began to penetrate the icy chill that encased her, the memories receded and with them, the last vestige of the love she had once felt for David Ackers.

David, poor David, had destroyed himself. He had made a wasteland of his life and had devastated hers. Now it was truly over. He would never hurt her again. She had never wished him dead, but now it was finally, completely over.

When her shudders abated, Jake leaned her limp body against the back of the couch and slipped away to the kitchen. A moment later he wrapped her fingers around a warm snifter of brandy.

"Drink this, sweetheart. It'll help."

Molly obeyed. She gasped as the fiery liquid burned its way to her stomach. But it helped. A moment later she felt her scattered parts coalesce into the familiar whole. Smiling gratefully, she lifted her face to Jake.

"Thanks. I'm all right now. It was just the . . . shock."

Jake searched her expression then returned to his chair and took a long sip of his drink. Molly watched him over the rim of her glass. His face was strained and taut. She knew he was bursting with questions, that the reporter in him craved answers. Well, it was time, past time, she told him everything.

For the next half-hour, she related the tale of her marriage to the handsome actor. Jake listened without comment as she described how David had changed as her career soared and his stagnated. His growing consumption of drugs and his jealousy of her success had led the failing actor to accuse her of becoming the character she played; a sly, treacherous, cheating woman who would do anything to get what she wanted.

"So you finally divorced him. Was that why you took a leave of absence from the show?"

Molly sighed. "That...I was close to a breakdown. That last year, three years ago, was a nightmare. David's tirades grew steadily worse. Then my mother had a stroke. She lived for five months but she didn't know me. The final straw was when I lost my baby. I discovered I was pregnant after the separation. The doctor said the miscarriage was caused by stress."

She blinked back tears and didn't see the look of fury that crossed Jake's face.

"So, I decided I had to get away. The show's directors allowed me to break my contract. I told everyone I would be away for an unspecified amount of time, and that I wouldn't get in touch with anyone until I returned. I didn't want David to find out where I was and follow me."

Wiping away her tears with the sleeve of her dressing gown, she forced a small laugh.

"I hadn't even chosen a destination. When I decided to take one more walk in Tom's Woods, the car was packed and ready to go. You know the rest."

"No wonder you spoke of Duncan's home as a sanctuary," Jake said softly. "I wish there was some way I could thank him for his kindness to you."

Then he frowned, his face ferocious. "David Ackers was a fool!"

Molly ignored his last words and smiled wistfully. "Duncan was the nicest thing that had happened to me in a long time. I'll never forget him. He was my salvation."

After a brief silence, Jake asked, "*Was* Ackers dealing drugs?"

"I don't know. I know his erratic moods were caused by drugs, but I never saw any evidence that he was dealing." Molly gestured toward the newspapers. "But why else would he be murdered? The police are probably right. Drugs and violence often go hand-in-hand."

She sighed. "David couldn't act, at least not well. If he had only faced that He was an intelligent man. He could have been a success in some other line of work. But he wouldn't accept the truth."

Jake nodded. Molly thought about her disastrous marriage for a few minutes more. What had happened, had happened. There was nothing she could do for David. That chapter in her life was over. She felt her insides settle.

A silence fell between them. Molly wondered what

Jake was thinking. Had she fallen in his estimation because she had misjudged the kind of man she'd married? No, he wouldn't do that. He was a fair man, well aware of the frailties of human nature. After all, he too had made a mistake in his choice of spouse.

They yawned in unison. Jake smiled.

"Bedtime, I think." Jake rose and extended his hand. Molly allowed him to pull her to her feet. She swayed with exhaustion.

"By the way," she managed, as Jake slipped his arm through hers, "don't you dare laugh, but my name is really Molly Malone. For career reasons, I never took David's name."

"Molly *Malone?*" Jake snorted in laughter. "Sweet Mol-ly Ma-lone," he sang, badly off-key. "I don't believe it."

"Believe it." Molly elbowed him in the ribs but had to chuckle with him. "My dad was Irish. What can I say?"

Jake pretended to be injured by the blow. They staggered through the bedroom door together. Mac followed, meowing in indignation at their antics. He leaped to the bed, wrapped his tail around his feet for safety, then sat regarding them alertly.

Just inside the room Jake released her and opened the closet door. Too tired at first to wonder what he was doing, Molly sat down on the edge of the bed and watched the play of his muscles clearly visible through the heavy robe. He pulled down a blanket and pillow from the top shelf, then closed the closet door.

With the bedding draped over his arms, he had almost reached the door when she realized he meant to bed down in the living room. For the first time, she consciously realized that the apartment had only one bedroom. And one bed.

A huge wave of tenderness swept over her. Jake was every bit as tired as she. He, too, needed a good night's sleep. The couch just wouldn't do.

She had no qualms that he'd take advantage if they shared the bed. She'd slept in his arms when they'd returned after answering Marge's call, but he hadn't presumed their relationship had changed. Jake Anderson was a gentleman. He'd returned to the cot in the pantry the very next night.

"Jake," she said to his retreating back. He stopped but didn't turn around. "You have two choices."

He pivoted slowly, his gaze dark and questioning.

"I refuse to put you out of your bed. Either I sleep on the couch or we both sleep here." Blushing, she added softly, "There's no reason why we shouldn't sleep in the same bed."

Jake caught her delicate emphasis on the word 'sleep'.

"You're sure you don't want to be alone? I mean, hearing about David—"

"David has been gone from my life for more than two years. I'm sorry he died the way he did, but I can't grieve for him. Grieving is for people who've lost someone they care about. I stopped caring a long time ago." She paused, and patted the bed. "I'll sleep better if you're beside me."

Jake's face lit like the sun at high noon. He dropped the blanket and pillow and kicked them out of the way. Three long strides brought him to her side. He lifted her hands and deposited a lingering kiss in each palm.

"I'll turn off the lights in the other rooms and put out some more food for Mac. You crawl in and get comfortable." At the door he turned again. "Do you think you'll be able to sleep on a water bed?"

"Oh, yes. I have one too, at my condo. Though I think I could sleep on stones tonight."

When Jake returned a few minutes later, Molly was sound asleep. He stood beside the bed and stared down at her. Midnight black hair lying like silk threads on the pillow made his fingers itch to tangle themselves in the lush growth. Her thick, black lashes fanned over the ivory skin of her high cheekbones. He longed to kiss her slightly opened mouth, to sweep his tongue over the sensuous fullness of her lower lip.

Jake felt himself grow hard and almost laughed aloud. "The sandman is going to have his work cut out for him tonight," he muttered under his breath. Not that he'd rather be anywhere than beside Molly—sleep or no sleep.

He turned out the light and slipped under the covers, smothering a groan when his thigh brushed her hip. He always slept nude, but tonight he'd put on the bottom half of a pair of pajamas his niece and nephew had given him on his last birthday. They'd never been used before.

Lying still to avoid disturbing her, he thought about the evening's revelations. As a reporter, he had heard the rumors about David Ackers. It seemed strange that the ex-actor had never even, as far as he knew, been taken in for questioning. The omission implied protection, as in someone running interference for him. Someone with power. In a political and cultural city like Ottawa, that could be anyone.

Obviously, the wall of protection around him had developed a hole. Why would a customer kill the goose with the golden eggs? Had he tried to blackmail the wrong person? Someone up for re-election? An entertainer whose career would be history if the public knew of his or her drug habit? Or maybe he had tried to cheat his supplier. Whatever, the man had made a fatal mistake.

Against his will, his mind replayed Molly's story of their marriage. Jake wasn't sorry the bastard was dead. He *was* sorry he couldn't personally punish the man for the way he had treated his wife.

Molly stirred and rolled over, coming to rest against his side. All thoughts of her ex-husband vanished when her arm fell across his waist and her foot snuggled against his ankle. He shifted slightly and slowly lifted her head until he could slide his arm under her neck. She murmured something unintelligible and nestled her face on his shoulder. When her body relaxed and grew limp against his, Jake emptied his lungs of the breath he was holding. He wrapped his other arm over her hip and drew her closer. Eyes closed, he contemplated their perfect fit.

It was a good thing his work had taught him how to get by without much sleep.

He kissed the top of her head and rubbed his cheek on the satin smoothness of her hair. He remembered his first sight of her, bending over him as he lay sprawled on her lawn. The pain in his leg and head hadn't prevented his heart from leaping with instant astonishment. He'd known he wasn't dead. Heaven held no angel as beautiful as Molly Malone Barnes. He felt a surge of satisfaction that she had never called herself Molly Ackers.

Even through the pain and subsequent fever, the sexual attraction between them had been strong. It had grown into so much more in the ensuing weeks—much more than mere chemistry—grown into something he had never felt for any woman before. With a bolt of insight, he realized he had been waiting for Molly Malone all his life.

Jake smiled. The smile grew until he thought his face would split in two.

"I love you, sweet Molly Malone," he whispered into her hair.

A few minutes later he fell asleep, the smile still huge on his face.

Chapter Eight

Molly woke slowly, aware of a heavy weight across her hip and the rise and fall of her warm pillow. Warm pillow? She opened her eyes and saw a forest of dark, curling hairs that thinned and narrowed in the distance. She frowned. A moment later, realization heated her cheeks.

Jake's deep, steady breaths told her he was asleep. She breathed deeply of the clean, masculine scent that had become so enticingly familiar. A contented smile crossed her face.

Jake sighed and shifted beneath her cheek. Her pulse began to hum and drive desire through her body. Was he completely naked? She longed to find out. Her hand curled around the edge of the covers . . . . No, she mustn't. It would be an invasion of his privacy. Not to mention too great a strain on her self-control. One by one, her reluctant fingers loosed their hold.

The sudden sound of a Heavy Metal rock group booming from the apartment below distracted her with its nearly forgotten familiarity. Without moving her head from his chest, she gazed around the brown and turquoise room. Jake's room. In their own time.

Desire dissolved into anxiety. Carefully, she eased away from him and rolled to the other side of the bed. Had they stayed marooned in another time, she felt sure they would have eventually made love. But they were home now. Things were different. They would pick up their old lives, not start a new one together. Jake had made it very clear that commitment wasn't for him. She had to accept that.

She knew he wanted her. But that was no more than normal male desire and perhaps gratitude for her nursing services. How embarrassed he would be if he knew her true feelings. She couldn't let him guess that she had fallen in love with him. She hadn't known it herself, not for sure, until he had refused to abandon Mac to the past.

She slipped from the bed and tiptoed into the bathroom.

After showering and dressing, she gazed out the kitchen window at the tops of the trees and watched the birds socializing, their conversations interrupted each time a squirrel invaded their space. It was hard to tell who was scolding whom. The confusion reminded her of the seeming chaos that transpired off-camera during a break in the taping. The memory sparked a sense of excitement, a longing to once again be a part of Canada's first daytime soap.

She thought about the possibilities. If they wished, the show's producers could bring back her character. Two years ago, when she demanded a leave of absence, rather than kill off Celia Chambers or introduce a new actor in the part, the writers had written in a plane crash in the North that had supposedly taken all lives aboard, though not all the bodies could be accounted for. If she returned, Celia's character would be faced with a charge of the murder of the fictional town's mayor. There was only one way to find out if the producer would welcome her back. She would have to visit the set.

But not yet. Molly knew she wouldn't be comfortable

slipping back into her old life if Marge Thomas' killer was still alive and free. The woman had been one of the first to accept her into the rural community. She owed the dead woman and she meant to uncover her murderer if at all possible. And alone, if necessary.

Would Jake help her? The reporter had problems of his own to solve. Someone had shot him. He didn't know who or why, and naturally he would be more concerned for his missing friend J.J. than for a long-dead woman whom he'd met only twice. It wouldn't be fair to ask for his help.

Molly wasn't sure just what she could do. First though, she needed to check out the condo she'd bought after the divorce, make some calls, renew her driver's license, buy or rent a car, and activate her financial affairs. She had no doubt that her lawyer, acting on her behalf, would have kept the bills and condo fees paid up to date. To restore her financial authority, she had to return to her own home.

The sound of the shower running ended her musings. She pulled bacon and eggs from the refrigerator and began to make breakfast.

When he entered the kitchen, Jake searched Molly's face. The depth of his disappointment, on awakening to find her gone, shocked him. A light sleeper, he had realized instantly that she must have taken great care to leave the bed without waking him. The thought made him uneasy.

"Good morning," he offered with a quizzical smile. "Coffee smells wonderful."

"Good morning." Molly gestured to the chair and placed a cup on the table. "Enjoy."

When they finished the almost silent meal, Jake helped Molly wash up. After some hesitation, she turned to him and asked, in a matter-of-fact voice, "If you wouldn't mind lending me cab fare, Jake, I'll get out of your way. I've already called The Royal Arms and luckily, the same security guard is there. He knows me, so I won't have any trouble getting into my condo."

Jake stared. She was going to walk out of his life? Just like that? He looked away and cleared his throat. Didn't the last three weeks together mean anything to her?

"You don't need a taxi. My car should still be in the garage. But," he reached for her hand and clasped it in both of his, "I thought we were going to find out what happened to Marge?"

Surprise and relief flowed across her face.

"I thought you wouldn't . . . . But what about J.J.? You need to find him. Unless you've remembered what—"

"No, I still don't know what breach of etiquette put me in line for a bullet—and I am worried about J.J. I've never known him to leave the Glebe area. But that doesn't mean I've forgotten about Marge. She was a kind, decent woman. The thought that her murderer might still be free is intolerable. First, though, we need information."

Molly's radiant smile took his breath away.

"Oh, Jake, thank you!" She flung her arms around his neck and kissed his mouth then immediately drew away. Her cheeks were pink. "I need to get sorted out at my place, then I thought I'd examine the back issues of the newspapers to see if her killer was caught. And we should check out the phone directories for the names of anyone from those days who may still be around. And—"

Jake's chuckle stemmed her flow of words. He took her hand and led her back to the table.

"You're reading my mind," he said. "I was going to suggest that you examine the back issues of *The Chronicle*. And we need to look over Doug Baylor's notes again." He paused and rubbed the back of his neck. "I have some contacts in municipal government, too. It's time to call in a few favors. I want to know exactly what happened to the people whose farms became the Capital Highway." One eyebrow rose. "And who had the amazing good luck to buy those farms before the government expropriated the land. It should be possible to discover who paid the taxes until the government took over."

Molly thought quickly. "The problems that forced the farmers to sell out—you think they were more than acts of God?"

"I think Doug thought so." Jake spoke slowly. "If the disasters *were* man-made and the wrong person discovered he was investigating...."

Molly shivered. "Maybe Marge was right when she said his death couldn't have been either suicide or an accident."

"It's possible. It would mean that someone in the Department of Highways leaked confidential information about the proposed route of the new highway."

"Someone connected in some way to the people who bought up the farms," Molly added. "It makes sense, Jake! With inside information like that, they could make a lot of money. But how would Doug have found out?"

"I don't know," Jake admitted. "But remember the markings on that piece of map. There are no straight lines in nature, so maybe he noticed the linear pattern of the affected farms. The disasters were reported in the local weekly newspaper."

"But according to Doug's notes, each farm was bought by a different person." Molly crossed her arms on the table and leaned forward. "If it were me, I'd hesitate to let so many people in on the scheme."

"Me, too—and maybe that's how Doug caught on to it. Someone was careless and let something slip. Or maybe most of the buyers' names are phony. Even the government would have to take notice, if nine of the parcels of land it purchased were owned by the same person."

"What puzzles me," Molly said, "is how the buyers found out about Doug's investigation. What tipped them off in the first place? Someone must have been following him, or keeping track of his activities."

Jake hesitated, choosing his words carefully. "It had to

be someone who was in a position to observe his comings and goings. Someone who knew of his close relationship with Marge."

"But who—" Molly inhaled sharply. "You mean Brad," she accused. "No, you're wrong. Just because you don't like him, doesn't mean he's involved in fraud or killed his own father and cousin. That's monstrous!"

"I agree, but just because you *do* like him, doesn't necessarily mean he's innocent," Jake returned. "You have to admit he was in the best position to discover what Doug was doing. It's a possibility, Molly."

Molly didn't answer, couldn't answer. Much as she hated to admit it, Jake was right. Brad could be involved in the fraud, though she was certain he hadn't killed his father.

Doug had made a mistake, perhaps questioned or trusted the wrong person, or somehow let slip information he shouldn't have had—and he'd paid for the blunder with his life.

Since it was still too early in the morning to start digging for information, they continued to discuss the possibilities for another half-hour, neither mentioning Brad again. When they began to repeat themselves, Molly reluctantly excused herself and left the room. She'd put off the moment of departure as long as she could. It was time to leave. She returned to the kitchen with the plastic bag of purchases Jake had made for her the night before.

Jake swallowed his disappointment. He was being foolish. Much as he'd like her to stay, he knew she had to return to her own life. He had no claim on her.

He drove her to her condo and tried not to be bothered by the security guard's enthusiastic greeting. The gray-haired man's narrow-eyed look was almost jealous when Molly introduced Jake. He agreed, reluctantly, to admit Jake whenever the reporter asked to enter the building. With difficulty, Jake refrained from smiling in triumph.

When Molly explained that she had lost her purse and

her keys, the guard immediately offered to accompany her to her door. Jake took his leave, assuring Molly he would return about seven to take her to dinner.

As he drove away, Jake's thoughts turned to J.J. Not only did the man's disappearance disturb him, he needed J.J. to repeat the tip that had led him to the vicinity where he'd been shot. What exactly had J.J. heard?

If only he could remember something, anything, about the shooting. What had he seen that made him a liability? And a liability to whom? Though Jake hadn't said anything to Molly, it occurred to him during the night that he could still be a target. The shooter couldn't know that Jake had no memory of the incident.

The back of his neck prickled at the thought. Somewhere there was a bullet with his name on it.

And he had no idea who owned the gun.

Forcing away the disturbing thought, since he could do nothing until he'd talked with J.J., Jake drove to the Glebe area, where his friend usually hung out.

One of the casualties of economic downsizing five years earlier, J.J. had discovered that the jobless life suited him much more than his former work. He had never married and had no living family. Unemployment insurance, then welfare, yielded just enough money to pay for a room in a boarding house, and enough time to read the daily paper from first page to last. He augmented his income by indulging his avid curiosity about the people around him. He watched and he listened. And at least once a week he heard some tidbit of information to interest the police or his friend Jake.

His appearance was average in every respect, his dress and manner designed to blend into the background. Few ever noticed him. To encourage verbal carelessness, he wore a conspicuous, old-fashioned hearing aid. His hearing, however, was excellent. He had never spent a dime on batteries.

Jake smiled. He was fond of the small man. But where could he be?

He decided to stop first at Andy's Eats, where J.J. spent a large part of his days. When a parking spot opened just as he arrived, he told himself it was a good sign. He fed the meter and entered the unprepossessing but immaculate restaurant.

One table was occupied by a tired-looking mother and a sulking toddler. Choosing a stool at the far end of the counter, Jake greeted the rotund owner and chief cook.

"Hi, Andy. You bake any doughnuts today?"

"Don't I always, man? You get a chocolate one today. I bin foolin' round with a new icing. Tell me what you think."

Andy slipped a doughnut on a paper plate and set it in front of Jake. Without being asked, he filled a styrofoam cup with coffee and passed it to the reporter. Then he did something he'd never done before. After glancing around he circled the end of the counter and sat down beside Jake, crowding close, his head slightly lowered.

Jake looked at him in surprise. "What's up?"

"Don't know, man. But I sure am glad to see you. You seen J.J. lately?"

"No, I've been looking for him. He's okay, isn't he? Do you know where he is?"

"I got a number, is all. He was in here 'bout three weeks ago. He called the next day, wanted to know if I'd seen you. Haven't heard from him since. Give me a number to pass on to you. He sounded worried, man. Kinda scared, too." Andy leaned closer and whispered in a gravely voice. "What's goin' on, Jake? Where you bin, anyway?"

"You wouldn't believe me if I told you. Have you got that number handy?"

"Sure." Andy dug a meaty paw into his apron pocket. As he handed the food-speckled piece of torn paper to Jake, he gestured with his head toward the back room. "Use my office. It's private."

Jake thanked him, swallowed the last bite of doughnut

and carried his coffee cup through the curtained entrance. Andy's office consisted of a battered desk and sprung chair squeezed into the corner of a room piled high with boxes of restaurant supplies. A glass-walled walk-in cooler contained crates of fresh vegetables and meats.

The surface of the desk was littered with invoices and files. Jake pawed through the mess until he found the buried telephone. He was surprised to see his hands shaking as he dialed the number. Without realizing it, he had begun to think that something terrible had happened to his friend.

His tension grew as the phone rang and rang. After ten rings he started to hang up. A rough growl stopped him just in time.

"Yeah, what?"

Jake inhaled deeply. "I'd like to talk to J.J. please."

"Jeez. Ya hadda call in the middle of the game, dinj'ya." The voice was heavy with disgust. "Hang on."

Jake winced at the sound of the receiver dropping to a table. A moment later he heard the disgruntled voice bellowing for J.J. Jake waited.

"J.J. here. Who's this?"

Almost lightheaded with relief, Jake managed to blurt, "Jake. Jake Anderson. Where the hell are you?"

"Oh God, Jake. You're alive. What happened? I was sure they'd killed you. Thank God you got away. Are you all right? I called all the hospitals and—"

Jake interrupted. "I'm fine. How did you know I've been shot? No, never mind that now. Where are you? We've got to talk."

"We sure do. I've been staying with a buddy in the west end. Meet me in thirty minutes behind the supermarket at Shopper's City. I'll wait behind one of the delivery trucks. And Jake, watch your back."

Before he could ask, *watch out for whom?*, the line went dead. Jake hung up. What was J.J. doing in the west end? He never left the Glebe area. What did J.J. know about that night? Stretching, Jake rubbed the back of his neck and cut off his speculations. He'd have his answers soon enough.

Her spirits lifted by the security guard's genuine pleasure at her return, Molly thanked Rudy and stepped into the home she had left two years before. With her back to the door, she snapped on the light and looked around curiously. From the entrance foyer she could see into the living room to the solar extension. It looked strangely different. Yet nothing at all had changed.

The air was musty and stale. Molly made a slow circle through her home, opening the vertical blinds and windows, caressing the few carvings scattered here and there, and admiring the moss green and rose of the thick carpet and nubby upholstery. Would Jake like her apartment?

The walk-in closet in her bedroom embarrassed her. There were clothes enough for three women, clothes enough for every conceivable occasion. Had appearance meant that much to her? She thought of the meager wardrobe that had more than satisfied her when she was Molly Barnes. How strange that she had never once missed this cornucopia of garments. With sudden insight, she realized the expensive clothing had served as her protection against David's attempts to destroy her self-esteem.

Well, she had no need for such armor now. She had Duncan and the healing interlude in his home to thank for that.

She sat down to make a list of the things she needed to do. By late afternoon, she had visited her bank, leased a car, arranged for the telephone to be reconnected and stocked her cupboards and refrigerator. Postal service and newspaper delivery would resume the next day. Her life would soon be back to its normal, familiar course.

No, not normal. How could it be? A career interrupted by

a vacation or bad health was one thing. A career break spent twenty years in the past was quite another. No, her life would never be the same again.

Molly glanced at her watch. Jake would arrive in an hour. She headed for her bedroom to get ready.

Molly drummed impatient fingers on the table. "Well? What did you find out? I swear, Jake, I won't wait another minute."

"Sure you don't want dessert?"

"Jake, I warn you—"

Jake threw up his hands. "Okay, okay, I'll talk." The teasing light in his eyes faded. He looked around the restaurant quickly, then leaned forward. "I found J.J. He's been hiding out."

"Hiding out? Why?"

"He's been afraid." Jake shook his head. "It seems he was worried and followed me that night. He hid in a doorway half a block back, so he didn't see whatever it was I saw. He told me he watched me slip through the gates of an abandoned warehouse. Then he heard a shot and saw me start forward, then turn around and run away when there was another shot. He figured I'd been seen."

"Did he see the person who shot you?"

"Yes, but he wasn't close enough to identify anyone. It was too dark. Someone—a man he thinks—chased after me and fired again. I went down, but then I got up and managed to disappear into Tom's Woods." He smiled at Molly. "I wish I could thank Duncan. Those trees are probably the only reason I got away."

Molly smiled back at him. "We both owe Duncan a lot. In a different way, he saved my life, too. I was at the breaking point. He saved my sanity."

Jake said softly, "I wish I could thank him for that, too." Then he fell silent.

A waiter appeared and filled their coffee cups. When

he left, Molly reached over the table and put a hand on Jake's arm.

"What is it? What aren't you telling me?"

Jake met her gaze. He covered her hand with his. A chill slipped down Molly's spine. She had never seen him look quite so serious. His glance darted around the room, then he leaned forward.

"J.J. said the tip was about a possible drug buy. I've been doing a series of articles about the drug scene in Ottawa. I had a lead on some local suppliers, but I needed to discover the route from the States that their suppliers used." He shook his head with regret. "Unfortunately, I still can't remember. But . . . "

"But?" Molly held her breath. She thought she knew what was coming.

"In the newspaper the next day, J.J. read of the discovery of a body. The paper reported the location and time of death. I must have seen the murder. Molly," he swallowed and went on, "I'm sorry. It was David."

Though she'd guessed as much, Molly shuddered. She stared at the flickering candle on the table and remembered the last time she'd seen her ex-husband. David had begged her to take him back, promising to give up drugs. When she refused, his abusive language had been horrendous. Even if she hadn't lost the baby, even if he'd stopped using drugs, she never wanted him to touch her again.

When she could speak again, she said, "David chose to live his life the way he did. He was too intelligent not to know how dangerous his associates were. I'm sorry he died that way, but I can't grieve for him."

Jake nodded and continued his story. "The next day, J.J. scoured the woods for me. He found a trail of blood and expected the worst—that I'd been caught and killed. He's kept out of sight ever since."

"Does he think he was seen?"

Jake shook his head. "He wasn't sure at first, but now that he knows I'm alive, he's moving back to the Glebe. I tried to convince him to stay away longer, but he won't listen. Somehow he's got it into his head that, since I'm still alive, he's in no danger."

"Do you think he's safe?"

"Probably," Jake admitted. "He didn't really see anything. He was half a block back. If J.J. couldn't identify the person who chased me, the reverse is probably true. It's possible he wasn't even seen."

Molly's eyes widened in shocked realization. "But *you* were seen. Jake—"

His grip tightened on her hand. "But probably not identified," he inserted quickly. "It was dark, remember. The only light was from an outdoor bulb over the door. I was twenty feet away at the corner of the building. I doubt the killer could identify me."

Molly wasn't so easily reassured. Dread flowed in her veins.

"You don't know that. Wouldn't a big supplier have bodyguards? Others you didn't see may have seen you. You could still be in danger." For just a moment, she wished they were safely in the past.

"I really doubt that," Jake lied. "They probably think I just crawled into a hole somewhere and died, or that they scared me off. Remember, no one's seen or heard from me in three weeks, so they know I didn't go to the police. No, nobody's looking for me."

"But now that you're going back to work...."

"Stop worrying, sweetheart. I'm not going after the drug story. We're going to concentrate on Marge. In fact, I've decided to do a series of articles about the Capital Highway. A teaser. An account of the disasters that led to the sale of the farms that were expropriated only months later."

Molly allowed herself to be distracted. "So you think Marge's death and the Highway are connected?" She gently tugged her hand free and put it on her lap.

He frowned but didn't comment on her action. "Doug

Baylor's papers certainly suggest some kind of fraud. The accident or suicide theory seems less and less likely, in view of his investigation. And why would he give them to Marge for safekeeping, unless he felt he might be in danger?"

A somber silence fell between them. Molly thought of the people she had met in the past. She couldn't picture any of them as a murderer. Of course, she hadn't known many very well. She and Duncan had been content with each other's company on his isolated farm. During the last months of his life, they had been virtually housebound. The only regular visitors had been Brad Baylor and Marge Thomas.

She sipped at her coffee and watched Jake from under her lashes. He looked lost in thought. An icy shiver slithered down her spine. No matter how easily he dismissed her fears for his safety, she sensed the danger was real. Even if David's killer didn't think he'd been recognized, he would want to be sure. Jake was a loose end. He had witnessed a murder and maybe a drug transaction. The more she thought about it, the more she was convinced Jake was still a target.

The set of his jaw told her it would be useless to suggest he leave the city. He wasn't the kind of man to run away from a problem. A problem! She almost laughed at the idiotic choice of word. That *problem* could kill the man she loved.

Unless . . . . She inhaled sharply.

Chapter Nine

Jake stared at the ceiling. The foliage outside his bedroom window swayed in the light breeze, the street light creating shifting shadows on the ceiling and walls. Further down the street, a solitary cat yowled his longing to the night sky. Jake felt a kinship with the lonely animal.

He wondered if Molly lay awake, too. Was she thinking of him? Probably not. He had no doubt that something was on her mind though. Something it seemed she didn't intend to share with him.

Shortly before they left the restaurant, a small, secret smile had hovered on her lips, then disappeared. She looked determined and studiously avoided his gaze and his questions.

It worried him. Surely there was nothing she couldn't say to him. They had been through so much together. But an insistent voice in the back of his mind pointed out that things were different now. They were back in their own time. Had she relegated their relationship to the past, as finished as her relationship with Duncan Barnes? The thought that she might consider their brief time together as a mere interlude never to be repeated set his stomach churning.

Just that morning she had slipped from his bed while he slept, and tonight, though she had invited him in for a nightcap, he heard the stiffness in her voice and knew she hoped he'd refuse. He'd mumbled some excuse about getting an early start in the morning and drove away as soon as Rudy saw her safely inside the entrance.

He'd struck out before. No big deal. But Molly's rejection hurt. Hurt more than he'd thought possible. Did she regret their closeness? Now that she had returned to her own time, maybe she meant to pick up the threads of her life and go on without him. When their investigation into the twenty-year-old crimes was over, would she say goodbye?

Nice knowing you, Jake. Have a good life.

The cat's forlorn lament echoed down the empty street. Jake groaned with brotherly rapport.

Molly shifted position for the hundredth time. Her queen-sized bed had never seemed so large before. Or so lonely.

She reminded herself that Jake had turned down her invitation for coffee. At the time, she'd been more relieved than disappointed. She knew he wouldn't approve her intention to look into the drug business in the entertainment field. With her connections, she might be able to uncover the name of David's supplier. Jake's safety depended on discovering who had tried to kill him. She was eager to concoct a strategy that would elicit the information she needed. Jake's presence would have been a distraction.

Now, she wondered why he'd refused. Not for a minute did she think he was concerned about the late hour. His reason must be the obvious one—he didn't want to spend any more time with her. His interest in her had begun and ended in the past. She had to accept that and go on.

Dawn was evicting the stars from the sky when she finally fell asleep.

* * *

"Molly Malone! Thank God you're back! And about time, too. We need you desperately. Did you know the ratings plummeted when you left? Never mind, you're back now. Get your agent to make out a new contract. Where have you been, anyway? No, tell me all about it later. I have to see the writers. I want them to start on a story line for Celia immediately."

He gave her a quick hug and started away.

"And get your hair cut," he called back over his shoulder. "The way you're wearing it isn't sophisticated enough for Celia Chambers."

Without giving her a chance to speak, Edwin Larch bustled off, his moon face wreathed in a Cheshire grin. Molly smiled after him. The short, tubby director hadn't changed his machine gun manner of speech or his habit of dressing like a sixties hippie. He still wore his long, thin hair in a braid, although the bare, tonsured circle on his head had spread in the two years since she'd seen him.

She picked her way carefully around the sound stage, accepting warm greetings from those she knew and being introduced to the newcomers. Within a half-hour, it seemed as if she'd never been away. The cast and crew had been her only family for a long time. She was truly home again.

Finally, she climbed the stairs to the small room used by the script writers. They welcomed her with enthusiasm. Only Gayle Everett's greeting held a hint of constraint. Molly made a concerted effort to treat the writer as just one of the group.

Molly accepted a cup of the ever-present mud they called coffee and allowed the voluble writers to bring her up-to-date on the various story lines. They bounced ideas against each other to account for the return of Celia Chambers and to devise a suitable plot for the conniving character. Frequent laughter echoed around the room as they brainstormed a variety of scenarios. Molly choked back a gasp when Winston Tuck, the most creative of the writers, suggested they add a science fiction element to the show by portraying Celia as having been tossed into the past at the time of the plane crash. Luckily, the others hooted in derision and the idea died.

Molly got up to leave an hour later. At the door, she stopped and looked over her shoulder. In a friendly, offhand manner, she called to the woman she had found in bed with her husband.

"Oh, Gayle, could I talk with you for a minute?"

The script-writer paled but rose from her chair and approached the door. "Of course, Molly. Can I help you with something?"

"I hope so."

Molly peered around the open door of the next room. It was empty. She stepped inside and waited for Gayle to join her. Closing the door behind the apprehensive woman, she gestured to the chairs arranged haphazardly around the scarred table.

"I'd like to ask you some questions about David."

Her freckles starkly visible against her milky skin, the petite redhead sank into a chair. When Molly sat facing her across the table, she shuddered, then straightened and faced the actor.

"Molly, I want you to know that David and I—"

"I'm not interested in that," Molly interrupted. "I need to know—"

"Please." The writer leaned forward. "Let me explain. I've wanted to tell you for so long. I've been so ashamed, all the more so when I realized you weren't going to tell anyone what I did."

Molly was moved by the anguished appeal on the scriptwriter's pretty face. The lump of bitter resentment she hadn't realized she still carried in her heart shifted and began to shrink. Until that terrible day, she had liked the vivacious and talented woman. Now she felt an unexpected surge of sympathy for Gayle. She nodded reluctantly.

"Thank you," Gayle sighed. She clasped her hands together and began to speak in a trembling voice.

"There was no affair. When you found us . . . it was the first and only time. I had gone to your apartment with some last minute changes in your script for the next day. David was alone. He invited me in for a drink. I was cold and tired, so I accepted. I only meant to stay a few minutes." Her gaze fell to her hands.

"I'd missed dinner, so the brandy went straight to my head. So stupid of me, though liquor never affected me like that before. Then when he...." She gulped and looked beseechingly at Molly.

"I understand. David could be amazingly charming when he wanted something." Molly suppressed a shudder of remembrance.

"Yes," Gayle continued, "but it wasn't all his fault. I knew better. It was just...I was so flattered, you see, that such a handsome man actually wanted me, and my head was swimming. I couldn't think." She lifted her face and looked straight into Molly's eyes. "It only happened the once. I swear. He called me a few times after that, but I refused to see him again. Molly, I *hated* what I'd done to you!"

Molly sensed Gayle was telling the truth. The bitter feelings she'd had for the writer evaporated. Gayle had been just another of David's victims. David, she suddenly realized, had also been a casualty. Her handsome, immature husband had fallen prey to the capricious regard of the viewing public. His insecurities and bruised vanity had sent him to drugs and other women.

"Forgiven and forgotten, Gayle. We're none of us perfect." She paused and returned the woman's relieved smile.

"Thank you." Gayle inhaled deeply and brushed away the moisture in her eyes. "What was it you wanted to ask me about?"

"Drugs," Molly said baldly. "David and drugs. He used

them and maybe sold them. Do you know anything about the people he dealt with? Or the person who supplied to him?"

Gayle opened her mouth, then hesitated. Finally she asked, "Molly, you do know that David was killed several weeks ago?"

"Yes. I found out last night. I suspect drugs may be behind his murder." She sighed. "Our marriage was good at the beginning. I can't forget the man David used to be. If I can get a line on the people he bought the drugs from, maybe—"

Gayle shook her head. "That's dangerous talk. Anyway, I don't think drugs were involved, in spite of what the newspapers said. You know how people talk about everyone else in this business? Well, they say David went into rehab shortly after you left two years ago. The word is that he cleaned himself up and never touched drugs again. Just last month someone told me that he was talking about going to California, to try to get back into acting. I don't know for sure if any of that is true, but . . ."

For a moment, Molly sat perfectly still, stunned by this picture of David. Had he given up drugs to prove he still loved her, as he claimed when they signed the divorce papers? She remembered the pain in his eyes when she had miscarried. Had he blamed himself for the loss of their baby? It seemed something had made him grow up and take a good look at himself—too late for their marriage, but not too late to make a new life for himself. A life ended by a bullet three weeks ago. Pity and regret surged through her.

"Hearing about David's death must have been a terrible shock for you. I'm sorry."

"Yes," she said faintly. Straightening her shoulders, Molly shook her head. "If he wasn't involved with drugs for the last two years, then why was he killed? I don't understand it."

The writer lifted her hands in a helpless gesture. "Some say he was in the wrong place at the wrong time. Or was mistaken for someone else. Or it was a random killing. According to the papers, the police have no suspects and no motive."

The two women sat without speaking for a few minutes. Finally, Molly sighed deeply and rose. Gayle stood and regarded her with a desolate expression. Impulsively, Molly reached for the other woman and gave her a hug.

"I've forgiven you, Gayle. Now you must forgive yourself. It's all in the past."

Tears welled up in the writer's eyes. "I feel so guilty."

"Don't," Molly chided. "From your description, I think it's likely David doctored your drink with something. So you see, you weren't to blame. If we're to work together again and be friends, you have to put it behind you. I have." She drew on her acting abilities to smile cheerfully at the other woman. "Just don't let Winston develop that time travel idea."

As she hoped, Gayle laughed. "Heavens, no. Even a soap opera has to draw the line somewhere. The audience deserves *some* credibility."

They grinned at each other. With a wave of her hand and a promise to see her again soon, Molly left the room and made her way downstairs.

Deep in thought, his steps lagging, Jake scarcely noticed the pedestrians flowing past him. He thrust his hands in his pockets and stared unseeing past the crowd of shoppers on Bank Street. His conversation with J.J. had made him question his theory about the purpose of the meeting that ended with David Ackers' death. Three weeks earlier, both men had assumed that the meeting involved drugs. J.J. had changed his mind when he'd learned the identity of the dead man from the newspapers. Street talk had it that the failed actor had never been a seller, just a user. And a user who'd quit using, at that. But if the meeting hadn't been about drugs, then what?

According to J.J., the ex-actor was to meet with someone heavy. The street gossip hadn't specifically mentioned drugs. What other reason would account for David's murder? An irate husband? Some kind of personal feud? A random mugging gone awry?

No, not a mugging. Though he still wasn't able to recall the incident, Jake knew that the meeting had been set up in advance. Drugs *must* have been involved. Why else would the actor have gone to such a lonely, isolated spot in the middle of the night, if not for some illegal enterprise?

Jake sighed and shook his head. He had no idea where to begin looking for the killer. Frowning in frustration, he turned the corner and started down the side street where he'd left his car.

He paid the charge and drove to the parking lot exit. As he waited for the chance to make a left turn out of the lot, Jake idly watched the passing traffic. Three teenage girls walked by, laughing together. Their fresh young beauty made him smile. He frowned when a heavy-set man, seemingly the worse for drink, stumbled into their path. When he clutched at one of the girls to keep his balance, Jake started to get out of the car.

The girl's shriek of fright was drowned by the squeal of brakes. Jake halted outside his car as a uniformed officer leaped from his car, strode over to the group and hauled the man away from the teenagers. Jake watched as he frog-marched the man to the patrol car and shut him in the back. The officer returned to the huddling threesome and began to question them.

Frozen to the spot, Jake's head whirled with a sense of déjà vu. This same officer had directed him to the right office at the police station a few months earlier, when he'd gone to report the break-in at his landlord's apartment. But why should his instant recognition cause the weird hitch in his chest? He had seen numerous officers that day, several of whom he knew. What was special about this man? Jake narrowed his eyes and searched the man's face.

Shock jolted through him. It was Brad Baylor, twenty years older than the last time he'd seen him. Three days before.

Jake told himself to get back in his car and hide his face. But he couldn't move, couldn't look away from the man whose cousin had been so brutally murdered.

As he waved to the girls and turned back to his vehicle, the policeman's gaze flickered over to Jake. His outstretched hand stopped just short of the car door, his brow furrowing in thought. Jake drew a deep breath. Surely Brad wouldn't recognize a man he hadn't seen for twenty years?

The two men faced each other for a long moment. Then, eyes narrowed, the officer walked over to Jake.

"Seems I know you from somewhere. And you know me. What's your name, sir?"

"Jake Anderson. I'm a reporter for the Ottawa Chronicle. I was about to help those kids when you showed up. Good timing, officer."

"Yeah." Brad's short nod dismissed the incident. "Have we met?"

"Not exactly. You pointed me to the right office at Elgin Street a few months ago. My landlord's home had been burgled and I was reporting it for him." Jake held his breath. Would Brad accept the explanation?

After what seemed like minutes the policeman nodded.

"I remember," he said. His brow smoothed though a touch of uncertainty lingered in his eyes. "Jake Anderson, eh? Think I've read some of your stories. Aren't you the reporter who uncovered that case of unemployment insurance fraud last year?"

Jake nodded. "You'd think someone who's cheating

the government would have the sense to keep his mouth shut, wouldn't you? He'd probably still be getting away with it if he hadn't gotten drunk and started bragging."

"How'd you get on to him anyway?"

Jake laughed. "Sheer luck. My sister and her husband were skiing at Mont. Tremblant. He was there, too. In the evening the jerk got drunk and started to brag about how he drew in unemployment insurance under three different names. So Gwen and Don played up to him and got his name. I just took it from there."

Brad chuckled. "I could use that kind of luck myself." His smile faded and for a second he looked much older. Then he shook Jake's hand. "By the way, my name's Brad Baylor." He jerked his shoulder toward the drunk sprawled in his car. "Guess I'd better take this idiot to the tank to sleep it off. See you again, Jake."

Jake watched as Brad pulled into the traffic. Slowly folding his big body back into the driver's seat, he heard his breath whoosh out in relief. The relief was short lived.

Brad was satisfied about his identity. But for how long? This meeting could prove disastrous, unless Marge's real killer had been found. Somehow, Jake doubted that.

Ignoring the caterpillar feet creeping down his spine, he headed for Rideau Street. It was time to check in with his boss. Reg Colfax, senior editor of The Ottawa Chronicle, would bluster and holler over Jake's absence. Tongue in cheek, the reporter would apologize and promise to keep in touch from then on. Finally, the editor's ire spent, they would get down to business.

It was a familiar scene, one they both knew would be repeated many times again. Despite the outwardly bombastic nature of their relationship, the two men liked and respected each other, though Jake occasionally wondered how long Reg would continue to cover for him. Now Jake vowed to curtail his independent streak. Reg didn't deserve the aggravation.

Jake parked behind the building and entered through

the back door. He climbed to the third floor and threaded his way among the crowded desks, returning the numerous greetings tossed his way.

"Well, how kind of you to visit," the editor growled, when he looked up and saw Jake lounging in his doorway. "Is there some particular reason for your presence? Like maybe, to work for your paycheck?" His voice got louder with every word. *"Where the hell have you been?"*

Jake grinned at his red-faced boss. The relief in Reg's eyes belied the angry words. Jake had never been out of touch for such a long period before, and he knew the senior editor had been genuinely worried. But to acknowledge that concern would have embarrassed them both. Instead, he hooked one buttock on the edge of the desk and spread his hands in apology.

"Here and there," he said. "Following a lead."

Reg's face cleared. "You got something good?" He knew from the past that the more casual Jake's attitude, the more important the story.

"Yeah." Jake leaned forward, his face intent. "I want to write a series of articles on the Capital Highway. I came across some information that—"

"The Capital? That's old news. We covered that when construction was going on. Why should—"

"Believe me, we didn't get the whole story. A lot more went on than just building a highway. If my leads pan out, we can blow the lid off some dirty dealings. And I do mean dirty."

"Like what?" The editor's eyes began to shine.

"Like just about anything you can think of, including, maybe, murder. I want to put a teaser article in tonight's paper. So how about it? Is it a go?"

Reg eyed the reporter. "You got names and dates? Proof positive?"

"Names and dates, yeah. Proof positive, not yet. But I will have. Is it a go?"

They both knew Reg would give his blessing, but as always, he hedged.

"Sounds like it could be dangerous. If you're right, there'll be some heavy people annoyed with you."

"Maybe," Jake conceded, "but they don't know I'm on the trail. After all this time, they have to believe they're safe. I can get a long way before they wise up." He paused, then asked again, "Is it a go?"

Reg drew in a deep breath and puffed out his thin cheeks. "Yeah. Okay. Check your info with the lawyers. And keep me informed this time."

Jake nodded mechanically, then caught himself up short, remembering how he'd wished he'd left some word with Reg about his destination the night David Ackers was killed. If anything had happened to J.J., Jake still wouldn't know that he'd witnessed a murder. Silently, he vowed to curb his tendency to keep his cards plastered tight to his vest. It could prove a fatal mistake, as Doug Baylor would testify, if only he could.

Halfway to the door, he turned back. "Have the police any leads on the David Ackers' killing?"

The editor looked startled. "Not that I've heard. Why? You think there's a connection with your story?"

"No, not likely. I just wondered."

Reg eyed him suspiciously. Then he shrugged. "The cops seem to think there was a witness. They found some blood close by that wasn't Ackers', but nobody came forward. And no report of a bullet wound from the hospitals. If there was a witness, he's probably dead, too."

"Yeah, could be. Or maybe there's some other reason for not coming forward." Frustration with the hole in his memory made Jake grimace. Too late, he remembered the editor's sharp eyes. Reg rose from his chair and blocked his exit.

"What's going on, Jake? You going to tell me what happened to your leg?"

Damn! He might have known Reg would spot the trace of limp. After a moment's hesitation, he knew he'd never get away with a lie. He saw Reg's eyes widen in comprehension.

"You were the witness!"

"Yeah." Resigned, Jake retreated deeper into the room and briefly explained what had happened, omitting all reference to time travel.

When he finished, the editor looked shaken.

"Amnesia! I never really believed in it." A grim look crossed his face. "You'd better take some holidays and get out of town. At least until the cops catch him. Or until you get your memory back." His hand shot to Jake's shoulder. "Don't shake your head at me. Now's not the time to be stubborn. You're a target, damn it! Get the hell away for a while."

"It was dark. The killer doesn't know me. Or if he does, he thinks I'm too scared to talk. After all, he knows I didn't go to the police. I'll be fine."

Reg searched his reporter's face and sighed. Experience told him there was no point arguing. "All right, all right. But watch your back."

"Will do." Jake headed for the door again. He stopped and looked questioningly over his shoulder when Reg called his name again.

"Where were you for the last three weeks? And who took care of your leg?"

Knowing he wouldn't be believed, Jake told the truth. "I've been twenty years in the past, and a beautiful soap opera star nursed me back to health."

At the editor's snort of disbelief, he laughed and hurried to his desk. A glance at the clock told him he'd have to hustle to get the first article in that day's paper.

Chapter Ten

Molly carefully folded the newspaper and set it on the bench beside her purse. When Jake said he'd write a series of articles on the Capital Highway, completed eleven years earlier, she hadn't expected anything quite so provocative.

The writing itself was matter-of-fact, prosaic even. But in spite of the absence of names and outright accusations, the implication of wrongdoing came through clearly. No thinking reader would miss the insinuation of conspiracy. The paper had protected itself by printing the article on the op-ed page, that space reserved for opinion pieces written by members of the public.

Conscious of Jake waiting for her comments, she avoided his eyes and busied herself gathering up the litter from their lunch. Silently, she stuffed the wrappers and napkins in the take-out bag and tossed it into the wire basket beside the bench.

For once, Tom's Woods failed to provide its usual magical balm. The cloudless blue sky and quiet evergreens promised a peaceful interlude they didn't deliver. Instead, the distant sounds of traffic and the small movements of scurrying animals cast an invisible atmosphere of pending disaster, at odds with the seeming serenity.

She shivered with dread and thought of the old saying that a goose walked over her grave.

"Well, that should stir things up, don't you think?" Jake sounded both impatient and piqued. He had been expecting her enthusiastic endorsement of this first step of their plan.

Molly finally faced him, her face pale and strained. "Yes, it should."

Bewildered, Jake took her hand. "I thought you'd be pleased. What's wrong?"

"I . . . I just didn't realize until now . . . " She shook her head, searching for words that wouldn't reveal the extent of her panic. "You signed the article as Jake Dune. I checked the back issues of The Ottawa Chronicle. They never found Marge's murderer and . . . and the police reported you as the chief suspect. Jake, if the killer reads that article—"

"Hush, sweetheart. You're worrying for nothing." He slid an arm around her shoulders and drew her close. "Remember, I can prove I'm Jake *Anderson*. Besides, when Marge was killed, I was only sixteen and you were eleven. Even if the killer thinks he recognizes me, he'll realize he has to be wrong."

"But if he panics, he may not think of that. He's been safe for twenty years. He won't take a chance—"

In his desire to reassure her, Jake spoke without thinking. "If anyone would recognize me from those days, it would be Brad. And he didn't." When she stiffened, he realized his mistake.

"Brad? You saw Brad Baylor?" she whispered in horror. "Are you certain he didn't remember you?"

"Well, yes and no."

Molly twisted out from under his arm and clutched his shirt with both hands. "What do you mean, yes and no?"

Jake quickly described the encounter. "So you see," he finished, "Brad thinks I look familiar because I reported a burglary three months ago. That's all."

He spoke with more assurance than he felt. Molly's anxious look only deepened. She wasn't convinced. She pointed a warning finger at him.

"Listen to me. I knew Brad for two years. He's very persistent. If he reads the article and sees the name Jake Dune on the very day he ran into you . . . " She shuddered. "And there's still the person who shot you three weeks ago. You can't be certain he didn't identify you. Oh, Jake! This investigation isn't safe for you. This *city* isn't safe for you."

A slow, sexy smile spread over his face. He cupped her head with his large, warm hands and looked deep into her eyes.

"You do care about me, don't you? I was afraid, now that you're home again and back in your glamorous life, you would forget me."

Molly stared back, dumbfounded that he could think such a thing. What she saw in his eyes made her forget that she had had similar thoughts about him. How wrong could one woman be?

Her hands slowly released his shirt and spread flat on his chest. Heat spread from her palms to every part of her body. Her gaze dropped to his lips. As if he'd been waiting for the invitation, Jake kissed her. Tenderly at first. Then the kiss deepened, became something more, something demanding and utterly sensual. Molly stopped breathing, her entire attention centered on his mouth.

"In a public place. And in daylight, too. Terrible! Alfred, stop smirking. What is the world coming to, I'd like to know." The indignant voice brought her back to awareness of their surroundings.

Startled, Molly drew back and looked up at the couple on the path. A chunky, blue-haired woman was looking down her nose at them, her lips tight in disapproval. Her razor-thin companion struggled to hide his mirth. He winked at Jake and drew the woman along the path.

"Now, Daisy, they're not doing anything outrageous. Don't you remember that time we sneaked away from the church picnic, back before . . . " His voice faded away as they disappeared around a turn in the path.

Molly felt a giggle bubble up in her chest. She slanted a glance at Jake. When she saw the sparks dancing in his eyes she grinned, then chuckled, then burst into laughter. A split second later, Jake joined her. By the time they recovered, her eyes were streaming. Jake pulled out a large white handkerchief and tenderly dabbed at her face.

"You know, I really like to see you laugh. Actually," he added easily, "I like you. Even though you do misbehave in public."

Molly quickly matched his lighthearted tone. She poked him in the chest with mock displeasure.

"Takes two to misbehave, buddy." She paused and said thoughtfully, "I wonder just what Daisy and Alfred did at that picnic."

Jake chuckled and hauled her to her feet. He slipped his arm around her waist as they sauntered back the way they'd come. When they reached the entrance to the woods, Jake glanced at his watch.

"I need to check on Mac. How about coming back to my place? We'll go over Doug's papers again, in case we missed something. Then we'll go out for dinner later."

She agreed and as they strolled the few blocks to Jake's home, Molly recounted her meeting with Gayle Everett.

"Is it really possible David might have kicked his drug habit?" Jake's voice was heavy with doubt. "Not many do."

Molly was silent for a moment as she forced herself to remember David's qualities. Finally, she nodded. "Yes, it *is* possible. He was stubborn to a fault. Once he made a decision about something, there was no changing his mind. He did what he wanted to do, believed what he wanted to believe, no matter what the evidence indicated."

She lifted one shoulder. "His obstinacy was a strength as well as a weakness. If he did decide to stop doing drugs, I'm certain he succeeded. But," she frowned, "if drugs weren't involved, why was he killed?"

Jake chewed over the possibilities as they turned down his street. "If we rule out a random killing or an accident, it seems to me it has to be blackmail. If he wasn't dealing drugs, or just buying them for himself, he might have been broke. If Gayle is correct, he wanted to make a new start in California. He would have needed money. A lot of money. But what could he have known and about whom? Blackmail is a risky business, and to try that on someone in the drug scene goes way beyond foolhardy. Was his judgment that bad?" He threw Molly a questioning look.

She shook her head quickly. "No, David wasn't that big a fool. At least I don't think so." She gave a wry half-laugh. "I could be wrong. When I married him, I thought I knew what kind of man he was. Talk about faulty judgment!" She sighed heavily. "But if his death had nothing to do with drugs, we're nowhere. He could have been blackmailing anyone, about anything. And his murderer is after you."

Jake pulled her to a stop. When she threw him a questioning look, he placed his hands on her shoulders and drew her close. Molly's breath caught in her throat when his face descended to within an inch of hers.

"We are going to find out what happened, sweetheart, to Marge and to Ackers. Believe that." Before she could answer, his mouth lowered to hers and deposited a light, warm caress on her lips. It was over almost before it began. He straightened, slid one arm around her waist and propelled her down the street.

Her knees trembling from reaction, Molly was grateful for his supporting arm. Her lips were still tingling when they climbed the stairs and entered his apartment.

To give herself time to gather her poise, she immediately headed for the kitchen. While she pulled mugs from the cupboard and started the coffeemaker, Jake retrieved Doug's papers from his safe and spread them out on the kitchen table. From a shallow drawer in the table, he produced two pencils and two lined pads. They settled down to reread the papers and make notes.

Two hours later, Jake stood and stretched, then wandered to the window to stare into the back yard. Molly leaned back in her chair and scanned her notes. Something nagged at her mind, something she'd missed, something . . . . Shaking her head in frustration, she closed her eyes. What wasn't she seeing?

When she opened her eyes again, her gaze fell on the green and white stripes of the wallpaper. She wondered if Jake's mother and sister had chosen the alternating pattern. Then it struck her.

She tore a fresh page from the pad and divided it into vertical columns. Quickly labeling each column, she scoured Doug's papers for the information she wanted. With growing excitement, she filled in the columns in a certain order. A pattern emerged.

"Jake, look," she called.

His attention caught by the excitement in her voice, Jake left the window and leaned over her shoulder. Except for the vertical arrangement, he saw the same data as before.

"What is it? I don't see—"

"Compare the dates of the disasters and the dates the farms were sold. In every case—"

"—only three weeks passed before the sales. The buyers must have really hustled the farmers."

"More than that," Molly exclaimed. "After each sale, only a week to ten days passed before another farm was hit by some kind of disaster. The pattern is so consistent, it can't be just chance. This alone would have made Doug suspicious. It's almost proof of wrongdoing."

Jake's lips stretched into a giant grin. He wrapped his arms around Molly's shoulders and pulled her to her feet. Turning her to face him, he gave her a resounding smack on the tip of her nose. Molly felt a hot flush stain her cheeks.

"Smart lady. I knew you were more than just a pretty face."

Flustered and thrilled by his approval, Molly laughed and wrapped her arms around his waist. Immediately, his warm hands dropped to her hips. He smiled down at her.

As their gazes met, their smiles faded. The air seemed to heat around them. A thundering silence enveloped them. Molly's breath caught in her throat. An intent look crept into Jake's eyes, a look she hadn't seen before. Suddenly, she was afraid, though she couldn't have told what frightened her.

Shaken, Molly dropped her arms and eased away from him. Fearing her legs would give way, she dropped into the chair and hid her trembling hands in her lap. To avoid Jake's penetrating gaze, her eyes sought out the revealing sheet of paper.

Jake sat down opposite her and cleared his throat. He wanted to talk about what had just happened between them, but sensed it was too soon. In any case, he didn't know the words to use. Instead, he picked up the sheet of paper and pretended to study it.

"You know, you've just given me my next article."

Molly's head snapped up. "What do you mean?"

"I'll write an article about the hazards and difficulties of farming. How each year the weather determines whether or not the farmer earns or loses money. The kinds of accidents that can happen on a farm. General statements at the beginning. Then I'll cite specific incidents, using only the nine disasters that occurred along the path of the Capital Highway. Doug's news clippings are all the research we need. The chart you've just worked out can be on the same page, as a sidebar. Some readers, at least, will see the pattern and start to ask questions."

A sense of foreboding raised goose bumps on Molly's skin. She wanted to argue that such an article would be too inflammatory, but she knew that the first article was not enough to stir the authorities into investigating. She had a sense of time slipping away from them. Someone was bound to connect Jake Dune and Jake Anderson. When that happened, they would find themselves charged with Marge's murder.

"We should fax a copy of your articles to the Toronto News and to the Department of Transport at Queen's Park. Someone might start investigating from that end."

"Good idea." Jake looked at his watch. "Unless you're hungry, I'll write the article now. I'll fax it to Reg as soon as I'm done, so he can get it in the morning paper. Okay?"

Molly nodded and gathered up the clippings and her chart for him. He disappeared into his office. She made another pot of coffee. When she tiptoed in and placed a mug on his desk, he grunted his thanks without looking up. Smiling at his fierce concentration, she carried her own cup to the living room and curled up on the sofa to relax.

Her mind drifting, she watched through the window as sunset bathed the sky in ever-shifting hues. Dusk fell, but she made no move to turn on a lamp. Only when she realized she was humming tunelessly under her breath did she acknowledge how right it felt to be here in Jake's home. Contentment flowed through her as she wallowed in the sense of being exactly where she belonged.

Jake stared at the woman bathed in the soft light from the hallway. When he saw her curled on the sofa, his heart had leaped with pleasure at the picture she made. She seemed a beautiful fantasy, an illusion created by his imagination. He stilled, afraid a noise or a movement would cause her to disappear.

How could he dare to hope that a woman like Molly would consider spending her life with a man like him? He was a man whose work entailed irregular hours, middle-of-the-night calls, even unexpected absences. He knew she was attracted to him, but attraction was a long way from love—and he wanted her love. He wanted all of her, in every way there was. He groaned silently. When all this highway business was over, maybe then….

Molly shifted on the sofa and sighed aloud.

"What was that for?"

The low voice in the doorway startled her upright. How long had Jake been standing there, watching her? She rose and faced him. "I didn't hear you come in."

"I know."

He walked into the room and snapped on the floor lamp beside his recliner. Handing the columnar sheet of paper to Molly, he smiled.

"There's another pattern. I didn't see it at first."

Molly's eyebrows rose. She took the paper and held it under the lamp he'd lit.

"I don't see—oh! The buyers' names." Her eyes moved down the page and up again. "Five of the nine names begin with the same initials and the other four with a second set And they alternate." She looked up, her eyes shining. "As if two people took turns buying up the properties, each time using a new name. Do you think—"

"Yeah. I think maybe there were only two in on the scam, not counting the person at Queen's Park who tipped them off about the route. And I think we should try to locate those farmers. Maybe they can describe the person who bought their property."

"That was twenty years ago, Jake—a long time to remember someone they may only have seen once or twice, if at all. And some of them may be dead or moved away. Still, if we could locate even a few descendants, we might get lucky."

Jake grinned at the eagerness in her face. "There

should be records of the sales somewhere. Didn't you tell me that Karen McLeod works in real estate? Maybe she would—"

Molly laid her hand on his arm. "I don't think we should contact another person who might recognize us. Besides, that was also twenty years ago," she reminded him gently. "We don't know if the agency is still in existence. Or if she still does that kind of work."

Jake groaned and rubbed the back of his neck.

"I keep forgetting," he muttered. "It all seems like a few weeks ago."

In an attempt to cheer him, Molly teased, "It *was* only a few weeks ago. *And* twenty years ago. What would the politically correct gurus call us? Time-challenged?"

She was rewarded by an upward curl of his mouth.

"Incredible, isn't it?" Bemusement gave his face a boyish look. "To step back in time. Some day science may discover the how of it, but I find myself wondering about the why of it. Why you? Why me? Were we accidental travelers or were we chosen, for some reason, to play a part in some plan?"

He shook his head in defeat and covered her hand with his. "One thing I *do* know—I'm glad we met, by accident or by design."

Molly's heart skipped a beat as she looked up into his warm brown eyes. Unconsciously, she leaned toward him, like a cat drawn to the heat of the fire. Her heart thumped at the intensity of his gaze. Jake's hand tightened on hers and he, too, leaned closer. Mac chose that moment to wind himself around her ankles.

She gasped and drew back. Snatching her hand away, she bent to lift the cat into her arms, not sure whether to cuddle or throttle him. Burying her flaming face in Mac's soft fur, she avoided Jake's gaze and murmured to the squirming animal.

"It's about time you said hello, cat. I suppose you want feeding." She glanced briefly at Jake and caught a look of disappointment before he wiped it from his face. "Have you finished the article?"

"I faxed it to Reg a few minutes ago. As soon as we feed the bottomless monster here, we're free for the rest of the evening. Where would you like to go for dinner?"

Molly hesitated. She really didn't feel like eating in a public restaurant. More important, she couldn't forget the unknown shooter, though she knew she couldn't keep the reporter hidden and safe forever. But at least for tonight . . .

"There are two filets in my refrigerator," she offered tentatively. "We could—"

"Great!" Jake's eyes lit up. "I'll bring the wine. Just let me feed Mac and we can be on our way."

He bent over almost double. Mac scrambled from Molly's arms and draped himself across Jake's broad shoulders. He dug his claws into Jake's sweater and purred loudly as his mount headed for the kitchen.

A few minutes later, they left the contented cat and set out for Molly's apartment. Neither noticed the gray sedan parked at the end of the street.

Despite Molly's objections, Jake insisted on helping her clean up the kitchen after their meal.

"For a meal like that one, this is the least I can do."

"Then you don't subscribe to the notion that preparing meals and doing dishes are strictly women's work?" Molly glanced over her shoulder at him as she stored the clean dishes away. She had to smile at the picture he made wearing her pink and tan striped apron.

"Nope. I see no reason why a man shouldn't do his share of the work, if he enjoyed his share of the food. He should help in the preparation, too. One day soon, I'm going to treat you to my utterly delicious, world-famous chicken cacciatori. It's m-m-m!" He kissed his fingertips and closed his eyes in pretended ecstasy.

Molly laughed. "Such modesty! Be warned, I intend to hold you to that invitation. And if the meal doesn't match the advertising, you'll do the cleaning up by yourself."

"Deal."

Jake removed the apron and hung it on its hook in the broom closet. When he turned to face her, Molly sensed a hint of tension in the set of his shoulders, a query in his dark eyes. Immediately, her feeling of well-being disappeared. For the first time since they'd entered her home, she was acutely conscious that they were alone together. The naked longing in his face stopped her breath in her throat. Heat spread over her skin to blanket her in sensual awareness.

Jake made no effort to hide what he wanted, but he made no move toward her. He simply waited. Molly knew that what would happen between them next—if anything—was up to her. She swallowed again and again, but her heart remained firmly lodged in her throat.

She stared at his impressive torso, his narrow waist, his flat stomach. When her gaze fell to his long, muscular legs, her heart lurched at the sight of the bulge straining the fabric of his slacks. She felt dizzy with desire, dizzy with the need to feel his arms around her, to feel his skin against hers. The intensity of her feelings frightened her.

She stood, marble still, locked in indecision. The idea of an affair devoid of any commitment or deep feelings had always repelled her. Lovemaking was too intimate, too precious, to be merely a recreational activity. Jake didn't want to marry. She knew he cared for her but that wasn't enough. One day he would walk out of her life and she would pay the price in heartache and loneliness.

Jake watched the ambivalent emotions flow across her face. Desire, reluctance, sorrow, fear. What was she afraid of? He waited. Still she didn't move. Then shame moved through him as he remembered the shocks she had endured so recently—Duncan's death, Marge's death, the death of her ex-husband. He was as bad as David Ackers, to pressure her when she was vulnerable. He cleared his dry throat and plastered a polite smile on his face.

"Well, uh, I guess I'd better be going and let you get some rest." Sheer willpower moved him past her and down the hall. He opened the door and forced himself to look back at her. "Uh, thanks for the meal, Molly. I'll be in touch."

Molly felt her heart splinter as he pulled the door open. *He was leaving.* Her mind cleared. With startling insight, she knew that if all she could have with Jake was an affair, so be it. At least she would have him for as long as it lasted. When he tired of her and moved on, she would still have her memories. Memories that, she'd no doubt, would be magnificent.

"Jake."

It was scarcely a whisper, but he heard. He turned around, not daring to hope.

"Please, stay with me."

Jake's heart lurched to a stop, then began to race. He searched her face. Her lips were trembling but the glow in her eyes rivaled the sun's light. He took a shaky step toward her.

"Are you sure?" The hoarse words hurt his throat.

Her arms opened in answer. He kicked the door closed behind him and with one long stride, gathered her against his chest, his relief as great as his joy. For a few moments they simply stood, their bodies straining together.

Jake spread his legs and with his hands cupping her bottom he pressed her against his iron hard need. Molly gently rubbed her hips back and forth. When he groaned she smiled into his sweater, thrilled by her feminine power. It was her turn to moan when his large hands slid inside her sweater and cupped her aching breasts. She gasped as his fingers stroked lightly across her nipples. A shudder ran through her as heat flooded her body. Her legs buckled.

Then strong arms lifted her. She pressed her face into his neck and breathed deeply of his aroused, masculine scent. Anticipation shot through her veins as he carried her into her bedroom and slowly lowered her to her feet. He straightened and stepped a few inches away. As one, they kicked off their shoes, their eyes never parting.

Smiling, his eyes glowing in the moonlight streaming through the window, Jake reached for the bottom edge of her sweater. Molly lifted her arms. He pulled it over her head, then folded it neatly and set it on the dresser beside the bed. His trembling hands rose to her shoulders and slowly, so slowly, slid down her arms. Molly wanted to scream at him to hurry, but the look of wonder and tenderness on his face kept her still.

His fingers grazed her skin as he unhooked her bra. Their heat sent shafts of desire deep inside her. Without taking his eyes from her chest, he dropped the garment to the floor.

"Your breasts are perfect," he whispered.

Molly felt her nipples harden as he gazed with an intensity that turned her core to molten fire. Her hands clutched his shoulders for support. Her head fell back when he took a nipple into his mouth and slowly caressed it with his warm, wet tongue. Pleasure-pain arced through her, drawing a cry from her lips.

"Jake!"

He would not be hurried. His mouth moved to her other breast and repeated its loving treatment. Molly's fingers dug into his shoulders as she whimpered with need.

When he finally lifted his head she reached for his shirt buttons. He shook his head.

"Not yet." Placing her hands around his neck, he unfastened her slacks. Kneeling in front of her, he lowered slacks and panties inch by slow inch to her feet, his mouth following after with feather-light kisses. Her legs trembled violently as her breath grew ragged.

She stepped out of the heap of fabric and kicked the

garments away. He looked up at her and sucked in a deep breath. Her naked beauty overwhelmed his senses. He had guessed she would look like this, but the reality put his imagination to shame.

Molly felt her insides turn to liquid at the sight of the fiery desire in his eyes. She tugged at his arms. "Hurry," she whispered.

He would not be hurried. Clasping her bottom in his large, firm hands, he lowered his head and laid a trail of hot, wet kisses over her quivering stomach. She moaned and twisted, but he held her easily.

And then his mouth covered her most intimate parts, his tongue sweeping in long, slow strokes. Her body rigid with shock, Molly plunged her fingers into his hair.

"No, Jake, no," she half-screamed.

He lifted his face an inch away from her curls.

"Yes, Molly, yes. Let it happen, my darling."

With tender fingers he nudged her legs apart. His face again buried at the apex of her thighs, he inhaled deeply of her woman's scent. His fingers parted her soft folds and planted a lingering kiss at the doorway to her center. The tip of his tongue found her nub of pleasure and softly teased it into tumescence.

With a shriek of delight, Molly arced as spasm after spasm of sensation coursed through her. She barely heard Jake's cry of triumph. Her body was still shaking when he stood, his hands moving up to her waist, caressing the slope of her hips. He pressed his hard, male torso against her soft flesh and waited for her breathing to quiet.

Gradually Molly's senses returned. She opened his shirt and melted against him, reveling in the texture of his smooth skin and prickly hairs against the softness of her breasts. She could feel the pounding of his heart against her cheek. Disbelief swirled in her mind. Not even David when they first married had ever put her needs before his, had ever given her such pleasure. She was stunned by the depth of Jake's generosity.

Her hands rose to caress the rough planes of his face, to wipe away the perspiration dotting his brow. She pulled his head down and gently dropped kisses as soft as summer rain on his face, his jaw, his mouth. It wasn't until she felt the rough fabric of his trousers against her bare hip that she realized he was still partially dressed. She drew back and met his gaze. Slowly, deliberately, she traced her lips with the tip of her tongue. When his eyes fell to her mouth, she purred.

"You have to pay for that. It's only fair. No," she whispered when his head dipped toward her. "It's my turn. I wonder, can you take as well as give? Let's find out. Don't move, Mr. Anderson." She smiled a wicked smile. "Take your punishment like a man."

Jake's body trembled with anticipation. Molly's blue eyes were alight with sensual promise. He loved pleasuring her, but his swollen manhood couldn't take much more. When she pushed his shirt off his shoulders and bent to nuzzle the small buds almost hidden by the mat of curls on his chest, he felt his pulse race. Grimly, he forced himself to stand rock-still.

Her hands palmed his shoulders and chest in long strokes that electrified his skin. When she fumbled with the buckle of his belt, he groaned aloud and bit his lower lip for control.

"This is just the beginning," she mouthed against his chest. He shivered with excitement and felt her smile against his skin.

Inhaling deeply, he filled his nostrils with the sweet scent of her and watched her hands. She pulled down his zipper slowly, so slowly, and eased his trousers over his lean hips. She looked down at him then and he almost lost it.

"Molly, sweet Molly, you don't know what you're doing to me." His whisper was a strangled moan.

But she would not be hurried. Her fingers slipped under the waistband of his briefs and bit by bit rolled them down, the backs of her hands caressing the flat, taut muscles of his stomach. When his rigid maleness sprang free, they both gasped.

His briefs slid to the floor. Molly stepped back and slowly, blushing at her wanton behavior, swept her gaze down his body. He was beautiful, so beautiful she might have thought him a dream but for the waves of heat flowing between them. He was big, a mountain of a man. His wide shoulders and broad chest narrowed to a slim waist and flat stomach. Her gaze fell lower. She sucked in her breath at the sight of the jutting power of his maleness. Her inner muscles tensed with need.

Reaching for him, Molly curled her fingers around his hard, male flesh. Jake groaned. The sound delighted her. Unaware of the devilish glint in her eyes, she smiled up at him and sat down on the edge of the bed. When she began to bend toward him, Jake grabbed her shoulders.

"Uncle," he mumbled hoarsely. "I cry uncle."

Grinning in triumph, Molly put her arms around his waist and tugged. They landed in the middle of the bed in a tangle of arms and legs. Jake rolled her under him and propped his weight up with his elbows. He looked down at the flushed face of the beautiful woman fate had sent him.

Molly's newly-styled hair lay like a black silken cape on the pillow. Her eyes seemed lit by starlight and kissed by moonlight. His heart turned over when she whispered his name. He loved the sound of his name on her lips.

With delicate care, he rained small kisses on her face, on her slender neck, on her eyelids. Finally, his mouth locked with hers. Her lips parted with a sigh, inviting him in. His tongue caressed hers as he deepened the kiss. Her slender fingers traced the line of his jaw, the slope of his strong neck.

He spread her knees and knelt between them. Leaning forward on his elbows, he kissed her deeply, rubbing his chest against her rigid nipples. His hands moved to her breasts, cupping and kneading the tender flesh. She reached down and finger-stroked his throbbing arousal. On the very edge of exploding, he drew back and gazed into her flushed face.

"I can't believe you're here with me."

Moaning, she wrapped her legs around his powerful thighs. "Jake Anderson, are you trying to drive me crazy? Conversation is not what I want from you at this moment."

He grinned and palmed the center of her femininity. She lifted her bottom, blindly searching for what only he could give her.

Jake guided his aching flesh to her entrance. She was hot and wet and more than ready to welcome him. At the first contact he shuddered with need.

"Molly, I can't wait any longer."

"Who asked you to wait?" she gasped, her voice as urgent as his.

He thrust into her with one long, smooth stroke, rejoicing at the wet heat of her. Panting, he waited until he found a measure of control. He withdrew, leaned forward to kiss her stomach, then thrust deeper than before.

Molly felt waves of pleasure spread further and further through her body until her mind was spinning. When he thrust a third time, the explosion inside her forced a cry of joy from her lips. Jake's body quivered in release, then collapsed on her, resting his head on the cushion of her breasts. He felt stunned by the depth of his pleasure and knew he could never willingly let her go.

He was heavy and she loved his weight on her. They lay still, slowly drifting back to earth, relearning how to breathe. Molly felt boneless, incapable of moving. Lovingly, she swept her hands down the sides of his massive body, her palms memorizing the velvet feel of his skin. If she could have frozen this moment in time, she would have.

Finally Jake rolled to his side and tucked Molly into

the curve of his body. He draped one leg over hers and wrapped his fingers around the firm globe of her breast. Sated and exhausted, surrounding each other, they fell asleep.

Chapter Eleven

Molly scowled at the silent telephone then looked down at her watch. Two minutes had passed since the last time she'd checked. She got up, dumped her untouched breakfast into the garbage, and filled her coffee mug for the third time. Her stomach roiled in protest, but she paid no attention. What was keeping Jake? Why hadn't he phoned?

He had left an hour before, stopping only long enough to gulp down juice and coffee. Jake. Her Jake. The thought left her breathless. For as long as it lasted, Jake was hers. Her mind drifted back to the moment when she had awakened in his arms.

Still half-asleep, only vaguely aware of a sense of warmth and comfort, she had stretched and turned over. And bumped her head. Her eyes popped open to see Jake's face inches from hers, his chocolate eyes sparking with amusement.

"Ouch." His throaty whisper puffed against her cheeks.

"Oh." Her hand rose to stroke his cheekbone and trail over the rough bristles of his morning beard. "I'm sorry. Did I hurt you?"

"I hurt." When her face fell he smiled and moved his lower body closer. "I hurt," he repeated.

"Oh."

Her pulse began to race as she identified the hard length of flesh that nudged her stomach. "Oh, I see." She tried to frown but the corners of her mouth twitched and one eyebrow rose. "Should I call for a nurse to ease your pain?"

"Only if Florence is available." His dark gaze scorched her skin.

Inspired by a feeling of deviltry she'd never experienced before, Molly pursed her lips and lifted an imaginary phone to her ear. She watched his smile widen as she described his symptoms in erotic detail to the supposed listener. By the time she completed the fictitious call, he was struggling not to laugh.

"Well, is Florence available?"

Molly smiled widely. "Oh, yes. She said she'd be delighted to . . . take care of you."

Jake leaned back from the waist and ran his hands down the slope of her hips. "What shall we do while we wait for her?"

Molly donned a contemplative expression and pretended to ponder the possibilities. "Let's see. I suppose we could . . . " She suddenly reached for the sheet covering them and swept it to the foot of the bed. Before Jake could move, she lunged to a sitting position and fell across his chest, her flickering fingers unerringly finding the ticklish spot she'd discovered the night before.

With a roar of laughter, Jake retaliated. The room echoed with their mirth as they rolled and thrashed in play. At last, breathless, they stilled, Molly stretched full-length on his massive frame. When she finally lifted her head to gaze at him, Jake's fiercely sensual expression instantly electrified her. Her heart began to pound.

They loved each other with the same wild abandon with which they played. In the exhausted aftermath, her limbs splayed and drained of strength, Molly knew she'd be Jake's for as long as he wanted her, and when his interest faded she would have her memories. But she wouldn't think about that time.

A rumbling protest from her empty, caffeine-abused stomach brought her back to the present. Once again, she checked the time and glowered at the phone. Drumming impatient fingers on the table, she remembered their excitement when Jake called his boss and learned that three people were waiting in the editor's office to speak to him. Three people whose surnames were among those on the list of farmers who had been forced to sell their properties after so-called acts of God had ruined their livelihood.

Now she waited, hope and apprehension jostling for position in her chest. Jake's first article had brought them to the newspaper office. With luck, this morning's article might entice others to come forward. Surely, one or more would remember *something* about the buyers of their property.

If only there was something she could do!

Suddenly, the name Carl Tipit surfaced in her mind. She drew in a sharp breath. Why hadn't she thought of him before? Her lawyer was known to brag that his investigator was the best in the business. With his own and his boss's connections, Carl Tipit would have methods of accessing information unknown to the average citizen.

A few minutes later, she hung up the phone with a satisfied sigh. Though he expressed concern that she had need of a private investigator, the lawyer readily agreed to send his operative around to her apartment. Molly adroitly sidestepped his questions. Her promise to tell him the whole story later finally appeased him.

Jake still hadn't phoned when Rudy called up from the entrance. The doorman's voice was laced with curiosity as he announced her visitor. Smiling inwardly at the fatherly man's nosiness, a trait easily tolerated by the building's residents who appreciated his kindness and devotion to his job, she assured him that Carl Tipit was expected. A few moments later she opened her door to the most nondescript man she'd ever seen.

Carl Tipit was the ideal investigator. Short, small, gray, forgettable. Nothing about him caught the eye. Only the most discerning might note the intelligence in the soft, gray eyes that surveyed her with a sweeping glance of appreciation. His attitude, however, was businesslike and formally polite.

Molly led him to the living room, where he perched on the edge of a chair, his expression both patient and alert. He gave the impression of a man confident of his abilities, yet showed no sign of pride or complacency. Molly liked him immediately.

When he declined refreshments in a voice as unexceptional as his appearance, Molly gave him a list of the original farm owners and the location their farms once occupied. Beside each she'd written the name of the buyer. Then she explained what she needed from him.

"Twenty years ago, these people bought up farm property that was later purchased by the government. It's probable, though not certain, that the buyers used false names and may represent only two real people. If at all possible, I need to know the present location of the former owners, and the identity of those two buyers and anything else you can discover about them."

The investigator nodded without speaking and slipped the list into his pocket.

Molly lifted her shoulders and spread her hands in a helpless gesture. "It's asking a lot of you, I know, but even a tiny bit of information would be useful."

"I'll do my best, Ms. Malone, but you must understand that it will take time—especially if the names are false." He stood up to leave. "Luckily, my desk is clear at the moment. I can get on this right away. I'll be in touch the moment I learn anything at all."

Relieved that he hadn't said the task was impossible, Molly quickly wrote out a large retainer check.

At the door he hesitated for a long moment. Finally, he spoke, his words telling her he recognized the farmers' names.

"I've seen the morning paper, Ms. Malone. You be careful. There may be some very unhappy people out there. It could be dangerous for you. I'll be as discreet as I can, but word of my inquiries will reach them eventually."

With a final promise to be in touch as soon as he had anything to report, the investigator shook her hand briskly and left.

Feeling that she'd done something positive that might help in their search for Marge's killer, Molly felt her appetite return. Her head was deep in the refrigerator when the phone rang. She whirled, slammed the refrigerator door and ran to answer.

It was Jake. "Good news and bad news."

"Come for brunch. I have news, too."

"On my way."

Molly hung up the receiver, telling herself the sudden excitement in her stomach was due to Jake's promised news. It was a lie. He'd been gone less than two hours, yet she felt like a teenager before her first date with the school hero.

She took a deep breath to collect her scattered wits and returned to the kitchen. Soon the table was heaped with salad, cold cuts and fresh rolls.

To her chagrin, she felt her hands tremble as she waited for him. This was so silly—a twice-married woman of 31 undone by a fit of shyness. Not even the television cameras made her feel so skittish and self-conscious.

Though she told herself to wait a suitably proper pause before opening the door, she flung it wide at the first knock. Jake stood in the doorway, his shoulders filling the space, his rugged face wreathed in a smile. The eager look in his eyes banished her nerves. When he reached for her, she melted into his arms with a sigh of pleasure and buried her face in his neck.

After a few minutes, they moved arm in arm to the kitchen. Jake began to talk while Molly made coffee.

"The good news is that the three people waiting for me are all related to the farmers who were bought out. Two of them are sons who expected to inherit the farms one day. They were too young at the time to really understand what happened, but they remember overhearing their fathers' insistence that the fires that destroyed the animals and outbuildings were deliberately set. Unfortunately, there was no proof. And neither farmer carried enough insurance to save his property. They were forced to sell at giveaway prices."

"That's terrible, Jake." Molly shook her head in sympathy. "Those families must have been devastated."

"Yeah." Jake's hands curled into fists. "One farm had been in the family for six generations, the other for five. One man said he can still hear the screams of the cattle trapped in the burning barn. The family had been at an evening service in their church. When they got back, it was far too late to save anything."

Molly shuddered. "How could anyone do such a thing? Those poor animals."

Jake was silent for a moment, then seemed to gather himself. "The third man, Bud Russell, had just taken over the family farm a few months earlier, after his father died of cancer. His illness left the farm in debt, but Bud managed to borrow enough money to buy a stud bull. He expected to recoup his money from stud fees. When the bull died, the bank called in the note. He had to sell. After paying all the debts, he and his mother were left with two thousand dollars and their personal items. His mother died six months later."

Molly dropped into a chair. "Does Mr. Russell suspect the bull's death was induced?"

Jake nodded. "He had the local vet in to examine the

bull as soon as it arrived. The vet gave it a clean bill of health. A week later Bud found it dead in the pasture. The vet had tests done but they came up empty. Bud still believes someone killed the animal, but he has no idea how. Or who."

Molly put her elbows on the table and dropped her chin in her hands. "I wonder if it would be possible to get a copy of the test results. It all happened almost twenty years ago. Knowledge has come a long way since then. Maybe today's vet could spot something the first vet missed."

"Hey, that's a great idea. Good thinking, partner." Jake reached across the table and clamped a large warm hand on her shoulder.

Molly blushed. Jake's compliment made her heart smile. Not wanting him to see how ridiculously pleased she was, she asked, "And the bad news?"

Jake grimaced. "None of the three can remember meeting the person who bought their farms. Well, two were just kids at the time, but Bud Russell says the sale of his farm was handled by a real estate agent. After he read my article, he tried to reach the man. He's no longer in business and no one could tell Bud his present whereabouts, or even if he's still living."

"I suppose once the buyer sold the property to the government, he disappeared too."

"Probably," Jake said. "If he was using a false name we'll never locate him. How do you find a man who doesn't exist?" He scowled at the plate of cold cuts.

"It may not be as bad as that," Molly protested. Then she told him about the private investigator.

"Mr. Tipit has incredible resources at his disposal. With the level of technology available today, keeping a secret is all but impossible. If he can prove that none of the nine buyers ever existed as real people, then that, by itself, is—"

"—proof of some kind of fraud." Jake brightened.

"The government would be forced to investigate. The cheated families might eventually receive some kind of compensation." His brow furrowed again. "A private investigation can cost a lot, sweetheart. Are you sure you..."

"I can afford it, Jake. And I want to do this for Marge. And for Brad. I've been thinking. Marge was so certain that Doug's death was neither an accident nor a suicide. Isn't it likely that Brad had the same suspicions? He knew his father even better than Marge did. With no leads and no proof, he might have kept quiet for his sister's sake. Sophie adored their father. If she thought someone might have killed him . . . "

"I've been thinking the same thing. Maybe we should have given Doug's papers to him. At the time, I figured he'd never believe Marge gave them to us freely then disappeared a few hours later. Especially since he would have grabbed any reason to make me look bad in your eyes." Jake raised his eyes to Molly. "He loved you, you know."

"I know." Molly met his gaze squarely. "But he knew I didn't feel the same way about him." *Not the way I feel about you.* But she couldn't say that aloud. Jake's whispered endearments the night before had not included a declaration of love.

And that was what she wanted from Jake Anderson.

She forced her thoughts back to the topic at hand.

"We could give him Doug's papers now. Although we'll need some kind of story to account for their reappearance after a twenty year lapse in time." She smiled wryly. "Still, the information might mean more to him than it ever could to us. If he believed his father was murdered, he may have discovered something after his father's death—something that wouldn't be in Doug's notes."

"I suppose it's possible." Jake rubbed the back of his neck. "But what if he was involved in the fraud himself?" He lifted his hand to forestall Molly's protest. "I don't believe he killed his father, but there had to have been two or more involved in the scheme. If his partner killed Doug, without Brad's knowledge, he'd have no reason to connect Marge's death with his own criminal activities."

Molly chewed at her knuckle. Much as she hated to admit it, Jake could be right. She thought of Brad's persistence despite her stated lack of interest. "He was a determined man. I hate to think he might be a dirty cop but if he once decided to work on the wrong side of the law, he would probably stick to the road he chose."

Sighing, she added, "Suppose we keep the originals and send him photocopies anonymously. Is there any way we can follow his movements?"

Drumming his fingers on the table, Jake thought a moment, then nodded. "J.J. can alert his fellow street buddies to keep an eye out for Brad's personal car. If he got rich back then, he's not throwing it around. He's married, has three kids and lives in an ordinary house in the Glebe. Of course, he may have invested his share of the profits."

Surprised, Molly stared. "When did you discover all that? And why?"

Jake smiled sheepishly. "When I ran into him yesterday, I remembered how much he hated seeing me with you at Duncan's. You've heard the old adage 'Know your enemy.' So," Jake shrugged, looking mildly embarrassed, "I did a little research. At the time, I wasn't thinking of him as a possible crook."

A warm feeling stole over Molly. Jake saw Brad as a rival. The thought pleased her, until she remembered David's unreasonable jealousies. But Jake wasn't making accusations.

"I'm certain Brad forgot me years ago. He probably doesn't even remember what I look like."

Jake leaned back in his chair and clasped his hands behind his head.

"Now that's the first foolish thing I've ever heard you

say, Miss Molly Malone. Don't you know that you are beautiful, sexy, fun to be with and totally, utterly, splendidly *un*forgettable?"

Molly blushed scarlet. Not trusting her voice, she pointed to his plate. "Eat."

Jake chuckled, deepening her blush. They ate quickly, both avoiding those topics that might ruin their lunch. When they had finished tidying the kitchen together, they discussed their next move.

"Come home with me," he suggested. "You can feed Mac while I change. Then we'll go over the newspaper clippings again, this time keeping Brad in mind. It's just occurred to me that I didn't notice if the articles named the investigating officers."

"The Ontario Provincial Police have jurisdiction outside Ottawa. I don't recall meeting any OPP officers. I probably won't recognize any names."

Jake nodded. "Even so, we can list the names and try to find out if any of them are still around." He frowned suddenly.

"What is it?"

"This act of God business," Jake muttered. "Some farms were burned to the ground. How could there not have been traces of arson? It doesn't make sense. The fires must have been started simultaneously in several places for the devastation to be so complete."

He paused. "It might be a good idea to have Tipit look into the lives of the men who fought fires at the time. With their training and expertise, one or more would know the best way to start a fire and be sure of total destruction. Or a corrupt inspector could hide evidence of arson."

Jake couldn't keep his gaze from the enticing sight of Molly's perfectly rounded bottom as she climbed the outside steps ahead of him. He pictured her as she had looked bouncing around the bed in childlike play that morning. There were so many sides to her, so much more than he'd suspected when they first met.

She had shown kindness and caring, even tenderness when she'd nursed him back to health. She'd understood his dismay when he'd first realized he had somehow returned to the past, his life lost to him. He couldn't imagine any of the women he'd once known displaying such bravery in the face of the mysterious green circle. He admired her loyalty to Marge, dead now twenty years.

She had the moral strength to forgive Gayle Everett and to feel pity for her dead ex-husband, despite the treatment she'd endured at his hands.

And she had passion. Her outward poise hid depths that would take a lifetime to explore. A year of lifetimes.

Molly reached the small porch at the top of the steps and moved aside. Curiosity stirred in her when she caught sight of the bemused expression on his face.

"What is it?"

"Mmm?" Jake fished in his pocket for his keys.

"What are you thinking?"

"Oh, uh," he stammered. "Well, I . . . " Needing time to think, Jake bent to fit the key in the door.

The sharp crack of a gunshot splintered the air.

Chapter Twelve

Jake heard a whining sound as a narrow breeze shifted the hair on the back of his head. Brick dust rained on his hand. A startled gasp burst from Molly's lips. Instantly, he grabbed her by the arms and forced her down on the landing, covering her with his body.

"Don't move!"

"What? What's the matter?"

"Keep still!" Over the thunder of his heartbeat, Jake heard the sound of squealing tires as an unseen car raced down the street and screamed around the corner. When the afternoon quiet descended once more, he struggled to his knees, looked cautiously down at the street, then helped Molly sit up. A tiny trickle of blood threaded down her cheek.

"Molly, are you all right?"

Totally dumbfounded, Molly stared at the man looming over her.

"I'm . . . I'm fine. Why did you—"

She got no further before he pulled her to his chest and, groaning, buried his face in her hair. With her hands trapped between them, she could feel the tremors that shook his huge frame. As she became aware of her stinging cheek, understanding seeped into her. She struggled out of his arms and lifted her shocked face to meet his eyes.

"Someone shot at us!" She looked up and saw the fresh gouge in the brick wall beside the door "Someone shot at *you!* If you hadn't bent just then—" Horror stopped her throat. The bullet had passed through the space where Jake's head had been a second before. She began to shiver violently.

"Molly, he missed." Jake shook her hard. "I'm all right. He missed."

"Truly?" Unaware her hands were roaming over him for confirmation that he was indeed unhurt, Molly blinked back the tears threatening to spill down her cheeks. Horror and relief churned in her stomach like the noxious brew in a witch's cauldron.

"Honestly, I'm okay—but your cheek is bleeding. Just a tiny scratch, probably from a piece of flying brick. Let's get inside and clean that up."

He rose cautiously to his feet and again checked the street. No one was in sight. Still, he unlocked the door quickly, pulled Molly to her feet and led her into the apartment. Closing and locking the door behind them, he sat her down in his old recliner and lifted her feet to the hammock.

"Jake—"

"Don't move."

Molly disliked the commanding tone in his voice, but one look at his grim face told her his order was prompted by concern. Surrendering to the chair's comforting embrace, she leaned her head back and closed her eyes. She wasn't sure her legs could take her weight anyway.

She couldn't remember ever being so terrified in her life. Even David's rages hadn't provoked such fear. Jake had come within an inch of being killed. Suddenly, fury flamed and burned away the fear. Her lips drew up in an unconscious snarl. She knew beyond certainty, that if anything happened to Jake Anderson, she wouldn't rest until she made the killer pay. And pay. And pay.

"Whoa! You look a mite vexed, friend."

Molly opened her eyes and found Jake bending over her, his counterfeit smile at odds with the uneasy expression in his eyes. With her woman's instinct, she knew he wanted to pass off the incident as lightly as possible, with no fuss. She inhaled deeply and reached for her acting talent.

"Reckon I am, partner," she drawled, "reckon I am. Never did cotton to cowards who shoot at unarmed folks. Plumb irritates me. Best we do somethin' to find that snake."

Relief flooded Jake's strong face. He dropped a quick kiss on the tip of her nose and knelt down beside the chair. Dipping a cloth in the bowl of cold water, he began to wipe the blood from her face.

"The bleeding's stopped already. It's just a superficial scratch. It won't leave a scar."

Although he kept his tone light, almost cheerful, a fine tremor shook his hands. He was well aware that only chance had caused the ricocheting bullet to miss her.

When the slight wound was cleansed, he smeared a dollop of antiseptic salve on her cheek. Setting the tube aside, he stood and plucked her from the chair. Molly marveled at the easy strength in his muscular arms.

Standing in the middle of the room, his legs braced, Jake held her against his heart. He felt overwhelmed by gratitude and relief. They were both alive. They were together. Nothing else mattered.

Reluctantly they broke apart when Mac stood on his hind legs and stuck his claws in Jake's thigh. Whether as an appeal for food or as punishment for neglect was uncertain; whichever it was, the cat's interruption relieved the tension.

"I'll feed the monster while you change," Molly offered. Now that the danger had passed, at least for the moment, impatience nipped at her heels. The sooner they figured out what was going on, the sooner Jake would be safe.

"Okay." Eager to review the newspaper clippings, Jake agreed and strode to his bedroom. They needed a lead. The sooner they uncovered the criminals involved, the sooner Molly would be safe.

With Mac curled in full-bellied contentment on the kitchen floor, Molly and Jake poured over Doug's papers. When every newspaper clipping had been read and reread, they compared notes. Harvey Streeter's name appeared three times, Doug Baylor's four times and Brad's twice. The names of the other investigating officers were unfamiliar.

"I wonder . . . Only two of the incidents occurred in the area where these three had jurisdiction." Jake rubbed the back of his neck. "Why were Streeter and Doug at the other scenes?"

Molly thought a moment. "They may have been called in to assist. Or maybe they knew the families and offered to help."

"Could be," Jake allowed. "But you notice that none of the officers from the other jurisdictions were involved in the investigations on Streeter's turf. That seems a little odd."

Before Molly could comment, Jake put his finger to his lips and cocked his head. Mac lifted his head. Belatedly, Molly heard footsteps on the outside stairs. She glanced at Jake and quickly swept the papers together into a pile.

The knock on the door made her start. Jake stood,

mouthed 'Stay here,' and left the kitchen. Molly quickly shoved the papers out of sight in a cupboard. Refusing to hide and leave Jake alone to face possible danger, she moved silently to stand in a spot near the kitchen door where she could see the outside entrance. Her pulse throbbed erratically.

The knock came again.

Jake approached the door and stepped to one side. "Who is it?"

"Officer Brad Baylor, Mr. Anderson. I'd like to speak to you for a few minutes, if I may."

Molly sucked in her breath. When Jake glanced back she nodded. They had known that sooner or later the meeting would happen. Jake's articles, signed by 'Jake Dune,' were bound to be arouse the officer's interest. To refuse Brad entrance now would only arouse his suspicions. Try as she might, she couldn't picture him as a killer. Still, anything was possible. She clasped her hands tightly together.

Jake opened the door and stepped aside to allow the officer to enter.

"I hope I haven't picked a bad time," Brad said. He smiled, but his eyes were wary.

"Not at all. Have a seat." Jake gestured him into the living room.

Molly hesitated at the kitchen doorway. Brad hadn't noticed her, but she had a good view of him before he left her line of sight. He looked much the same. His hair had grayed and thinned on top and he looked meatier around the shoulders and waistline. Would he recognize her? She hadn't changed, but then, twenty years had passed since he'd seen her.

Well, there was no sense in procrastinating. Thankful that she'd had her hair cut and styled in Celia Chamber's sleek, chin-length bob the day before, she stepped into the living room, smiled at the policeman, then looked at Jake, as if waiting to be introduced. Once again, her acting skills assisted her. Her face and bearing showed only the polite curiosity of someone meeting a stranger for the first time.

The policeman rose when he caught sight of her. One eyebrow lifted quizzically, but Molly noticed he didn't look surprised that Jake wasn't alone. Could he have been the one who shot at them earlier?

Jake made introductions. Molly offered her hand, ignoring the totally male look of appreciation in his eyes. It was a look she'd seen many times and had come to disregard. She couldn't claim credit for her features—she hadn't earned them. Outer appearances, her own included, were mostly a matter of genes and revealed little of the real person within.

"Would you care for a cup of coffee, Officer Baylor?"

"Coffee would be welcome," he answered. "Black, one sugar please."

Biting back the words 'I remember,' Molly nodded and returned to the kitchen. As she made another pot, Molly could hear the rumble of male voices from the front room. A few minutes later she served the coffee and sat down on the couch beside Jake. They sipped in silence for a minute. Baylor complimented the coffee. His next words caught her off balance.

"What happened to your cheek, Ms. Malone?"

Molly glanced at Jake before she could stop herself. It was a mistake, she knew.

"It's just a scratch," she stammered.

Baylor's gaze swung between them. His friendly, noncommittal expression turned watchful. He leaned forward and placed his elbows on his knees. The pose told them better than words could, that the time for social chitchat was over.

"I wonder," he said softly. "I wonder if the scratch has anything to do with the fresh gouge in the brick by the door. Or with the bullet I found in the grass."

Molly's heart sank like a brick in a tub. She looked at

Jake. Not having the benefit of her training and experience, the reporter's pained expression was the only answer the policeman needed. Jake knew it and shrugged. Brad Baylor was sharper and more perceptive than he'd thought.

"You're very good at this, officer. How did you happen to find the bullet?"

It was Brad's turn to shrug. "Sheer luck," he admitted. "The sun hit it. The glint caught my eye." He paused, then surprised them again.

"I take it someone was . . . perturbed by your articles on the Capital Highway. You've made yourself a target. I need to know where you got your information."

"Articles?" Jake stalled for time. "Those were written by a Jake Dune, if I remember correctly. What makes you think—"

"Please." Brad gestured brusquely. "Don't waste my time denying it. I've spoken with your editor. I also want to know how you came to choose that particular byline."

"What does that matter?" Jake's mind was whirling.

Brad hung his head for a moment. When he looked up, it was clear he had made a decision.

"I'm probably making a mistake, but I'm going to take a chance and trust you, both of you, with a story. It's been twenty years now and I'm desperate. Your articles make me think there might be a chance after all. I'd about given up."

Molly recognized the sadness deep in his eyes and knew he was thinking of his father and cousin. Suddenly, she felt certain he had nothing to do with the murders. When Jake draped his arm on the back of the couch behind her, she knew he had come to the same conclusion.

The policeman swallowed a large gulp of coffee, leaned back in his chair and began. He told them of his father and of his certainty that his death was neither accident nor suicide. Grim-faced, he expressed his belief that his father's last case was behind his murder.

Here Jake interrupted. "Why do you think his investigation and his death were connected?"

"I knew he was working unofficially on something. The morning he died he told me that he needed one more piece of information and expected to get it that day. I got stuck at the station later than usual and when I got home I found his body." Brad's face showed the effort it took to speak calmly. "You have to understand—my father was a meticulous investigator. He would have had a file on the case. I found nothing. It's probable that whoever killed him stole the file."

"If you're correct, wouldn't the killer destroy the file? Its existence would have been a danger to him," Molly reasoned.

The policeman shot her an approving glance. "You're right, he would have destroyed it. *If he found it.*"

"I don't understand. Have you some reason to believe the killer didn't find it?" Jake asked, trying to inject a note of puzzlement into his voice.

"Three reasons," Brad said. For a moment he remained silent. A faraway look came into his eyes. Then he shook his head and focused on the reporter.

"Three months after my father's death, my cousin was murdered. Someone beat her up, then shot her."

Molly gasped in horror. Jake hadn't told her how Marge had died and she hadn't asked. She was grateful when Jake's hand squeezed her shoulder.

"There was no reason for it." Brad hurried on, forestalling their expressions of commiseration. "At least, no personal reason. She was very well-liked. But she and my father were close. It occurred to me that he may have given her his notes for safekeeping. Unfortunately, I didn't think of that possibility until after Marge—my cousin—died. Then, of course, it was too late to ask her. If I hadn't been such a fool, I might have prevented her death."

"Was your cousin's killer found?" Jake knew the answer, but he felt Brad would expect the question.

"No. There were two suspects, a man and a woman, though there were those who believed the woman couldn't have had anything to do with it. Some said the man must have forced her to leave with him. In any case, they both disappeared into thin air. Neither have been heard of since. Nor were we able to find any information about either of them. It was as if they'd never existed."

Molly felt her skin prickle with apprehension. Brad's gaze had turned to her when he started to talk about the woman suspect. Something moved deep in his eyes. Was it recognition? She couldn't tell. If he said she looked familiar, she would identify herself as Celia Chambers and hope that he watched the soap at least occasionally.

She sighed silently in relief when Jake drew Brad's attention from her.

"And the second reason?"

"When I read your articles, something clicked in my mind. My father had been disturbed by the rash of farm accidents at the time. Four of the families who lost their farms were friends of our family. It seems to me now, in hindsight, that dad was more upset than even the friendships would warrant." His eyes narrowed. "Your articles imply something illegal was going on. He may have been working on that when he died."

He inhaled deeply. "So you can see why I want to know where you got your information and what put you on to it in the first place. And before you ask, the third reason is the name you used as a byline. Jake Dune was the name of the man suspected of killing my cousin. An incredible coincidence, wouldn't you say? There's still a warrant out for his arrest. An unsolved murder case is never completely closed, regardless of how much time passes."

Brad picked up his mug and drained it, then for the first time, leaned back in the chair. Clearly, he meant to stay until he got some answers.

Molly turned her head to look at Jake. His eyes held a

question. She nodded. They had to take a chance on Brad. Jake cleared his throat and gave the policeman a direct look.

"I'm willing to show you my information but there is one condition. No, two. First, you share what you know with us. There's no way I'm bowing out of this thing."

Brad hesitated, then nodded. "And the other condition?"

"I won't explain how I came by the papers I'll be showing you. You have to accept that."

The policeman frowned. "I realize you want to protect the names of your sources but—"

"No, it's not that. You'll understand when you see the papers. I'll only say that you wouldn't believe the truth and I'd rather not lie." Jake paused. "Agreed?"

Finally nodding, Brad agreed, although it was obvious he didn't like it.

Molly got the papers from the cupboard and set them on Brad's lap, the newspaper clippings on top. Then she sat down beside Jake and took his hand. They watched the policeman's face closely.

He skimmed the top pages quickly and lifted his head.

"Twenty year old newspaper articles? I read them when they were first published. I don't see—"

"Keep going, Br—uh, Officer." Molly said.

He stared at her for a long moment then bent over the papers again. Jake squeezed her hand but didn't say anything. They waited, hardly breathing, for Brad to reach the papers written in his father's hand.

"What the hell!" Brad's head snapped up. "Where did you get these?"

"Are you asking me to lie?" Jake met the policeman's eyes, willing him to remember the agreed-upon conditions.

There was a long, still moment. Brad's mouth was tight, his anger and frustration unmistakable. Finally his face cleared. Muttering something under his breath, he shook his head and began to scan the rest of the pages. When he was finished, he gazed at them with pain-filled eyes.

"These are my father's own notes," he whispered.

Both Jake and Molly nodded.

Brad looked from one to the other, suspicion alive again in his eyes.

"How did you know?"

"Know what?" Jake asked.

"My father died over twenty years ago." Brad's words were harsh. "He didn't put his name on these notes. So how do you know his handwriting?"

Molly froze. Jake replied, praying his hesitation was too brief to be noticed. "We don't, of course. We were told by someone whose word we had no reason to doubt. Don't ask who that was."

Brad stared, then his lips turned up slightly at the corners. "Another detail I wouldn't believe, I suppose?"

Jake returned the smile. "'Fraid so."

Molly made more coffee while the policeman again turned his attention to his father's papers. When he had read every paper twice, they discussed the contents of the file. Brad's conclusions as to the meaning of his father's investigation matched theirs, even before Jake told him of the conversation with three of the farmers.

"This couldn't have been a one-man operation." Brad tapped his finger on the arm of his chair. "Nine farms were destroyed, although in different ways. There was never a trace of evidence to suggest deliberate sabotage. That suggests criminal experts, professional arsonists, were used. The average citizen wouldn't know how to locate people like that." He paused. "It must have all started when someone discovered the proposed route for the new highway. We need to find out who had access to the information."

"It was likely someone who worked in Toronto and had a relative or friend in southeastern Ontario," Molly added. She told Brad about Carl Tipit and promised to have him obtain a list of those employed by Queen's Park at the time. If Brad recognized a name they would have a starting point.

Jake had been silent for some minutes. His long legs stretched out before him, he sat rubbing the back of his neck. Suddenly he spoke.

"The money," he blurted. "The farmers were forced to sell out at bargain basement prices, but even so, the buyers needed seed money. Quite a lot of it, I'd say—to buy the farms and then to hang on until they could sell to the government. That involved paying taxes for a number of years. So the buyers were rich already or they borrowed money."

"But," Molly protested, "even if the buyers obtained bank loans, how does that help us? There must be dozens of banks in southeastern Ontario." She turned to the policeman. "I suppose there's no hope of searching bank records?" She wasn't surprised when Brad shook his head.

"No, not a chance. I'd never be able to get a warrant based solely on my dad's papers and our suspicions."

The discussion continued another half hour, then Brad got up to leave. Though they hadn't come up with a plan of action, his eyes no longer looked as haunted. At the door, he repeated his promise to share anything he managed to learned and thanked them for the photocopies of his father's notes. He shook Jake's hand and turned to Molly.

"I can see why Jake, as a reporter, is interested in this. But I don't understand why you're so involved, Miss Malone."

"Please call me Molly," she answered. "I believe in justice and—" She broke off abruptly when the policeman went still as a marble statue. His eyes widened.

"Molly? Molly and Jake?" He looked from one to the other, his mouth agape.

Molly reached for Jake's hand and edged closer to his large body. She glanced up at him, but if he was flustered, it didn't show.

"Yes. Molly and Jake. Is something wrong?"

For a tense moment, no one spoke. Then the policeman blinked and shook his head. His rigid posture relaxed.

"Sorry," he muttered. "You two look a lot like the couple that's wanted for my cousin's murder. They had the same first names, too. But of course, twenty years ago you were just kids." He inhaled deeply and grinned. "All this has turned me upside down and sideways. I've been trying for twenty years to find out what really happened to my dad. Finally, after all this time . . . ." With a final smile, he started down the stairs, his steps almost jaunty.

Molly and Jake waved as he drove away. They reentered the apartment and closed the door.

A figure stepped out from behind the neighboring house and gazed intently up at Jake's apartment, then made his way across several back yards. He reappeared on the next block and drove away in a nondescript gray sedan.

Chapter Thirteen

"Did we do the right thing?" Molly couldn't prevent the trace of anxiety in her voice as she gazed up at Jake. She felt exhausted from the effort to guard her tongue in front of the policeman.

Jake drew her into a loose embrace and kissed her forehead. "I think so. I hope so. One thing is certain. He had nothing to do with his father's death, or Marge's."

"I'm sure he didn't," Molly agreed. "Poor Brad. These past twenty years must have been so difficult for him."

"Yeah. But now that he knows about his father's last case, he's found a place to start looking for the answers. Actually, I'm glad he showed up today because he has resources even Tipit can't use. I just hope he'll share what he learns with us."

"He will," Molly said firmly, "if only because he wants to know how we came to have his father's papers. Sooner or later he's going to insist we explain."

Jake grinned widely. "Maybe we'll tell him when it's all over. He won't believe us, but I'd love to see his face when we claim to be time travelers."

Molly shook her head and clasped her hands behind

his neck. "I can hardly believe it myself. I mean, when I really think about it, I wonder if I'm asleep and dreaming all this."

But she knew Jake was no dream image. In her most extravagant fantasies, she could never have imagined a man like Jake. He was too real, too solid, too wonderful.

And he was in terrible danger. Despair invaded her heart.

Immediately sensing her changing mood, Jake tipped her face up with a gentle fingertip. Her wide gray eyes shimmered with unshed tears. "What is it, sweetheart?"

For a moment she couldn't speak. "You," she finally whispered.

Understanding coursed through him. His furrowed brow smoothed. In a low, teasing voice, he tried to reassure her. "They missed, remember?" He gathered her tightly to him. "And now we've got Tipit and Brad on our side. The four of us make a winning combination. It'll be all over soon."

"But we've no idea who wants to kill you," she cried. "And now there may be two of them out there."

"Two?"

"Don't play dumb," she snapped, knowing she was overreacting but unable to control her tongue. "You know exactly what I mean. A few weeks ago you witnessed a murder. The person who killed David tried to kill you today. He'll probably try again. And if Doug Baylor *was* murdered because of a land fraud scheme, your articles will bring *his* killer after you, too."

Jake's mouth thinned. "I can take care of myself."

"What? You can dodge a bullet?" Molly jerked free from his arms. "*Macho Man*. Is that the name of the game?"

Jake's face hardened and Molly knew she'd gone too far. Immediately contrite, she cupped his face in her hands. "I didn't mean that. But please, Jake, let Brad do the rest. He's a trained officer of the law. Promise me you'll stay in the apartment. At least for a few days."

He backed away. Molly's hands dropped to her sides. Jake looked affronted, as if she had called him a coward.

"I can't do that." His tone was impatient. "I'm glad of Brad and Tipit's help, but this is my job, my story. I finish what I start."

Frustration flared again. "Your *story*? Is that all it is to you, a *story*? I'm afraid for your life and all you can think about is your *story*? Is that all Marge's death means to you? A *story*?" Bitterly angry, Molly whirled around and started down the hall.

Jake's hand closed over her upper arm, bringing her to a sudden stop. He swung her around to face him and leaned over until his face was only inches from hers. His features were tight with resentment and outrage.

"If that's what you really think of me, then I guess we don't know each other as well as I thought. I care about Marge, but I also care about my job. The two aren't mutually exclusive, whatever you may think."

He drew in a deep breath and dropped his hand. "I'm a reporter. It's what I do. I thought you understood."

Molly stared up at him. He looked big and tough. But size and strength had no chance against a bullet. Why couldn't he admit he was as vulnerable as any hunter's prey?

Knowing she was being unfair, she couldn't stop herself from lashing out at him.

"Oh, I understand. I understand bull-headed, arrogant men. Men vain enough to think they're invincible. Oh, I understand all right. I was married to one, remember?"

Shocked by her tirade and resenting the insulting comparison with David Ackers, Jake was stunned into speechlessness. By the time he recovered his equilibrium, Molly had snatched up her purse and was clattering down the outside steps. He called after her, but she didn't slow or look back. He followed her out to the landing and descended a few steps, then halted.

What did she want from him? He had a job to do. He

couldn't hide like a terrified mouse in its hole. A malicious inner voice reminded him of his ex-wife's refusal to accept the conditions of an investigative reporter's working life. He told himself Molly's unexpected attack was merely a delayed reaction to the shooting. She just needed some time to calm down.

The reassurance wasn't convincing. Depressed, he reentered his apartment, closed the door and slammed his fist into the wall.

Arms wrapped tightly around her middle, Molly paced the length of her condo and back. Her frantic anger had faded, leaving her distraught and despondent. She wished now that she had kept her mouth shut. The hurt in Jake's eyes haunted her.

The telephone drew her eyes again and again, but it wasn't in her to call and say she hadn't meant her wild words. Because she had. In the past, she had kept her mouth shut in the face of David's unreasonable rages. She couldn't—wouldn't—do that again.

Eventually, her emotional turmoil faded, leaving her tired and rumpled. She filled the tub, poured in a handful of bubble bath powder and sank into the soothing water. While her muscles gradually relaxed, she forced her thoughts from Jake to David.

Poor, self-destructive David. To have won the battle against his addiction—if indeed he had—only to be murdered just when life looked promising again. Yet it was typical of David to grab at the easy way, to blackmail someone rather than work at a job to raise money for a new start. How could he not have seen the danger? Were all men so careless with their lives? Were they all such fools?

Molly didn't realize she was crying until her eyes began to ache. She sat up in the cooling water and covered her face with her hands, sobbing for everyone she'd ever lost; her mother, her baby, Duncan, Marge. Most of all, she cried for Jake. Knowing the main reason for the failure of his marriage, she was certain he'd never forgive her for the terrible things she'd said. Like his ex-wife, she'd attacked him for being what he was, a reporter, a man who loved his work. How could she have been so stupid?

She'd lost him, even if the assassin's bullet never found its mark—and she had no one to blame but herself. Their affair was over almost before it began.

When she had emptied herself of tears, she washed her hair and dressed in an old, comfortable sweat suit. Disgusted by the wan face and red-rimmed eyes in the mirror, she applied makeup with a lavish hand, then padded to the kitchen, determined to cook herself a proper supper.

Life went on—a cliché and a hard lesson, but one she had learned several times over. Soon she would have her work to fill her days. She loved acting. Her work—and her memories—would be enough. They would have to be.

Later, curled on her sofa with a huge mug of hot chocolate, she found her thoughts returning to David. What had he learned that led to his death? A sudden insight flowered in her mind. David had been impulsive and would have acted on the information immediately. If she could trace his movements that last week of his life, maybe she could uncover the source of whatever information he'd used for blackmail.

She shivered, remembering that Jake had witnessed David's murder. If only he could remember. But she couldn't wait for something that might never happen. Her knowledge of David's activities was more than two years out of date, but one of his acquaintances might know something of his actions the last week of his life.

Cheered by the prospect of positive action, she made a list of the names she could remember, most of whom, like David, were unemployed actors. About to phone the Central Casting Agency for phone numbers or addresses, she checked her watch and realized the office would be closed.

It was too early for bed. She didn't expect to sleep anyway. By focusing on her late husband and his friends, she had managed to crowd Jake from her mind. But his image, ever present on the periphery of her awareness, clamored for attention. Sleep would be impossible.

Resigned, she snapped on the television and searched the channels for something to occupy her mind. Nothing appealed. Finally, she left it tuned to CTV News and went to the kitchen for more hot chocolate.

Only half-listening to the news reports, she almost dropped the pan of hot milk when she heard a familiar name. Her pulse pounding, she dashed back to the living room and stopped abruptly at the sight of ambulance attendants maneuvering a stretcher through the doorway of a rundown tenement house. On the stretcher was an ominous-looking black bag. Uniformed policemen held back the crowd of people on the sidewalk. The bright sunshine indicated the scene had taken place earlier that day.

When the camera swung back to the announcer, she waited, tense as stretched wire, for him to repeat the name she'd heard.

"According to Mrs. Alice Simms, the landlady, the body being removed from the house is that of Dr. Alexander Harrison, a retired veterinarian who specialized in farm animals. Dr. Harrison was found a short time ago, allegedly dead of a gunshot wound to the head." The announcer's thin face managed to look grave and bored at the same time. *"The police are unwilling to say, at this time, if foul play or accident is suspected."*

Molly didn't hear what else was said. A man in street clothes stepped into the doorway and beckoned to one of the uniformed officers. Ignoring the whispering crowd, he disappeared back into the house. Her heart pounding, Molly stared at the empty doorway.

The last time she'd seen that figure she'd been racing

through the trees with Jake, in a desperate bid for freedom. It was Harvey Streeter, heavier, mostly bald, but looking just as tough as he had twenty years earlier. Goosebumps peppered her skin as she remembered the look of belligerent suspicion in his eyes when Marge disappeared.

Harvey Streeter believed that she and Jake were responsible for Marge's death. Almost certainly he would have kept their fingerprints on file. A premonition of impending disaster cramped the muscles of her stomach.

When the program turned to the latest news about Quebec's language issues, she remained riveted to the carpet, staring blindly at the screen. An image of the middle-aged, smiling Alex Harrison hung before her eyes. He had been one of Duncan's most frequent visitors the last few months of his life and a staunch friend to her after Duncan's death.

The man must have been in his early seventies. Had he committed suicide? Perhaps he was sick and in pain. With a sudden start, she remembered a conversation early in her marriage to Duncan, in which the vet expressed his abhorrence of firearms. Molly found it hard to believe that he would choose that method to end his life.

Possible foul play, the announcer said. It was ludicrous to imagine that pleasant old man with a deadly enemy. It must have been an accident. He had been a country vet, widely respected for his rapport with farm animals and for his willingness to answer a call for help at any time, day or night.

A thought niggled at the edge of her mind. Molly frowned. She held her breath, searching her mind for . . . something. Something important. Something . . . . But it wouldn't come.

She released a long, quavering breath, only then realizing she still held the pan of milk. Feeling deeply depressed, she returned to the kitchen. The shrill sound of the telephone startled her, jerking her hand just as she reached the stove. Milk splashed over the edge of the pan and sizzled on contact with the hot element.

Ignoring the stench of burning milk, she switched off the burner and dashed to the phone. *Let it be Jake!* But it wasn't Jake. Swallowing her disappointment, she managed to greet Brad Baylor in a steady voice. Had he learned something about the past?

He hadn't.

"Miss Malone? Molly? Are you there?"

"Yes, I'm here." Her voice was a faint whisper.

"I'm sorry to hit you with this, but I think it's important that you know. We just got back a preliminary report on the death of Doc Harrison and—Did you know about the body found in a rooming house this afternoon?"

"Yes. I've just seen it on the news."

"You wouldn't have known the man, but he was a friend of my father's and well-known and liked when this area was still rural. The thing is . . . " He inhaled noisily. "The gun that killed Harrison is the same one used to kill your ex-husband."

Molly felt her knees buckle. She dropped into the nearest chair. "But that doesn't make sense. David lived in the city all his life. According to the news report, this Dr. Harrison was a retired country vet. It's highly unlikely they ever met or knew anyone in common. There must be some mistake."

"I'm afraid not. The bullets were fired from the same gun. I phoned to warn you to be careful. Whoever killed your ex-husband may think he has reason to kill you, as well."

Nonplused, Molly shook her head. When she realized that Brad couldn't see her, she said, "I haven't seen David for almost three years. In fact, I've been . . . away . . . for two years. I've no idea what he was doing or with whom. Why would anyone come after me?"

"I don't know," Brad replied. "but his killer may think you know something. That shot today—maybe it had nothing to do with Anderson's articles. It's just possible the bullet was meant for you."

Jolted, Molly couldn't speak for long seconds. Finally, remembering that the officer didn't know that Jake had witnessed David's murder, she changed the subject.

"Why did you call me? I mean, my name is Malone. How did you know I was once married to David?"

"Jake called me about an hour after I left his place. He wanted to see the police file on David Ackers. When I asked why he was interested, he told me who you are. When we found Harrison—well—I'm not sure why, but I asked the ballistics expert to compare the bullets retrieved from the two bodies. They matched. God knows what it all means." The policeman sounded tired and frustrated.

Molly's mind was working again.

"David was once involved in the drug scene. I've been told that he got himself straight recently but maybe he didn't. Do you think Dr. Harrison—"

"—took drugs? I doubt it, though we won't know for sure until after the autopsy. And you're right about Ackers. No drugs were found in his body. But there has to be some connection between them. We'll keep digging until we find it. Doc Harrison was once the finest vet in southeastern Ontario, until he started drinking heavily and stopped practicing. These last years, he's been just one step up from a street bum."

"Could he have killed himself? Maybe he was drunk and didn't know what he was doing."

"No. This is off the record as yet, but the gun was missing from the scene. It's almost certainly murder."

Molly sighed, remembering the man who'd been such a good friend to Duncan. "That poor old man."

It was Brad's turn to be silent. Molly didn't realize what she'd said, until he slowly repeated "That poor old man? You sound as if you knew him."

She hesitated, silently calling herself all kinds of fool. Finally, she said the only thing she could. "No. No, we never met. I just feel very sorry for anyone who ruins his life with alcohol."

She wasn't sure he believed her, but he contented himself with repeating his advice to be careful, then hung up.

Mechanically, hardly aware of her actions, Molly trailed back to the kitchen and began to clean up the mess on the stove. She felt numb. Why would someone try to kill her? It didn't make sense. If the killer knew she had once been David's wife, he must also know that the marriage ended years ago—and that she had been away from Ottawa for the last two years. It would be ridiculous to presume her ex-husband would have confided in her, especially if his actions were illegal.

She simply couldn't see it. No, Jake was the target, either because of the articles or because he had witnessed David's murder. Or both.

Briefly, Molly considered reporting the latter incident to Brad. Almost immediately she discarded the idea. The fact that Jake hadn't come forward at the time would place him in a bad light. How could he excuse himself, when his only defense lay in the fact that he had been trapped twenty years in the past? That excuse would never fly! She concluded that, in any case, the decision to speak up or not rested with Jake alone.

Feeling dejected and lonely, she decided against another cup of hot chocolate and went to bed. Somehow, although she had walked out on Jake, she felt like the one abandoned. The quiet apartment no longer seemed the comforting haven it once had. Without Jake's massive presence, the rooms echoed with sad silence.

Emotionally and mentally exhausted, she fell into a restless sleep.

Chapter Fourteen

Jake woke up clutching the extra pillow to his middle and thinking of Molly. A vast loneliness swept over him, a feeling he'd never experienced before. Last evening's anger was only a memory. He was aware only of the pain of her rejection and the silence of his empty apartment. He groaned and covered his eyes with his forearm.

How could she accuse him of not caring about Marge? The articles about the Capital Highway were intended to unmask the woman's murderer. That they might also serve to uncover corruption and graft was a bonus. What was wrong with that? He was a journalist, after all. Stories were his business and his livelihood.

He knew the shooting had upset her badly, but that was no excuse for equating him with her ex-husband. From all accounts, David Ackers had been weak, cowardly and completely self-centered. Jake knew he was far from perfect, but David's flaws were not his. It hurt that she would bracket them together.

After Molly walked out, he had stayed up to write a third article. He was more determined than ever to expose the people involved in the land swindle. Not least for the sake of the families who had been cheated of their property. When the last sentence was typed he faxed it to the office. Standing, he stretched his cramped muscles and decided to skip the eleven o'clock news. After a long shower, he went to bed and spent the night trying not to think of Molly.

Morning sunlight pried insistently at his closed eyelids. He rolled over to be greeted by an indignant meow. Forcing one eye open, he found Mac staring into his face. The cat yawned widely, showing pointed white teeth, then twisted his hind leg into position and began to bathe himself.

"I suppose you want breakfast?" Jake mumbled.

The cat stopped his ablutions long enough to lick his human's cheek with a rough tongue.

"Okay, okay." Jake rolled to a sitting position and stood up. He shrugged into a terry towel robe and trudged to the kitchen. After a cautious look around through a window, he opened the door and retrieved the morning paper from the small porch. Then he padded barefoot back to the kitchen, opening the paper as he went.

Quickly scanning the front page, he was about to turn to the sports section when his eye was caught by the picture of an elderly man. The skin on the back of his neck began to prickle. He forced himself to read through the article, while a part of his mind recalled the friendly, middle-aged veterinarian who had worked beside him in the past to repair the Stewarts' storm-damaged home.

Though the article stated merely that Alex Harrison was found dead in his room, his landlady described the retired vet as a sad, quiet man who drank too much. "Mind you," she was quoted, "he never bothered nobody and he paid on time. Nobody had no call to hurt him."

Hurt him? Jake frowned. The man must have been in his seventies. If his death was due to natural causes, why had his landlady used that phrase?

Mac chose that moment, with a barbed swipe to his bare knee, to remind him of breakfast. Jake tossed the paper on the table and obediently opened a tin of cat food. As he scooped the fishy meal into a bowl, he muttered aloud to the smugly purring cat.

"Who's boss in this house anyway? You whack me with your claws. I punish you with a meal. There's something wrong with this picture, Mac."

The cat didn't answer. Jake dropped the empty tin in the garbage and poured a mug of coffee. Back at the table, he reread the disturbing article. The coffee grew cold as he stared into space, reliving the days spent helping at the Stewarts.

Something didn't jibe. For a moment he couldn't put his finger on it. Then he had it. Late every afternoon, Tory Smithson had disappeared for a half-hour, only to return with a case of cold beer for the tired men. To the best of his recollection, Doc Harrison never took a bottle. Never. What had turned him into a man who drank too much?

He looked down at the dead man's picture. His instinct told him there was more to the vet's death than the paper reported. Suddenly, he recalled Molly telling him that Duncan and Alex Harrison had been good friends. Chances were, Molly was well acquainted with the man. She would be saddened by his death.

He found he wanted to comfort her, to put his arms around her and hold her close. But Molly had made it clear she wouldn't appreciate the effort. He shook his head. She needed him, whether she admitted it or not. He would go to her. And if she refused to see him, well, at least he tried.

He pushed back the chair and headed for his bedroom. Anticipation churned in his stomach. He didn't try to deny that he wanted to see her as much for his own sake as for hers. Sometime during the long, sleepless night, the stark truth had slapped him in the face.

Molly meant everything to him. Everything. He refused to let her go over one misunderstanding. She was right about one thing. He was bull-headed. She just didn't know how much.

Dressed and whistling tunelessly under his breath, Jake started and scowled when a knock sounded on his door. *Damn!* Well, whoever it was could just come back later. He was out of here.

He jerked open the door. "I'm just leav—" Taken aback at the sight of his visitor, his mouth dropped open as he stared at Molly. With the screen door between them, they stood for a long moment, neither speaking. Then Molly shuffled her feet and cleared her throat.

"I . . . May I come in for a moment? Unless you're in a hurry...." Her voice trailed away.

Jake's mouth snapped shut. He opened the screen door and gestured. Eyes downcast, Molly stepped past him. Now that she was here, the speech she'd rehearsed disappeared. Remembering how she'd compared him with David made her cringe with shame. It wasn't true. God knew it wasn't true. Her fear for Jake's life had made her crazy. She was still afraid for him.

She felt the heat of Jake's body at her back. What was he thinking? Slowly, she willed herself to turn around and meet his gaze.

"Jake, I'm sorry." She searched his face. His expression told her nothing. She swallowed and fought to keep from throwing herself in his arms.

"The things I said—they were stupid. I know you care about Marge. And you're nothing, *nothing*, like David. I was . . . way out of line."

He didn't answer or move. Her heart sank like a brick in a bathtub. "It's just that . . . I'm so afraid for you."

Knowing she had lost him, Molly bit back a sob. "I'd better go now," she whispered. She stepped sideways to go around him to the door. He stepped into her path and reached out to tip her face up.

His mouth descended on hers. His lips were soft and tentative at first. Then they firmed, became demanding, possessive. One warm hand tunneled into her hair, the other slipped to the lower curve of her back and drew her against his chest and thighs. Almost faint with relief and instant desire, Molly melted against him and filled her senses with his scent.

When lack of air threatened to fell them both, they broke apart and stood smiling at each other. Jake took her hand and led her to the kitchen.

"Coffee?"

"Yes, please," she answered. Then she stopped. "But you were going out. I don't want to keep—"

Jake tugged her forward. "I was on my way to your place. I thought you might need to talk about Doc Harrison to somebody. And . . . I wanted to tell you not to leave me ever again. Because I won't let you go." He raised her hand to his mouth and deposited a moist kiss in her palm.

Molly gasped as heat darted from her hand to flow into every crevice of her body. David had once made the same declaration, but his words had been a threat. The dark yearning in Jake's eyes was a promise.

She inhaled a shaky breath. Then she remembered the other reason for her visit.

"Doc Harrison. Jake, he never, *never*, drank when I knew him. I can't believe—"

"Me neither," Jake interrupted. "But people do change. In this morning's paper, his landlady said he's been a heavy drinker for years. What would drive a teetotaler to turn to drink? Something smells."

"More than the drinking, Jake. Brad called me last night. Doc didn't commit suicide. He was murdered with the same gun that killed David."

"*What?*"

Molly repeated Brad's revelation, including the forensic report that had discovered no drugs in David's body and only alcohol in Harrison's. Jake looked stunned. Finally, he shook his head, led her to a chair and busied himself with the coffee maker. When they were both seated, his first words echoed the policeman's.

"If David was killed because he was blackmailing someone, that person may think you hold the same information."

"No, I don't think so." Molly repeated her reasons for believing she was safe from David's killer. Jake, like Brad, wasn't convinced. He had to bite his lip to keep from ordering her to leave town. He knew she wouldn't run any more than he would. He forced himself to address the puzzle of the matching bullets.

"This doesn't make sense. David and Doc Harrison. An actor and a retired veterinarian. Where's the connection? Did Doc try to blackmail the same person? Maybe he and David were working together. But how could they even have met?"

Molly shook her head. "It must have been a chance meeting of some sort. Still, I can't imagine Doc involved in anything illegal." She propped her elbow on the table and rested her chin on her fist.

Suddenly she jerked upright.

"I just remembered! This morning I called a few of David's friends. I thought if I could trace his movements . . . Anyway, one man told me David spent three days in jail, a week before he died, for fighting in a bar. Suppose—"

Jake remembered his encounter with Brad and the man the policeman had taken off to the drunk tank. "I'll bet that's it! If Doc was arrested for drunkenness, they may have been placed in the same cell. Brad can easily check." Jake felt his excitement fade. "Even if we're right, what does it prove?"

Molly chewed at her knuckle and stared at the table. She didn't like the ideas that flowed into her mind. Finally she raised her head.

"It proves, or at least suggests, that Doc might have been the source of the information David used for blackmail. And whoever killed David for it realized that the information could only have come from Doc. So he shut him up to prevent him from telling someone else." She sighed. "But what did Doc know? And about whom?"

Jake watched Molly's downcast face. She hadn't yet seen the implications of her reasoning. He hated to add to her grief, but if their suppositions were fact, it was necessary to take the next step. He cleared his throat and reached for her hand.

"If Harrison had knowledge of a crime, he didn't go to the authorities." Jake paused. "He was killed after David. Someone realized he could no longer be trusted to keep silent."

Molly caught the implication immediately. "Oh, no. You think Doc was an accomplice in some crime? Oh, Jake!"

"It makes sense. It might also explain why he drank so much."

"Guilt, you mean." Molly moaned low in her throat. "I don't want to believe that!"

Jake squeezed her hand tighter and forced himself to go on. "We know he frequently acted as an expert consultant all over the region, as well as running his own practice. And," Jake swallowed, "according to Brad, the drinking started years ago."

Molly blanched as she remembered Doug Baylor's notes. Not all of the farmers were ruined by fire. Some lost whole herds of dairy cattle to disease and a very expensive bull died. Who better than a veterinarian could accomplish that?

Molly shuddered. She wanted to protest, but everything fit like the pieces of a puzzle.

"We could have it all wrong," she finally whispered, "couldn't we?"

"Maybe." His tone denied the qualifier. "We need

more information before we can be certain of anything. Have you heard anything from the private investigator yet?"

"Not yet, but I'm sure Mr. Tipit will be in touch soon. Jake, we must warn Brad. If we're right, he could end up like his father. And Marge."

Jake frowned and rubbed the back of his neck. Unless they were way off track, someone out there had killed twice in the past and again in the present. That person wouldn't balk at killing Brad if he thought the policeman was a threat. Nor would he hesitate to add a reporter to his death list.

But was Molly safe? He met her eyes, unaware of the speculative light in his own.

"What?" Molly's eyes narrowed. She sensed she wasn't going to like what he said next.

"I don't think we should be seen together for a while." He held up his hand to stop the protest forming on her lips. "Think, Molly. By your own reasoning, you're not in danger. That no longer holds if the killer sees you with me. He has to figure I'd tell you everything I discover. I won't be able to do my job properly if I'm worried about your safety."

Her face tightened. "You mean I'd get in your way."

"No! I mean I couldn't bear it if anything happened to you." He grasped her forearms and leaned across the table. "Please, sweetheart. Stay with a friend. Spend some time at the studio. I promise I'll keep in touch by phone. Do it for me, Molly."

Molly ground her teeth together. She didn't know whether to be happy that he was so concerned for her or angry that he denied her the same privilege. Before she could sort it out, a heavy hand pounded on the door.

Their eyes met. Then Jake stood up and pushed his chair away from the table. "Stay here," he muttered.

The moment he left the room, Molly moved to the counter, quietly opened a drawer and picked up the largest knife she could find. Holding it behind her, she began to edge her way toward Jake. Not that she really thought the killer would come after him in broad daylight. Still . . . .

She almost dropped the knife when she heard the voice at the door.

Chapter Fifteen

Are you Jake Anderson?"

"Yes. What can I do for you?"

"I'd like to talk to you for a few minutes. May I come in?"

"That depends. Who are you and what is this about?"

Molly backed into the kitchen, darted to the utensil drawer and replaced the knife. She was reeling with shock.

The screen door opened and two sets of footsteps entered the living room. Leery of allowing Harvey Streeter to see her with Jake, she silently eased back into a chair and prepared to wait in silence.

Why was he here? He had, she remembered, tried to arrest her and Jake for Marge's murder and had been one of the policeman who investigated the fires so long ago.

He must have read Jake's articles and, like Brad, would want to know Jake's source of information. The sound of masculine voices reached her ears, but she couldn't make out the words. Her mind turned back to the earlier brainstorming with Jake.

Incredible as it sounded, it appeared that the events of the past week were connected with those of twenty years earlier. Even more implausible, she and Jake were linked to both periods. It had to be coincidence. Didn't it?

But somehow, it all felt . . . arranged.

For just a moment she wondered if she was dreaming. A preposterous dream. She was jolted rudely back to reality when she heard Harvey Streeter's raised voice ask for a cup of coffee. She held her breath. There was no polite way Jake could refuse.

"Sure. Just be a minute." Jake's voice held a carelessly cheerful note.

He entered the kitchen and blew her a kiss, then turned to the counter. They both stiffened when a chair creaked in the living room and footsteps approached the kitchen. Molly threw a Jake a look of panic, then drew on her talent to arrange her face into a mask of polite interest.

"I take black, with three sugars," Streeter was saying as he entered the room. When he caught sight of Molly, he bobbed his head. "Sorry, Anderson, didn't know you had company. Or is this lovely lady your wife?"

Molly noticed he didn't look surprised to see her. What did that mean? She stood and waited for Jake to introduce them.

"Molly Malone?" The policeman raised one eyebrow and pouched his lips. "You look kinda familiar. Have we met before?"

"I don't think so, Mr. Streeter. You may have seen me on television. Until two years ago, I played a part on *Tangled Lives*."

"Oh, yeah, that must be it. My wife watches that show

all the time." He chuckled, but Molly heard no amusement in his voice. "She talks about those characters as if they were real." He laughed derisively.

Molly gave him a vague smile and refused to rise to the insult. He was acting like a jerk, but she remembered the look on his face when he questioned them about Marge. He might be a buffoon in some ways, but he could make trouble for them.

He sat down at the table without waiting for an invitation. Nothing more was said until the coffee was on the table. Streeter turned to Molly again.

"Maybe you can tell me where your boyfriend got the information for his articles. Or did he make it all up?" He grinned when Molly stiffened. "Come on. It wouldn't be the first time a reporter manufactured a story. I was there, you know." He glanced at Jake. "You're barkin' up a dead tree. All them tragedies were thoroughly investigated. There weren't nothing suspicious goin' on back then. I know."

Jake shrugged. "Maybe not, but that many coincidences are hard to swallow."

The policeman nodded. "To tell you the truth," he confided, "I thought the same thing at first." His gaze swung to Molly and back. "But I couldn't find a scrap of evidence that suggested foul play. Remember, several dozen farms along the path of the Highway had no problems at all. Those that did, well, farming's a chancy business. Between the weather and acts of God," he shrugged, "it's a wonder more of them don't go under."

"I suppose that's true enough."

The conversation turned to baseball, then to the upcoming federal budget. Finally, the policeman drained his cup and rose to leave. He thanked Jake for the coffee, then fumbled in his pockets.

"What the heck did I do with my notebook?" He bent to look on the floor under the table.

"It's in the living room," Jake said. "I'll get it."

Not wanting to delay the policeman's departure, Molly went to the sink and began to rinse out the coffeepot. A few minutes later, the door closed behind him. She slumped against the counter in relief. When Jake entered the kitchen she turned to face him, the coffeepot still in her hand.

"I don't think he associated us with Jake Dune and Molly Barnes," she began. "He seemed—"

She broke off abruptly, the blood draining from her face. The coffeepot fell from her hand and smashed on the tiled floor.

Heedless of the glass crunching beneath his shoes, Jake strode toward her and gripped her shoulders.

"What is it?" When she didn't answer, he turned to follow the direction of her gaze. She was staring at the table, a look of horror on her face.

"What? Talk to me, Molly. What's wrong?"

She dragged her eyes back to his face. "Your cup," she whispered hoarsely. "He stole your cup."

For a moment, Jake didn't get it. Then it hit him.

The man who believed Jake Dune had murdered Marge Thomas, twenty years earlier, now had Jake Anderson's fingerprints. Fingerprints that would match those of Jake Dune. Fingerprints found on the trunk of the car where Marge's body had been found.

Molly pushed open the heavy door of the bar and looked around. A hand waving in a dimly lit corner caught her eye. She slipped past a figure slumped at the bar and approached the thin blond man in the corner.

When he rose unsteadily to pull out a chair for her, she knew he'd been there for some time. His mouth had a loose look, though his eyes were bright with curiosity.

"Hello, Molly girl. Long time no see. You're looking prime."

Hiding her distaste, Molly sat down and smiled into the sharp-edged face.

"Thanks, Kurt. You haven't changed either. How's the business been treating you?"

His face contorted, making him look like a petulant child. "Nothing recently." Then he brightened, a sly look in his eyes. "Say, now that you're back in town, maybe you can do me a favor. For David's sake, you know."

"If I can, Kurt. As you say, for David's sake."

It was an effort to keep smiling. Kurt Riddle had hooked up with David on his downward slide. The two failed actors spent hours together, bemoaning the short-sightedness of casting directors. At the beginning, David's looks had carried him, but neither man could act his way out of a paper bag. And neither man would admit to that deficiency, preferring to blame their failure on others.

Ignoring the underlying whine in his voice, Molly listened to Kurt's appeal that she put in a good word for him with the casting director of *Tangled Lives*. She had expected something of the sort and had no difficulty projecting a sincere interest.

When he finished, she assured him she would speak to Edwin Coulter on his behalf. Looking smug, Kurt leaned back in his chair.

"Thanks, sweetie. Now what can I do for you?"

She took a deep breath. "It's about David. Even though we were divorced, his death bothers me. The police say they have no leads to his killer. I got the impression that they're not looking very hard. You were a close friend. Did they question you?"

"Yeah. But I didn't tell them anything. Figured David's plans were none of their business."

Kurt's tone held contempt for the police but greedy speculation gleamed in his pale eyes.

Molly stamped down a surge of excitement. He knew something. How could she convince him to share that knowledge? She looked down at the scarred table, then raised her head and met his eyes.

"David was once my husband. The marriage was good

at first, though it ended badly, as I'm sure you know." She spoke slowly and candidly. "The thought that his killer is still free really hurts me. I'm no investigator, but if I could just find some kind of clue, some lead, to force the police to keep searching...." She let her voice trail away. "I want to do this for David. And to be honest, for me, too. I feel I owe him that much."

To her surprise, Molly found she meant every word. David, whatever his weaknesses, hadn't deserved to die the way he had.

Sensing she'd said enough, she waited for Kurt's reply. He fumbled in the pack of cigarettes on the table and took his time lighting the crumpled cigarette. Then he leaned forward.

"My name won't come into it?"

"No, I promise."

"And you'll speak to Coulter?"

"Yes."

He stared at her a moment longer, then made up his mind.

"Okay. I don't know much and it may not help. But I do know that he met someone in the cooler, a drunk. Don't ask me his name, David never said. Anyway, the drunk talked in his sleep. David said he didn't listen at first, until he heard a name he recognized. He paid attention then."

Molly held her breath, curbing her impatience as the actor stubbed out the cigarette and lit another. He grimaced, a look of petulant disappointment crossing his face.

"It was supposed to be our big chance. David said he knew where to scrounge some big cash. We were going to try our luck in California. I was waiting for him at the airport with our bags, but he never came."

Kurt swallowed the last of his beer and stared at her. Molly waited, then as the silence became protracted, she shook her head.

"That's all?"

Kurt didn't answer, but a small smile hovered on his mouth. Molly caught her breath in sudden understanding. She thought quickly, then smiled apologetically at the man who professed to be David's friend. And swallowed the bile that rose in her throat.

"I'm sorry, Kurt. I was thinking of David, but you suffered a loss, too. Since I can't guarantee how much influence I'll have with Coulter, suppose I give you enough money to get to California. With extra to live on while you get established. I'm sure David would be pleased to know that at least one of you made it."

Kurt grinned. Obviously, he had no scruples about blackmail himself. Or was extortion the correct word?

"I won't say no. You're right, David would be pleased."

Molly dug in her purse and pulled out her checkbook. Not trying to hide his eagerness, Kurt reached immediately for the check. His eyebrows rose and his mouth pursed in a silent whistle. Molly knew he would have settled for less, but she wanted him sweet. The figure on the check guaranteed he'd hold nothing back.

"You know," he said casually, as he folded and tucked the check into his pocket, "now that I think of it, I seem to remember David mentioning something about the Capital Highway. Something about corruption. The drunk was crying in his sleep, muttering about dead cows and how sorry he was."

"Any names? Did David mention any names?" Molly felt close to exploding. Kurt's account seemed to confirm what she and Jake had surmised, but they needed more than that.

Kurt closed his eyes. "Yeah." He rubbed at his forehead. "Give me a minute to think."

Molly closed her eyes, too, and prayed fervently. A name would give them a place to start digging. Her eyes popped open when Kurt suddenly brought his fist down on the table.

"Got it! I mean them. Two names. Baylor and McBride. One of them may be a banker. The drunk mentioned a third name, but David refused to share that one. I figured that was the person he . . . ah . . . planned to approach for some . . . capital. I didn't want to hear that name anyway. He must be the one who shot David."

Kurt broke off abruptly when he saw Molly's face.

"Hey, I'm sorry. I didn't mean to—"

Molly waved a hand helplessly. "It's okay. I just didn't . . . I'm okay." She didn't tell him that the name Baylor was responsible for the nausea that swept over her. "Can you remember anything else?"

Kurt rubbed his mouth. "I don't think so. If there was, David played it close to the chest. I'm sure he didn't tell me everything." He leaned forward. "Look Molly, I appreciate the check, but I don't want to cheat you. You got to realize something. Most of what the drunk said was mumbled garbage. David may have got things wrong. You know, like maybe the drunk said Taylor or Brainer or whatever." He paused and grimaced. "I guess he must have got the third name right though."

Molly nodded. She softened a little towards the actor, appreciating his warning that David's information might not be accurate. She gave him a genuine smile and stood up.

"Thanks, Kurt. I really hope things go well for you in California."

The actor stood up and patted his pocket. "I should have a good shot now, thanks to you. And Molly, I want you to know, David never really believed you cheated on him. He was jealous of your career. He told me once, after the divorce, that he knew he was the one who blew it. Actually, I think he was pretty proud of you, deep down."

Molly blinked away sudden tears. The accolade was unexpected and touched her heart. She smiled her thanks, shook the actor's hand and left.

* * *

Jake exhaled softly and straightened from his slouch when he saw Molly exit the bar. He climbed out of the car and walked around to open the passenger door. She climbed in without a word. Her expression gave nothing away. His heart dropped. Evidently David's friend had been a dead end.

When he slid behind the wheel again, he reached for her hand. Before he could speak, Molly squeezed his hand and smiled widely, though her eyes glittered with unshed tears. Surprised, he smiled back uncertainly.

"We've got a lead, a definite lead," she said. "But let's go somewhere for a coffee. I'll fill you in on the way." Aware of the danger facing Jake on the open streets, she added, "It's such a beautiful day. Let's drive out of the city."

"Sure." Jake nodded and turned on the engine. "Take your time," he said, sensing that Molly needed some time to digest what she'd learned and gather her composure. He swallowed the questions crowding his throat.

When they'd driven south on Bank Street and turned west on Hunt Club Road, Molly began to speak. Calmly, she related everything she'd learned from Kurt. Jake listened without interruption, but his face tightened when he heard the familiar name.

"No first name?"

"No." Molly knew what he was asking. "He might have been talking about Brad or Doug. But we have Doug's notes. If he was part of the scheme, he wouldn't have needed or wanted to conduct a private investigation." She shook her head. "Even if we knew for sure which of the two Harrison was referring to, we don't know the context."

Jake heaved a sigh. Maybe Brad was involved after all. Not in the murders—he still felt certain about that—but they couldn't rule the officer out of the scam.

"Let's not jump to conclusions about Brad," he said. "What about this McBride person? Did you ever meet anyone of that name?"

"Not that I recall," Molly answered, "but at least we have a name to investigate."

She tried to look enthusiastic, but Jake was learning to see through her acting. The name Baylor had shaken her. He knew she wanted to believe that the policeman was an honest man. Hell, he did, too. Aside from his misguided early jealousy, he liked Brad Baylor.

"We're getting there." He patted her knee. "If Brad confirms that David and Doc Harrison shared a cell, we can assume we're correct about corruption playing a part in the land appropriation deal. We'll be that much closer to discovering who killed Brad's father and cousin."

"I know." Molly sighed loudly. "But it's all still supposition. We have no proof." She met Jake's concerned eyes. "I really, *really* hate the idea that Doc Harrison was part of the conspiracy. I liked him a lot., and Duncan spoke so highly of him. To imagine that he would kill whole herds of animals...." She shook her head in denial. The idea was just too big and too horrible to get her mind around.

Jake had no response to that. He wanted to pull her into his arms and assure her it wasn't true. But he was very much afraid that it was. What, he wondered, could drive a good man to commit such despicable acts?

They drove out to The Swan on the Rideau on Highway 19. When they were comfortably seated in the beamed, English-style pub, he ordered coffee and trifle. Their table overlooked the water. A gentle breeze tickled the surface of the river, jostling the anchored yachts and pleasure boats. The view was restful, painting a picture of innocent recreation and freedom. By the time she had swallowed the last spoonful of the scrumptious pudding, Molly had her emotions under control.

When the waitress approached again with the coffee pot, Jake checked his watch then shook his head at her. It was time to leave, if they were to be back at Molly's apartment when Tipit arrived with the results of his investigation.

* * *

As Jake and Molly had anticipated, the investigator had been unable to find any records to prove the existence of the reputed buyers of the farm properties. Evidence, if not quite proof, that the names were phony. It seemed they were on the right track.

Molly's exhilaration faded as she watched Jake clear the coffee table after Tipit left. His action seemed so natural, as if he'd been sharing her domestic chores all his life. From the beginning, as soon as he'd been back on his feet at Duncan's, he'd insisted on helping her. David had refused to undertake what he called 'women's work'. She suspected laziness and selfishness had as much to do with it as chauvinism.

What would a child of Jake's look like? Dreamily, she pictured a sturdy little boy with chocolate eyes and short curly hair careening through her life, driving her mad with his energy and curiosity. Unaware of the soft, wistful expression on her face, she stared unseeing out the window. Lost in the daydream, she jumped when Jake sat down beside her on the sofa.

"Penny for them." His voice was a caress.

Molly glanced at him and blushed scarlet. "Nothing," she said, a little breathlessly. Disconcerted, she looked away, afraid he would read her mind.

His hand rose to cup her chin and turn her head to face him. When their gazes met, his eyes darkened to pools of liquid tenderness. Molly thought she could gladly drown in their depths and be content. His head dipped until their lips met and melded, his warm breath mingling with hers, shutting out the world and all their problems, as if this moment alone were reality.

She melted against him. With Jake, she felt safe and beautiful and loved. Even in the early days of her marriage, she had never felt so feminine, so complete. Jake was her other half, the half she needed to be whole.

She whimpered a protest when Jake's mouth left hers,

then purred with delight as he dropped sweet kisses on her face. He trailed his mouth along her jaw and pressed his lips to her rapidly beating pulse. She shivered as tiny flames of pleasure danced on her skin. Her head dropped back, allowing him access to the soft skin of her neck. Shivers of anticipation skipped down her spine when she felt his fingers at the buttons of her blouse.

He smoothed the fabric from her shoulders. The straps of her camisole followed, to pool at her waist. Moist kisses wet the thin satin and lace of her bra and tightened her nipples to throbbing peaks. Jake cupped her swollen breasts in his hands and marveled at her responsiveness.

Some minutes later, the intrusive sound of the phone pierced their absorption. Jake belatedly realized it had been ringing for some time.

"Better answer it," he muttered. "It may be important." Then he grinned wryly. "It had *better* be important!"

"I'll second that." Molly returned his grin. She hurried to the phone, shrugging her blouse back on her shoulders and fumbling with the buttons.

The voice on the line wiped away all sensual awareness. Brad sounded so urgent the hairs rose on the back of her neck.

"Molly, is Jake there?"

"Yes, he is. What's wrong?" At her tone, Jake moved to stand beside her. Molly gave him the phone. Jake held the receiver away from his ear so they could both hear.

"I'm here."

"Jake, you've got to get out of there right away. Harvey Streeter is on his way to arrest you."

"What? Why?" Beside him, Molly inhaled sharply.

"For my cousin's murder. Never mind that now. He'll go to your place first, then to Molly's. Go to the Starlight Motel on Bank Street, it has underground parking. I'll meet you there in an hour. Register under the name of… of…McBride."

"McBride?" Jake's eyes widened in surprise.

"I'll explain later. Get moving *now*. I just hope to God I'm not making a terrible mistake!" He hung up abruptly.

For a few seconds Jake stood, dazed, staring at the equally stunned Molly. Streeter must have matched his fingerprints with those of Jack Dune, taken twenty years earlier. He had managed to half convince Molly, and himself, that their ages would preclude any serious consideration that they could have murdered Marge Thomas.

"He must be crazy!" Molly gasped.

"He's obsessed. Or something." Jake replied. "Maybe he had a soft spot for Marge." Suddenly he whirled and headed for the door.

"I'm coming with you," Molly cried after him.

"No!" He looked back, his hand on the doorknob. "It's me he wants. You stay here and play dumb."

"I won't, Jake. If you leave without me, I'll just follow."

There was no time to argue. A few minutes later, they were blocks away, Jake hidden on the floor behind the driver's seat. Molly's heart beat a mad tattoo in her chest. The trip seemed to take forever. At every moment she expected to see a flashing light in the rearview mirror and hear the harsh wail of a police siren. It didn't happen.

Molly parked in the underground lot, then followed Jake to the motel's foyer. Requesting and receiving a room at the back, away from traffic, he registered them as Mr. and Mrs. McBride. Molly's knees gave way the moment the door closed behind them. Jake scooped her into his arms. His own knees none too steady, he dropped into one of the stuffed chairs, Molly on his lap. They clung together, each silently contemplating the suddenly very real possibility of separation and prison.

Chapter Sixteen

Forty minutes later a soft knock on the door announced Brad's arrival. He slipped inside and quickly closed the door. Leaning against it, he silently scrutinized Jake's face and then Molly's. Finally he shook his head.

"I must be as crazy as Harvey Streeter. Damned if you two don't look exactly like Jake Dune and Molly Barnes. But you couldn't be, could you." It was a statement rather than a question.

When they didn't answer, he straightened and looked at Jake. "I don't suppose you can explain how your fingerprints match Jake Dune's, taken twenty years ago."

Clearly not expecting a reply, he continued. "I've done some checking. The summer Marge died, you were fourteen and with your family at Disney World in Florida." He looked at Molly. "And you were eleven." He sighed. "I tried to tell Harvey that, but he wouldn't listen. He kept insisting that fingerprints don't lie. And I have to admit they *were* a perfect match." He shrugged. "I can't begin to explain it."

"What I don't understand," Jake said, "is Streeter's behavior. The man's deluding himself. As you found out,

I was too young at the time and I wasn't even in the country. What's Streeter's problem?"

Looking distressed, Brad shrugged. "I don't know. He and my father were good friends for years. They went through training together. Since dad died, Harvey has taken me under his wing and been like a mentor, a father, to me. Actually, I'm worried about him. When the two suspects in Marge's case vanished, he was upset for weeks. I don't think he's ever fully accepted his failure to bring her killers to justice."

There was nothing to say to that, so Jake outlined the theory about Doc Harrison that he and Molly had devised. As he spoke, Brad's face slowly crumpled. He inhaled deeply and nodded.

"I was thinking along the same lines," he agreed. "But Doc Harrison . . . damn, that's hard to swallow. He was a wonderful man. After his wife died, he began to drink heavily. Finally, he couldn't be trusted with the animals and people were forced to find a new vet."

"How did she die?" Molly asked.

"Slowly. It was a terrible thing. She died of a progressive muscular disease. For six years they both knew she was dying. Doc kept her at home but he had to hire full-time, live-in nursing. I imagine his life savings were...." He stopped, as understanding moved over his face.

"Of course," he breathed. "He needed money for Aggie's medicine and nursing bills. I should have thought of that. Nothing else could have persuaded him to kill innocent animals."

Molly felt a wave of relief and sympathy wash over her. Duncan's friend hadn't acted out of mere greed. What he'd done was wrong, but how many others in the same situation would have done the same thing?

Jake cleared his throat and shifted in the uncomfortable chair. "How did you happen to choose the name McBride?"

"McBride?" Brad looked puzzled for a moment, then

his face cleared. "Oh, no reason, really. I was thinking about Doc Harrison and then I got to thinking about some of his friends. Duncan Barnes. Jason McBride. Tory Smithson. Jim Stewart. Some others." He shrugged. "The name just slipped out when I called you."

Jake and Molly exchanged glances. Brad looked from one to the other.

"What?"

"Was McBride a banker?" Molly asked.

Brad looked stunned. "How did you know that?" His voice was edged with suspicion.

Too elated to sit still any longer, Molly got up and began to pace around the room. "It all fits. McBride must have provided the seed money to buy the farms." With growing excitement she related everything Kurt had told her. "If the police records show that David and Doc were together in a cell, then we have proof," she finished with triumph. She plopped down on the edge of the bed and turned to face Brad.

His gaze on the ugly brown carpet, the policeman silently digested her story. When he looked back at her, some of the tension had left his face.

"Not proof, Molly, only hearsay." None of them noticed his casual use of her first name. "Still, I think you may be right about McBride. The last I heard, he's still alive. Lives pretty high on the hog, too. Retired now, but twenty years ago he was in a position to make the loans. No one would question the transactions, not if the loans were paid back."

The policeman broke into a grin. "At last, I've got a real lead."

Jake stood up and begun to pull on his jacket.

Brad frowned. "Where do you think you're going?"

"With you, of course. To find McBride." Jake's voice vibrated with determination. "Don't think you can leave me out of this. Without my articles, you'd be nowhere."

"I know that." Brad stood and stepped over to block

Jake's path. "Have you forgotten that Harvey Streeter is looking for you? Not to mention whoever took the shot at you on your porch? Don't be stupid, man!"

"He's right, Jake." Molly took his arm and gazed beseechingly into his face. "Let Brad handle it from now on. What good will it do if you're arrested or killed?" When he hesitated, she tightened her grip. "*Please*, Jake."

She choked back the torrent of words that filled her mouth and waited, the breath suspended in her chest.

Jake searched her face and knew her appeal was based on genuine concern for his safety. He didn't want to risk another quarrel with her. Besides, he reminded himself, this time they had Brad's help.

"All right," he muttered gruffly. "I'll stay here for now. But," he turned and pointed a warning finger at Brad, "you keep us informed of what's happening."

"Agreed. I'll check the arrest records and look into McBride's financial affairs. The more information I have when I tackle him, the more likely he'll crack. And I need to visit the evidence room. The bullet from the gun that killed Marge is still there. I've got a feeling it will match the ones taken from Doc and David Ackers."

He shook hands quickly and left. Exhaling in relief, Molly shut and locked the door behind him. For a moment, she leaned her forehead against the door and said a silent prayer of thanks that Jake had agreed to stay in the motel room. Her world seemed suddenly brighter.

When she turned around, she found Jake standing only inches away. She looked up. Her heart jumped at the sensual expression on his craggy face. Immediately she remembered what they had been doing when Brad's call interrupted.

Jake, too, remembered.

The fire in his eyes lighted a conflagration that seared every inch of her body. Without hesitating, she reached up and wrapped her arms around his neck.

"Do you remember where we were?" she murmured, her voice a husky whisper.

"How could I forget?"

Jake buried his face in her neck and inhaled her womanly scent. "I'm a man who doesn't like unfinished business. So I suggest," he picked her up in his strong arms, "we get back to what's important."

"Mmm," Molly purred and pressed closer. She was amazed that Jake hadn't insisted on accompanying Brad, to follow up on his story. Instinct told her it wasn't fear that kept him with her. He had stayed behind to prove to her that she was more important than a story. Did that mean he loved her? If only he would say the words.

But he didn't give her time to ponder the question. Suddenly they were on the bed, their clothes gone, their naked bodied touching from mouth to toes. Passion erupted between them and blocked out all thoughts of murder. Much later, when their breathing finally slowed, they dozed off, their limbs still entwined.

Jake opened his eyes. There was a moment of confusion, then he remembered where he was. The room was dark, except for the neon light shining dimly through the window curtains. Molly was cuddled up against him, her head on his arm, one leg flung over his. He felt a rush of love so strong, his breath caught in his throat. Their coupling had been fast, wild, abandoned, like nothing he had ever experienced before. He had tried to go slowly, to make certain she achieved the same pleasure he did. But she was as ready as he and no more able to wait. They had exploded together in a shimmering fireball of sensual ecstasy.

He knew instinctively that Molly Malone was not a woman for casual affairs. Yet she was here with him, sleeping naked in his arms. Did that mean she loved him? If only she would say the words.

Molly's nose twitched. She stretched and rolled over on

her back. Her nose twitched again. Still half asleep, she lifted a hand to rub her nose. A chuckle rumbled close to her ear. Her eyes popped open. Inches from her face, a large hand was waving a cardboard box back and forth. The delicious odor of pizza made its way to her empty stomach and shot her upright.

By the light streaming through the bathroom door, she saw Jake's teasing smile. Her heart turned over with love. He handed her the box, stripped off his clothes and climbed in beside her. With the pillows propped behind their backs, they gulped down the food.

At last, sighing in satisfaction, Molly set the empty box on the floor. In the light from the bedside lamp, Jake's powerful shoulders and broad chest were incredibly fascinating. Suddenly, she remembered her wild behavior a few hours earlier. She blushed, and for the first time, realized she was uncovered from the waist up. She reached for the sheet.

"No you don't," Jake whispered. "I like to look at you."

It was too late for false modesty. Molly shook an admonishing finger at him. "You make me crazy, you know. Look at us. Two grown adults misbehaving in a sleazy motel room."

"Just think of it as another episode in *Tangled Lives*," Jake teased. Then his smile faded. "I take that back. This is for real."

At his last words, Molly's mind skittered back to the reason they were there, though she knew that wasn't what he meant. Hiding from an obsessive policeman. That was for real. Running from a killer, a killer three, maybe four times over. That was for real.

Molly shivered. She threw Jake an apologetic grimace and climbed out of the bed. Thankful for the toiletries Brad had thoughtfully provided, she showered, cleaned her teeth and put on her underclothes, then returned to the bedroom, wishing there was something she could do to lessen the dark foreboding that wrapped itself around her.

Jake hadn't moved from the bed. Now he patted the space beside him, then reached for the remote control for the television anchored to the wall facing the bed. Molly curled up against him and dropped her head on his shoulder. He draped one heavy arm behind her neck.

The eleven o'clock news started with the usual short survey of the wars and catastrophes plaguing the world. Her attention wandered. She could smell the heady odor of their lovemaking, taste the flavor of Jake's unique scent. She snuggled closer. Her fingers burrowed into the crisp curls on his chest. His body radiated a sensual heat that drew her like a cat to a fireplace.

Suddenly, Jake sat upright, almost knocking her sideways off the bed. He snatched at the remote control and raised the volume.

"What—"

"Sh! Look!" Jake gestured with the control.

Bewildered, Molly turned her gaze to the television set. For a long moment, nothing registered. The area seethed with uniformed men. Some were busy holding back the sightseers, others searched the ground with powerful flashlights. A police cruiser, its front end buckled against a lamp post, sat like a wounded animal sprawled amid shards of glass. Through the gaping driver's door, they could see a dark stain shimmering in the light from the lamppost.

Then she heard the sound of an ambulance pulling away, its siren almost drowning out the voice of the reporter speaking into the camera.

"Once again," the reporter said, *"a member of our police force has been assaulted. This time, on the very grounds of the station. The condition of Officer Bradley Baylor is unknown at this time. It's generally believed that he was shot while exiting the station, approximately fifteen minutes ago."*

The camera left the reporter and slowly panned the

area. Knots of people, many in pajamas and dressing gowns, stood huddled together, their expressions both fascinated and anxious. A few children raced unheeded among them.

When the camera switched back to the announcer in the studio, Jake switched off the set. Silence thundered in the room. A shudder shook Molly's body. Jake drew her into his arms and pressed her ashen face against his chest. He palmed her back in slow circles and stared blindly at the blank screen.

Who had shot Brad? Why? Was the shooting related to their shared investigation? Or was some other case involved? Was the shooter out for revenge? He thought of the random drive-by shootings of the last few years. Was Brad the victim of some spaced-out crazy? Could it be a case of mistaken identity? The possibilities were endless.

His mind slowed and settled as one thought emerged. Brad was out of the picture. McBride was Jake's baby now. Only one chance remained to find the killer and expose those involved in the land expropriation scheme. McBride had to be found and made to talk.

Molly pulled herself out of his arms and wiped her damp cheeks with the back of her hands. She stood up and inhaled deeply. Her lips were narrowed in anger and her eyes were hard. She headed for the clothes closet, determination in every line of her body.

Jake gaped at her. "What are you doing?"

"I'm going to find McBride."

"Molly, we don't know that Brad's shooting has anything to do with Doc and Marge. Besides, it's almost eleven o'clock." Jake swung his feet to the floor.

"I know that. But it doesn't change anything." She stopped and faced him. "I should have warned you earlier. I have a temper. It's seldom on display, but when I'm really angry, I can be the quintessential screaming shrew."

She paused. "I have *never* been as angry as I am at this moment."

Jake searched her face and knew nothing he could say would change her mind. Reluctant admiration filled his heart.

"All right," he conceded. "But it's late. Shouldn't we wait—"

"No. This is the best time. He'll be easier to intimidate if I drag him out of a sound sleep." She began pulling on her clothes. "Will you check the telephone book for his address? I'll—what do you think *you're* doing?"

Jake flashed her a grin and began to dress. "You don't think you're going alone, do you?"

"Jake, no! It's not safe for you to be out on the streets. What if—"

"—Jason McBride is the killer? What if he has a gun?" His grin faded. "Don't argue with me, sweetheart. You're not leaving this room without me hanging on your shirttail. And that's final."

Molly's eyes narrowed. Her lips pursed, she looked him up and down. "Is that an order?"

Something in her voice made Jake hesitate momentarily. Then he placed his hands on his hips and scowled. "Yes, that's an order. So?"

Molly stared at the massive, half-dressed figure and waited for resentment to rise in her. It didn't come. She felt something tight break loose in her chest and disappear. A kind of contentment took its place.

"So okay," she drawled. The smile in her heart escaped to her face. "But see that you don't make a habit of ordering me around."

Jake smiled back, sensing a landmark had just been reached, though he wasn't altogether certain what it was. "Of course not," he teased. "Not now that I know about your awesome temper."

Molly laughed and disappeared into the bathroom. Feeling amazingly light-hearted, Jake pulled on the rest of his clothes and reached for the phone book.

Ten minutes later they were in Molly's car, headed for

one of the more exclusive bedroom communities on the west edge of the city.

"There it is." Molly pointed to an imposing, red brick home set thirty feet back from the road. A streetlight directly in front of the house illuminated much of the front yard. All of the windows were dark. "Maybe he's not at home."

"Only one way to find out." Jake parked the car directly under the cone of light.

They closed the car doors quietly. Jake led the way, keeping to the grass beside the walk. When he reached the house, he veered to the side and peered through the window of the double garage, then nodded in satisfaction.

He crept on silent feet to the front door and flattened himself against the wall beside the door handle. The top half of the heavy door was inlaid with glass. At his signal, Molly approached the door, making no attempt to muffle her footsteps.

She took a deep breath and pushed the doorbell. Nothing happened. She rang again, then a third time. Finally, she put her finger to the bell and left it there.

A light in an upstairs room snapped on, illuminating a patch of grass. Briefly, her mind resurrected the memory of the night Jake had stumbled out of Tom's Woods and collapsed in the square of light from her room. Molly Barnes' room. So much had happened since he toppled into her life.

She glanced quickly at Jake when a light suddenly lit a wide inner staircase. At the top of the stairs, she could just make out slippers and pajama-clad legs. She pressed the buzzer again. The legs descended until she could see the figure of a white-haired man clad in a rich dressing gown. He moved slowly, suspicion in every line of his spare body.

Molly inhaled deeply, ready to act out the most

important role of her life. Her face assumed the contorted expression of a desperately frightened woman. She hunched forward and looked over her shoulder nervously, as if watching for an unseen assailant. Rattling the handle of the screen door, she mouthed, *Please!*, at the approaching figure. The porch light snapped on above her head.

Wary eyes ran over her, then peered beyond her to the car. Finally, the heavy door opened.

"What do you want?" His tone was brusque, annoyed. He spoke through the locked screen door.

"Oh, please, let me in. A car has been following me for ages. I'm afraid to go home. He'll know where I live then." Molly looked fearfully over her shoulder again. She whimpered. Her big gray eyes dripped tears down her face. "Please, let me in to call the police. Help me, *please*."

His eyes swept over the empty car and lawn again. Finally, grumbling under his breath, he unlocked the door and shoved it open.

Molly slipped inside quickly. Before the door swung closed, Jake lurched into the opening, stepped inside and pulled the door closed. The middle-aged man backed up, his hands flung out in front of him.

"Who are you? What do you want? Get out of my house." In the overhead light, his face was milk-white. Fear edged his blustering voice.

Jake closed the heavy door and moved forward, until he towered above the quaking man. He didn't answer. Through the door on his left he could make out the dim shapes of furniture. Hooking his thumb, he motioned for the terrified man to move.

McBride stumbled backward in his haste to put some distance between them. When Jake pointed, still without speaking, to a leather recliner, McBride backed into it and pressed himself deep into the chair. Molly pulled the handle at the side that lifted the foot rest, then shoved down hard on the back. McBride began to keen in fear. He was as immobilized as firmly as if he'd been tied.

"What do you want?" he wheezed. "I've got money, lots of money. Just don't hurt me. Please don't hurt me." His thin frame shook.

Molly felt sick. She wanted to run, to pull Jake away. But she remembered Marge and David, poor Alex Harrison and now maybe Brad. She remembered the attempts on Jake's life. She held her tongue.

"We don't want your money," Jake growled. He towered over the helpless man. Even to Molly, he looked menacing, dangerous.

"Wh . . . what then?" McBride squirmed in the chair, his hands clasping the arm rests in white-knuckled terror.

"Information. We want information. And you're going to give us what we want. Here. Now. Whatever it takes." No one seeing Jake's grim face would doubt him.

"Information? Yes, yes, whatever you want. Just please don't hurt me!" In his fear, the ex-banker didn't realize that Jake hadn't laid a finger on him. Molly suspected it wouldn't matter if he did. Jake's massive physique promised untold violence.

"That's a very good boy." Jake produced a wolfish grin and pulled up a chair. His mouth trembling uncontrollably, McBride watched as Jake made himself comfortable.

"Have you a good memory, Mr. McBride?" Jake's change to a casual, conversational voice made the banker shrink deeper into his chair.

He nodded rapidly, obviously anxious to please.

"Wonderful." Jake smiled cheerfully. "Right then, I want you to cast your mind back, oh, say twenty years."

The banker's face steadily whitened as Jake rhymed off the names of the farmers who had lost their properties and then the names of the long ago buyers.

"I see you're familiar with those names. You're doing just fine, Jason." Jake paused. His eyes hardened.

"I've one more list for you. Then you're going to carry the conversational ball." He leaned forward, his stance again hostile. McBride swallowed hard, his eyes huge with fear.

"First, there's Doug Baylor, an honest policeman, murdered with his own gun. Then there's his cousin Marge Thomas, a good, kind woman. Also shot to death."

The banker's ashen face looked bleached. He began to shake his head in denial.

"Then, more recently," Jake plowed on, "David Ackers died. Alex Harrison died. Both shot with the same gun that killed the other two twenty years ago." The latter point was as yet unverified, but Jake felt sure he was right.

"Doug B . . . Baylor com . . . committed suicide," McBride whispered. "S . . . suicide."

"No!" Jake thundered. "Doug was the first victim of your greed. And then you killed Marge, when you discovered Doug had given her his notes for safekeeping."

"I didn't kill her, I didn't!"

Jake ignored the man's cry. His voice dropped to a whisper. "For twenty years you've lived in luxury. You didn't care about the farmers you and your partners cheated. You had what you wanted."

The banker pressed his hands to his mouth and moaned.

"But now it's all starting to come apart, isn't it? Suddenly, someone else wanted a share. So you killed David Ackers. Only one person could have told him about the blood and grief spilled along the path of the Capital Highway. One person. Alex Harrison. Your friend, your partner. So you shot him, too. After all, if Alex talked once, he could talk again. Who can trust a drunk, right?"

"I didn't, I didn't." McBride clutched Jake's shoulders and tried to pull himself up. "I didn't! You've got to believe me. No one was supposed to get hurt. He promised no one would be hurt. We . . . we just wanted the money."

Jake tamped down a flare of excitement. McBride thought they knew it all. Another minute and he would name the other partner. He flung the man's hands from his shoulders with a contemptuous shrug.

"Then I was to be your victim, too. But you missed." He shook his head slowly. "I don't like it when people shoot at me, Jason. I get peeved. Extremely peeved. That was a very stupid thing to do. Almost as stupid as using the same gun that killed Marge and David and Alex."

"But I didn't shoot at you. I don't even know you." McBride's voice was a thin wail laced with panic and a desperate thread of truth.

"Did you use that same trusty gun to shoot Brad Baylor tonight, Jason? Another good man, dead by your hand. That makes five who've died so you can live in luxury. All that greed. All that blood. Do you see a monster in the mirror when you shave, Jason?"

A stillness came over the banker at the mention of Brad Baylor. The fear in his eyes changed to horror. He clutched the arm rests and pulled himself upright. His gaze moved to Molly, as if for confirmation. She nodded. When he spoke again, his voice was dead.

"I thought Doug committed suicide. The police said Marge was killed by a stranger passing through. I never heard of David Ackers. Alex . . . I figured street punks killed him for whatever he had." He turned to Jake. "I don't know who you are. I didn't kill Brad Baylor. I've never killed anyone."

Jason McBride had aged before their eyes. There was no passion, no fear left in him. And no lies.

"Who killed them, Jason?" Jake asked softly.

For a moment he thought the old man didn't respond. Then he blinked, as if the answer had just come to him.

"Why, the man who started the whole thing. It must have been—"

The name was lost in the sound of shattering glass and Jason McBride's hoarse cry. Jake jumped to his feet but tripped over a footstool. He reached the front door in time to hear tires squealing out of sight around the end of the block.

Chapter Seventeen

Jason McBride lay twisted in the chair, his upper torso draped over the armrest. Molly grabbed his shoulders and pulled him back on the recliner. Choking with revulsion, she snatched her hands away from the warm wet blood soaking one side of his dressing gown. Swallowing the sickness in her throat, she forced herself to probe for a pulse.

Don't let him die, she prayed, *don't let him die*. Finally she felt a faint movement beneath her fingertips. For a moment, relief made her dizzy. But she couldn't fall apart now.

She pulled open his dressing gown and pajama top. Blood welled from a ghastly-looking hole in his shoulder. Willing her stomach to behave, she whipped off her sweater and cotton-knit camisole, then folded the undergarment into a pad and pressed it against the wound.

Behind her, Jake returned to the room, took in the situation with one glance, and quickly dialed 9-1-1. When he hung up, he yanked off his belt. A moment later it was bound tightly over McBride's shoulder and under his arm, effectively holding the makeshift bandage in place. He covered the man with an afghan. It was all they could do.

He looked up and opened his arms to a white-faced Molly. She backed up a faltering step, holding her hands out from her sides.

"Blood," she croaked, "my hands are . . ."

She swayed. Her body went limp and began to topple forward. Jake caught her under her shoulders and half-carried, half-dragged her to a velvet settee. He shoved a pillow under her head and kneeled anxiously at her side, patting her cheeks gently. The breath he didn't know he was holding whooshed from his lungs when her eyes fluttered open.

"It's all right, sweetheart. I'm here."

For a moment, confusion fogged her eyes. Then she gasped and tried to rise. Jake gently pressed her down.

"McBride. Is he . . . ?"

"He's alive. The ambulance should be here any minute. Relax, darling. We've done all we can."

"Oh, Jake. He didn't tell us who the other person is. What are we going to—" She broke off abruptly as she suddenly became aware of the draft from the shattered window. She looked down to see the pink and white lace of her bra. A blush rose from her shoulders to her hairline.

Jake saw it and grinned. He cupped the sweet mounds in his large hands and dropped a kiss on the tip of her nose.

"Jake, you idiot," she protested, twisting away and trying not to smile. "Find my sweater before the ambulance gets here."

"Good idea. No one gets to see my woman except me." He wiped the worst of the blood from her hands with a small throw pillow, then pulled the sweater over her head. Deep inside, he was awed at her resilience. Most people would have fallen apart, even become hysterical. Not Molly.

He had never met a woman like Molly Malone. Never even knew such a woman existed. Cool yet passionate, tough yet tender, compassionate yet level-headed. Brave. Intelligent. Generous.

And beautiful. So beautiful.

He knew he would never, *could* never, stop loving her.

The wail of an ambulance interrupted his musings. By the time McBride had been loaded onto a stretcher and slid into the ambulance, two uniformed officers were spilling from a cruiser. Jake climbed into the ambulance before they saw him, and turned to whisper tersely to Molly.

"One of us has to be with him in case he regains consciousness and talks. Tell them the story you told McBride. Don't mention me. Then join me at the hospital. *Be careful!*"

Then, telling the medics he was a close friend of the wounded man, he retreated into the ambulance before the officers spotted him. Molly walked toward the policemen, talking rapidly and pointing to the damaged window. One officer took her elbow and began to walk her back to the house. The other returned to the cruiser and took off in a squeal of tires in the wake of the ambulance.

It took an hour and several repetitions of her story before the officer accepted her tale of an unknown pursuer. Molly wasn't a good liar, but by acting the part of a woman as quarry, she managed to convince the policeman that chance alone had placed her in McBride's home. She didn't mention Jake.

It was past two a.m. when she arrived at the hospital and found Jake slumped in an uncomfortable-looking chair in a waiting room on the fifth floor. His eyes were closed. His head rested at an angle against the back of the chair. Molly stopped in the doorway. He looked so tired, so vulnerable. Sleep hadn't smoothed the lines of anxiety from his face. Had McBride died on the operating table? If he had, the killer's name was lost forever.

The moment she stepped forward, Jake's head snapped up. His tension eased instantly when he saw her. He was on his feet and in her arms before she reached the middle of the room.

"Are you okay?" he asked, his voice muffled against her hair.

"Yes. The policeman bought my story." She leaned back to search his face. "What's happening?"

He led her to a chair and sat down beside her. "McBride survived the operation, but his condition is listed as critical. The bullet missed his heart. The surgeon's main worry is his age, although his general health is good. The next twenty-four hours are crucial."

Molly gripped Jake's hand tightly. "Even if he makes it, he won't be able to talk for a day or more. He's our only lead to the killer. Oh, Jake, what are we going to do?"

Jake was silent a moment. He rubbed hard at the back of his neck, then pulled her to her feet.

"We'll go back to the motel and get some sleep. But first, we'll see if we can sneak in a visit with Brad. He's on the third floor. He's going to be fine. The bullet just grazed his head. He's got a hell of a headache though. The nurse says he'll be discharged in the morning."

"Thank God," Molly murmured. "I don't believe he had any part of the land expropriation deal. But—"

"—why was he shot?" Jake asked. "If he wasn't one of the partners like Harrison and McBride, why kill him?"

"I don't know," Molly sighed. "Unless it had nothing to do with this investigation. Or," she paused, "the killer knew he was getting close to the answer and was afraid McBride would talk. He'd try to stop Brad from reaching McBride. Getting rid of both of them would stop the investigation for good."

"That would make sense except for one thing." Jake shook his head. "How did the killer know he was getting close? In fact, how did the killer even know Brad was investigating? Unless," he answered his own question, "he's been keeping an eye on Brad all these years. It wouldn't take a genius to figure that, as a cop, Brad would never stop searching for his cousin's killer, even if he believed his father's death was suicide."

"That sounds reasonable. I think." Molly gave a small laugh. "Right now, I can't think at all. Let's get moving before we fall asleep on our feet."

As they passed the nurses' station, Molly noticed the coy smile the blonde nurse directed at Jake who seemed oblivious to the seductive invitation in her eyes. When she looked at Molly, her expression held envy. Then she shrugged and smiled. Molly smiled back. The silent exchange warmed her. Despite the circumstances, she felt proud to be the woman at Jake's side.

When they turned a corner, Jake ignored the elevators and cautiously opened the door to the stairwell. He listened a moment for the sound of footsteps and heard nothing. They met no one on their silent trek down. A small window in the door to the third floor showed an empty corridor. They slipped through the door and moved quietly down the hall. The silence seemed unnatural. From further down the corridor, the soft-toned conversation of the night staff provided the only sign of life.

Brad's room was the third door on the left. Jake pushed it open and placed a hand on the small of Molly's back to usher her in. He winced when it squeaked in protest. They froze, listening intently. When the nurses' conversation continued uninterrupted, he exhaled softly and eased the door closed.

The room was small. To Molly's relief, it contained only one bed. By the light shining in from the hall through the small square of glass in the door, she could just make out the figure on the bed. The stark white bandage circling the patient's head seemed to glow in the dimness. With Jake a pace behind her, Molly approached the bed.

Before she could whisper his name, Brad spoke without opening his eyes.

"Oh, no you don't. Just go away. I'm fine. If you shine that light in my eyes again, I'm going to arrest you for assault."

Jake chuckled. At the sound, Brad's eyes snapped open. He blinked several times, then a broad grin spread across his face.

"You two! I might have known. You just couldn't stay put, could you? How did you know I was here?"

"You made the news, buddy. How are you feeling?"

"About what you'd expect. Like a construction crew is hammering in my head. Other than that, top of the world." Brad rolled his eyes, then winced. "What are you two doing here anyway? I thought we'd agreed to leave the rest up to me."

Jake and Molly exchanged glances. Brad caught the exchange.

"What?" He pushed himself to a sitting position.

Stalling, Jake asked "You didn't speak to McBride?"

Brad started to shake his head. He stopped abruptly and swore under his breath.

"Sorry, Molly. No. I went from the motel to the station. I was just leaving to brace McBride. He looks like a good bet to be involved. Next thing I knew, I was here. But," he added, " there's bad news. The file on Marge is there, but the bullet is missing from the evidence room. It probably got lost in the move to the new station."

"Damn," Jake swore softly.

Molly felt a black cloud of depression settle on her shoulders. Some capricious god seemed to be playing with them. One step forward, two steps backward. And Jake still the target of an unknown gunman.

"Our news is worse." She gave the policeman a brief, concise account of their encounter with Jason McBride. Brad's face grew grimmer and grimmer as she told him of McBride's confession and verified Doc Harrison's involvement.

"Do you think McBride is the killer?" he asked heavily.

Jake and Molly shook their heads in unison.

"He must have been aware of Harrison's part in the killing of the animals," Jake spoke slowly, "but we don't think he even knew about the murders. He'd never heard of David Ackers and he had no idea who I was."

Jake paused. "He was pretty convincing."

"He seemed genuinely horrified at our accusations," Molly confirmed. "That has to be why the other partner tried to kill him. He had to know McBride well enough to realize he'd fall apart if he found out he was an accessory to murder. Murders."

Brad groaned. "So McBride's the key. He's all we've got. If he lives."

Gloom pressed thickly in the dim room. Finally, Molly patted Brad's bowed shoulders.

"You get some sleep. Call us at the motel when you get out of here."

The policeman looked up and nodded. "At least now, the province will have to launch an official investigation into the matter of land expropriation—and hopefully change some procedures to make sure this doesn't happen again."

Jake's eyes brightened. "I can use the paper to push for provincial compensation for the families. That'll be something anyway, even if McBride doesn't make it."

Brad's face relaxed slightly. "Thanks, you two. For everything. I promise never to say anything nasty about the press again."

They laughed softly. Jake padded to the door and found the hallway clear. With a final wave to Brad, they slipped from the room. A few minutes later Molly led the way to her car. Traffic was almost non-existent. In ten minutes they were safely back in the motel room. In twenty minutes they were in each other's arms, sleeping the sleep of the exhausted.

* * *

Molly's eyes fluttered open. For a moment, she stared at the green-tinted ceiling. What had awakened her? Beside her Jake sprawled warmly, his long body touching hers from shoulder to foot. She smiled to herself. He had fallen asleep kissing her. Or had she fallen asleep kissing him? Whichever, she felt loved and protected. It was a deliciously feminine feeling.

Birds scrabbled outside the window, greeting the new day with noisy babble. Fingers of morning light poked through the cracks and chips in the blinds. It was much too early to think of getting up. Yawning, she turned to her side and snuggled back against Jake.

Sleep eluded her. Her mind jumped from the present to the past and back again. Somewhere there had to be a clue, a hint they were missing, something that didn't fit. Something subtle. Or was it something so obvious they couldn't see it, like Poe's purloined letter, overlooked and unrecognized.

A trickle of excitement shivered down her spine. The answer was there, just beyond her reach. She was sure of it. Breathing deeply and releasing the air slowly, Molly willed her mind to relax, to calm like the surface of a pool on a windless day. The yoga technique had stood her in good stead when stage fright threatened her nerves. She imagined a gigantic wire whisk slowly stirring up the debris at the bottom of the pool. Facts, questions, suppositions, rose like bubbles from the depths of her subconscious, to float on the surface. She examined each bubble carefully.

Whoever recruited Alex Harrison and Jason McBride had to have been aware of both the veterinarian's desperate need for money and the banker's greed. Alex, as a successful veterinarian, would have been widely-known, but Jason McBride's acquaintances were probably limited to his own community. Was the other partner a member of the same community?

Marge had been beaten before she was killed. To make her tell about Doug's notes? And disclose their whereabouts? No, that didn't fit. If the killer was the peeping Tom at Marge's window, he would know that she'd handed over Doug's notes. Unless the curtains had been closed or the person too far away to see.

But that didn't explain how the killer knew the notes even existed. Had Doug told him before he died? Why would he? Unless the officer hadn't yet identified his killer as a member of the conspiracy. There was no sign of a struggle in Doug Baylor's home. That implied the killer was someone he knew and didn't suspect.

Brad was shot on his way to question McBride. Who knew where he was going? And how? But maybe the killer had simply been waiting for a chance to shoot him and had no idea where Brad was headed.

Molly sighed. Was it mere coincidence that a few hours later McBride was shot? That was a possibility. After twenty years of secrecy, the third partner must have been shaken when David tried to blackmail him. With Doc Harrison dead, only Jason McBride remained with the power to bring the killer down. So he acted to destroy the last loose end. The action may have had nothing to do with Brad's investigation.

Who was the anonymous tipster who informed the police of their presence in Marge's home the night she disappeared? Doug had been dead three months before the harassment began. Marge seemed to think the calls were linked to Jake's questions about Doug during the days spent helping the Stewarts rebuild their home. But no evidence supported that belief.

Why was Harvey Streeter so determined to arrest Jake for a twenty-year-old murder? He had to know the charge wouldn't stick. Had his fellow officer's death broken something in his mind? Or had he been in love with Marge? If so, his determination to charge the couple he believed responsible would be understandable.

She remembered Kurt's description of David as keeping his cards close to his vest. It was unlikely that her ex-husband would have revealed the source of his information to the person he tried to blackmail. How then did the killer know that Alex, and not McBride, had talked?

Molly still hadn't put it together when Jake awoke an hour later. A single fact lurked just below the surface of the pool. No, not a fact. A simple comment, a throw-away line. Yes. Someone said . . . . Someone said . . . . It wouldn't come.

She rolled into Jake's reaching arms. He kissed her good morning and tucked her head into the curve of his neck. They lay quietly, remembering the shocking sound of the shattering window and the sight of McBride's unconscious body.

Finally Jake disentangled himself from Molly.

"I'm going to call the hospital."

Molly sat up and hugged her knees. She thought of the unknown killer who wanted to rob her of the man who had become her life. A cold, dark anger rose and clouded her vision. He must not succeed. He *would not* succeed. She trembled with the violence of her fury.

Slowly, she became aware of the hands on her shoulders, shaking her roughly. She blinked and lifted her head. Jake was calling her name, a touch of panic in his voice.

"Molly, what's wrong? Speak to me."

"Oh, Jake. Don't let him take you away from me." She scrambled to her knees and flung her arms around his waist.

Jake wove his fingers into her hair and pressed her head to his chest. He was awed by the fierce passion that blazed from her eyes, and thrilled that the threat to his life could fire her with such rage. The slender body of this beautiful woman housed the soul of a warrior. He felt unworthy even as his heart swelled with pride. What a fool David Ackers had been to let her get away.

When she stirred and leaned back, he sat down on the edge of the bed.

"McBride's still alive. Still in ICU. That's all the nurse would tell me. He should be safe as long as he remains there."

"Thank God," Molly breathed. Then she caught his meaning and gasped. "Safe. But when he's moved to a regular room... Jake, the killer will go after him again. He'll have no choice. We should call the police—"

"No one would listen to us. But relax, sweetheart. McBride is safe in ICU at least until tomorrow morning. In any case, I'm sure Brad has already thought of the danger. He'll arrange for a guard on the door."

Molly chewed on her knuckle. "What if he doesn't? A headache like his doesn't make for clear thinking."

Jake had no doubt that Brad would grasp the necessity for posting a guard, but he wanted to ease Molly's fears. "Maybe you're right." He checked his watch. "He should still be there. I'll call and light a fire under him. He'll probably want to do the guard duty hims—"

He broke off when Molly gave a strangled cry and grabbed his arm.

"*Light a fire*. That's it. Wait, wait a minute. Let me think."

As Jake stared at her wide, unfocused eyes, he felt a thrill of excitement race down his back. Hectic red flags rouged her cheeks. Her fingers dug into his arm. He waited.

Finally, her eyes cleared and a satisfied smile lit up her face.

"I know who the other partner is. It's been staring us in the face all this time." She waved her hands in the air and scrambled off the bed. "We've got to warn Brad. Since the killer can't get to McBride yet, he might decide to have another go at Brad."

She snatched up her clothing. In her frenzied hurry, her fingers fumbled with the fastener of her bra. Grinning, Jake did it for her, then put his hands on her waist and turned her to face him.

She backed out of his grasp and stamped her foot. "Why are you just standing there? Get dressed. We've got to hurry."

Jake folded his arms across his chest and shot her an indulgent look. "Aren't you going to share your brainwave with me?"

The teasing note in his voice brought her up short. For a moment, she stared questioningly up at him.

"What? Oh!"

When she'd outlined her theory, Jake had no objections to offer. He felt the truth of her reasoning settle in his mind. Without speaking again, they dressed, then headed for the hospital.

Chapter Eighteen

Molly preceded Jake into the hospital. She passed through the ground floor waiting room, her eyes moving constantly in search of danger. They had worked out a signal. If she dropped her purse, Jake would dive for cover. But there was no sign of their enemy.

The hospital bustled with white-coated men and women and a few visitors. It was still early morning. No one paid them the slightest attention as they climbed the stairs to the third floor.

At Molly's insistence, Jake ducked into the men's washroom. She had promised to knock on the door as soon as she knew the coast was clear. Disgruntled, but knowing she was right, Jake agreed.

Brad's door was open. Molly peeked inside. Brad was alone, fully dressed, sitting on the edge of the bed and looking impatient. She knocked lightly. He looked up and waved her in.

"Jake's waiting in the men's room. Is it safe for him to come in?"

"Should be," he answered. "Everyone knows I get out this morning so I don't think there'll be any visitors."

Molly nodded and left. After a cautious look around, she signaled Jake. They slipped quickly back into Brad's room.

"McBride's still in danger," Jake said immediately.

"I know. My partner and I are going to take turns guarding his door when he's moved from ICU." Brad grimaced. "If only we knew who to watch for. In the movies, the killer always gets in by dressing in doctor's clothes. We're going to be mighty unpopular, forcing hospital personnel to show identification."

"This killer won't need a disguise," Molly said. "No one would question his right to enter McBride's room."

Brad looked puzzled. "What do you mean?" He looked from Molly to Jake and back.

Before either could explain, a woman walked in, stopping in surprise at the sight of the two visitors. She studied their faces with a frown, then turned to her the policeman.

"You're right. If I didn't know better, I'd swear these people are Jake Dune and Molly Barnes." She smiled at the couple. "The similarity is incredible."

Brad introduced Nora, his wife of eighteen years. Inside, Molly wanted to laugh at the ridiculous situation. She had spoken with Nora less than two weeks before. Nora had last spoken with *her*, Molly, twenty years before. It took a real effort not to ask Nora Baylor if she still made her wonderful peach pie.

Nora sat beside her husband and picked up his hand. Curiosity filled her eyes.

Brad said, "Go ahead. Nora knows everything."

As he pulled up the visitor's chair for Molly, Jake said, "Molly figured it out. It's her story. Go ahead, sweetheart."

First warning the tense pair that what she had to say was pure conjecture, Molly took a deep breath and began.

Nora and Brad glanced at each other once, then locked their gazes on the woman who looked so familiar.

Brad's expression slowly changed from disbelief to uncertainty and finally to an appalled acceptance.

"But there's no proof," Molly cautioned at the end of her narrative. "And of course, I could be entirely wrong."

Brad shook his head, his face a white mask of grief. "No, you're right. Every piece fits. To think I trusted that *bastard*...." He choked and buried his head in his hands.

Nora put her arms around her husband. "He's not going to get away with it any longer, darling. We'll find a way to prove everything."

Four heads turned when a nurse pushed a wheelchair into the room. She looked a bit taken aback at the sight of the grim faces. Then Brad forced a smile. "At last. I'm outta here." He signed the release forms and surprised the nurse by climbing without protest into the wheelchair. A few minutes later they stood in the parking lot.

Molly laid a detaining hand on Nora's arm. "I think Brad should stay with us for now. His life is still in danger. And you have the children to think of."

"Of course." Nora nodded, her voice brisk, though laden with disappointment. As a policeman's wife, she accepted the situation. The danger was all too real. "Where will you be?"

"Let's go to my place," Jake said. "Streeter has already checked and knows I'm not there. It should be safe, at least for awhile. The cat will think he's been deserted, and he'll be hungry by now."

The others agreed. Nora embraced her husband and drove away. Brad, Jake and Molly stopped to check out of the motel, then picked up some take-out lunch and drove to Jake's. Brad immediately called the hospital, gave Jake's number and left orders that he be notified when McBride was scheduled to be transferred to a regular room.

Looking tired and strained, he sat at the table with Molly while Jake set out plates and opened the food packages. Mac came to the doorway and began to chastise his humans for abandoning him. He broke off in mid-scold when the scent of chicken drifted past his nose. With a mew of delight, he leaped to an empty chair and placed two eager front paws on the table.

"Patience, Mac. You'll get your share." Molly chuckled and reached out to scratch the cat's head.

"Mac? Mac?" Brad sounded disbelieving. His mouth worked silently for a moment, then he shot Molly an incredulous glance. "Duncan Barnes had a cat named Mac. He looked just like this one. Sat at the table the same way." He gulped. "Mac disappeared the same day as Molly Barnes and Jake Dune. This is... this is . . . ." He shook his head and laughed shakily. "I must be out of my mind. You wouldn't believe what I'm thinking."

Jake and Molly grinned. They had a pretty good idea what Brad was thinking.

After they'd eaten, Brad stifled a yawn and massaged his forehead. "If you two don't mind, I'm going to stretch out on the couch. Do you happen to have anything for a headache, Jake?"

"Sure, in the medicine cabinet. But help yourself to the bed, you'll rest better there. There's nothing we can do until McBride is out of ICU. We'll wake you when the hospital calls."

With a look of gratitude, Brad nodded and disappeared down the hall, Mac trailing after to keep an eye on the man who used to visit his lady human. Molly and Jake remained in the kitchen, drinking coffee and rehashing their theory, looking for a way to prove it. With no witnesses to the killings and no way to obtain the gun, only one possibility remained. Jake voiced it first.

"He has to get rid of McBride. Brad, too, but McBride is of more immediate danger to him. He can't afford to sit by hoping his partner will die without ever regaining consciousness. Our only chance is to catch him in the act."

"And he's got to do it soon. At least we can testify to

McBride's confession," Molly said. She shuddered, remembering the confrontation between Jake and the ex-banker. Between Jake's great size and his menacing manner, she had been almost frightened of him herself.

But not really. With her, he was a gentle man, a man who respected her for herself, a man who knew his own strength and controlled it. Jake would never permit himself to indulge in rages, as David had. If only his ex-wife hadn't turned him against marriage. She could understand how he felt, though. Marriage was a risky business, as she knew so well. The potential for failure was always present.

The telephone rang, making them both jump. Jake answered. Molly saw his body tense. She was on her feet when he turned and relayed the gist of the call.

"That was the hospital. There's been a three-car pile-up on the Queensway. They need all the beds in ICU, so McBride will be transferred to the fourth floor in a few minutes. He's still unconscious, but his vital signs are good. I'll wake Brad."

They were on the way in minutes. When they arrived, McBride was settled in the bed and a nurse was just leaving. She frowned at them and pointed to the No Visitors sign on the door.

The sight of Brad's badge and his abbreviated account of the danger still facing her patient persuaded her to let them in. With a strict warning not to disturb him, she at last moved away.

Jason McBride lay still on the bed, an intravenous tube taped to his wrist. He looked sick, old, and vulnerable. Molly stifled a surge of pity. He had felt none for the families he and his partners had cheated. Justice had finally caught up with the crooked banker.

The room contained an extra bed, thankfully empty. After a whispered discussion, Jake climbed into the empty bed and pulled the blanket up to his chin. Brad pulled the curtain partly closed between the two beds, then took up guard duty in the hall, blocking access to the room.

Against her will, Molly retreated to a small waiting room that permitted a view of the elevators and a partial view of the stairwell door. Neither man would permit her to remain in McBride's room. In any case, there had been nowhere to hide.

Her stomach was churning. Jake had no gun. His only advantage would be surprise. She could only pray that the killer wouldn't inspect the occupant of the second bed too closely. She tried to relax, though she didn't think it would take long for the killer to realize McBride had likely been moved.

From where she sat she couldn't see Brad. She worried he wouldn't be able to carry out his part in the deception. It was necessary to allow the killer access to McBride. Brad's role was to play the unsuspecting policeman. Would he be able to hide his feelings for the man who had killed his father and cousin and tried to kill him? With McBride the most important target, Brad should be safe, at least temporarily, as long as he could play his part convincingly.

Seconds seemed to pass like minutes, minutes like hours. Doctors and nurses passed in the hall, all busy, all oblivious to the drama waiting to happen. Molly watched for the killer to arrive.

Jake grew more and more tense as the minutes passed and nothing happened. Had they misjudged the killer? Would he wait until the next day, on the assumption that McBride would still be in ICU? No. By now, the whole city knew about the horrendous accident on the Queensway. Common sense would suggest that McBride would be displaced by one of the crash victims.

Through the closed door he could hear the rattle of the meal wagon making its halting way down the hall. An increase in the number of voices and footsteps indicated that visitors were beginning to arrive. Jake tried to think like the killer. Would he feel safer when the halls were crowded? Or in the evening after visiting hours were over?

He was still trying to figure the odds when he heard muffled voices at the door—Brad's voice and one other. He tensed. Then Brad raised his voice.

"I don't need a break, really."

"Yes, you do. You look terrible, son. Go on down to the cafeteria and grab a bite. I'll wait here until you return. Go on, I insist."

Jake heard Brad's footsteps receding down the hall. He would have to go far enough to get out of sight, then wait until the killer entered the room before he could return. Jake tried not to think just how alone he was, against a killer with a gun. He waited, scarcely breathing.

An eternity passed. At last he heard the quiet click of the door mechanism. For a moment, the hall noises penetrated the room, then faded as the door closed. Soft footsteps approached the bed. Jake concentrated on breathing evenly and heavily, like a man dosed with sedative. The curtain rings rattled as the dividing curtain was shoved aside. Silence.

Jake's skin prickled. He could feel the eyes watching, waiting for him to show signs of awareness. He continued to breathe noisily, expecting any moment to feel a bullet enter his back. When he thought he could remain still no longer, the curtain dropped. The killer turned his back and stepped to McBride's bed.

Jake waited. This was the tricky part. He knew Brad was listening outside the door for his yell. He had to catch the killer in that second before he actually killed his old partner. They wanted McBride alive, if possible. He waited.

Finally he heard the unmistakable sound of a gun being cocked. Jake leaped from the bed with a yell and plunged at the figure on the other side of the curtain. The gun went off, its bullet smashing harmlessly into the wall above McBride's head. Jake wrapped his arms around the curtain-shrouded killer and knocked him to the floor.

The door burst open. In the hallway, people began to scream. Brad took in the situation but didn't dare shoot. The curtain obscured each face in turn as Jake rolled with the killer, trying to break his grip on the revolver. The gun fired again, the bullet passing close to Brad's head. He ducked and moved in, circling the struggling, grunting pair, waiting for a clear shot.

An outflung leg caught his knee. He stumbled against the bed, lost his balance and landed on the floor with a crash that knocked the gun from his hand.

Molly dashed in the room just as the killer swung his right arm. The gun caught Jake on the forehead, loosening his grip. The killer bucked, knocking Jake away. In an instant, Molly found herself held by a rough arm at her waist, the barrel of a gun digging into her ear.

Jake and Brad struggled to a sitting position at the same instant. Both froze at the sight of Harvey Streeter dragging Molly backward to the door. Brad reached for his gun. In an instant Streeter swung the gun around and fired. Brad twisted away. His head crashed into the metal bed frame with an audible thunk. His body went limp.

"You hurt her, Streeter, and you're a dead man." Jake snarled in impotent rage. "I'll hunt you down forever."

"You move and she's dead," the lawman jeered. "I'm outta here. Maybe, just maybe, I'll let her go. Then again, maybe not." Molly winced as he ground the gun in her ear. "Don't bother calling for help. If I see a cop anywhere near me, I'll kill her." He tightened his grip on Molly's waist. "Come on, sweetie, let's travel."

He dragged her through the door. People screamed and scattered. Molly didn't hear them. Her gaze was welded to Jake's. Would she ever see him again? Just before Streeter swung her around, she mouthed *I love you* to his anguished face. The next thing she knew, elevator doors opened in front of her. Horrified faces gaped, then surged from the elevators at Streeter's growled command. He pushed the button for the ground floor, but the elevator continued up to the fifth. The elderly woman waiting gasped with shock when the door opened. She backed away, while Streeter cursed. The doors closed again. This time they descended without interruption to the ground floor.

Streeter shoved her forward, using his shoulder to keep the elevator door open while he looked around. No one noticed them at first. Then a couple approached the elevator. They halted abruptly when they caught sight of the gun jammed in Molly's ear. The woman's scream turned heads. Again people scattered like cats sighting a pack of dogs.

Streeter laughed. The maniacal note in his voice chilled Molly through. The small hope she'd been nourishing, that he would let her go, evaporated. Another murder wouldn't bother him. *If she could just see Jake one more time.*

The crowds parted like the Red Sea as he pushed and dragged her through the main waiting room and out the door to the parking lot. Molly was barely aware of the blood trickling down her neck from her ear. Streeter's head swiveled constantly to scan the parking lot. His harsh, ragged breathing was all she could hear.

He dragged her toward a small, gray sedan parked facing the exit. Would he kill her here? She felt a sudden certainty that he would. *Oh Jake, I loved you so much.* Tears welled in her eyes.

A movement on the far side of the car behind the gray sedan caught her eye. She blinked. Then a figure darted across the space and ducked down behind Streeter's car. *Jake!* She bit off her gasp.

Streeter hadn't seen. When they reached the car, he turned her in a circle, his eyes searching for any sign of pursuit. He grunted in satisfaction and loosened his grip on her waist. The gun barrel left her ear, although Molly could sense his hand still close to her head.

"Open the door. Slowly." His head was turned toward the hospital.

Obediently, Molly leaned forward. She looked through the window to the other side. Jake's hand was visible, his index finger pointing down. Molly took a deep breath and pulled on the handle. Simultaneously, she made her body go totally limp. Her dead weight slipped through Streeter's grasp. He staggered back as she pushed against his legs. The sudden movement flung his gun hand into the air. He whirled around and stopped dead.

Fear contorted his face as he gazed into the barrel of a gun three feet from his face. Jake was leaning over the roof of the car, his arms stretched forward, both hands gripping a gun. A gun aimed at Streeter's head.

"Move and you're dead." Jake repeated the lawman's words with quiet promise. "Over here, Molly."

Molly scooted around the car. She sat down and leaned against the fender. Her legs had turned to rubber.

"Are you all right?" Jake asked without taking his eyes from Streeter's hate-filled face.

"I am now, Jake."

"All right, Streeter. Drop the gun. *Now*." Jake's voice was harsh with menace.

A sly look moved across the lawman's face. "You haven't got the guts, reporter boy," he sneered. "I'm going to turn around and walk away from here. You won't shoot a man in the back."

"You're right. I won't." Jake moved his hand slightly and fired. Streeter's gun flew into the air. He screamed and grabbed his hand. Blood streamed down his wrist. He fell to his knees, sobbing and cursing. Jake dropped Brad's gun on the roof of the car and quickly circled around to the lawman. He grabbed Streeter's shirt and hauled him upright. Then his fist crashed into the killer's stomach. Streeter fell to his side, keening like an animal.

Jake held the gun on him until uniformed help arrived. When Streeter had been led away in handcuffs, Jake hauled Molly into his arms and held her so tightly she could scarcely breathe. She didn't complain.

That evening, after a celebratory meal in the most expensive restaurant in town, the two couples were wreathed in smiles as they entered Molly's apartment for after-dinner drinks. Molly hung up their wraps and entered the living room to find Brad's wife turning in a slow pirouette in the center of the room.

"I expected something more like Celia Chambers' mansion," Nora confessed. "You know—lavish, ostentatious, done up by some fabulously expensive interior decorator. But your home is lovely, Molly."

She smiled at Molly's flush of pleasure and joined her husband on the overstuffed sofa. Harvey Streeter's bullet had missed Brad, but he sported a bump on his forehead where his head had struck the metal bed. His bandages gave him the look of a battered pirate. A kind of peace had replaced the dark sadness in his eyes.

Jason McBride had wakened and was expected to live. Though still weak, he readily agreed to tell everything about the criminal activities surrounding the land expropriation deal. He had been genuinely horrified by the murders.

McBride's promise of cooperation and Streeter's witnessed attempt on the ex-banker's life, as well as his public kidnapping of Molly, broke the lawman's will. He confessed to everything—fraud, four murders and two attempted murders.

The Ottawa Chronicle carried all the details of the policeman's murderous career. Reg Colfax was a happy editor.

After Jake passed drinks all round, the four friends settled on Molly's comfortable furniture, their conversation light and relaxed. Then Brad leaned forward and looked at Molly.

"You haven't told us what made you realize Streeter was the one."

"It was something Jake said that reminded me of something you said." Molly nodded when the policeman's eyebrows rose. "You said that the average person wouldn't know how to locate a professional arsonist. It didn't hit me at the time, but later I realized that a policeman would know how to find a particular kind of criminal. It all fell into place then. David and Alex Harrison shared a cell. Streeter would know that, or could find out. He probably kept track of Alex. And of you. That's how he knew you were investigating McBride. He tried to kill you and then McBride. The killer had to have been in a position to know what you were doing. That, too, suggested he was a policeman. And Streeter was around in the past as well as in the present."

Brad shook his head. "Lord, I should have seen it long ago. Some cop I am."

Nora brushed her fingers on his cheek. "It's understandable, honey. You were too close to it all. With Streeter being Doug's friend and a fellow policeman, there was no reason to suspect him. So don't you dare put yourself down!"

Brad's brow smoothed as he gazed at his wife's stern expression. "Okay, boss." She smiled and kissed his cheek. Brad turned to Jake.

"I think it's time you told us that story you said I wouldn't believe. Start with how my father's papers came into your possession."

Molly and Jake exchanged grins.

"Okay," the reporter said. "But remember, you asked." He paused. "Marge Thomas gave them to us."

Brad and Nora stared blankly at the reporter. Then their faces fell into matching expressions of disbelief.

Molly laughed. "It's true," she insisted. She filled them in on her background, then explained how she became Molly Barnes.

"Time travel? Not likely!" Brad pointed an accusing finger at Molly. "You're pulling my leg."

"Not at all. Remember the time you picked up my glasses in town for me? Remember how Marge defended me when people thought I was trying to take advantage of Duncan?" She paused. "Let's see, what else? You and Sophie gave us a set of ironstone dishes for a wedding present. Cream-colored, with yellow dahlias. Marge gave us the matching teapot, cream and sugar."

Brad and Nora shook their heads, intrigued but not convinced. Jake took up the story, recounting his appearance in the past, two years after Molly's arrival. He explained how and why they had run away after discovering Marge's body in Molly's car."

"Brad, the first time you met me at Molly's, you invited her to a Lion's Club dance to raise money for the Stewarts. Remember? And Nora, your peach pie was a favorite with everyone who helped rebuild their home after the storm." He grinned as their mouths dropped lower and lower. "Ah, let me think. Oh yeah, you and Tory Smithson nailed the new shingles on the south-facing side of the roof. The pharmacist—I forget his name—and I did the other side. Is that enough?"

Smiling widely, Molly and Jake watched the speechless couple. Finally, Brad raised his hands in surrender.

"Either that's the tallest tale I've ever heard, or . . . or . . . or I don't know what." He looked at his wife, then back at the two grinning faces watching them.

"Time travel? You expect us to believe that?" He threw back his head and laughed. "Now really, come on," he coaxed, "you can tell us the truth. How did you learn all those details?"

"Brad." Nora spoke for the first time. "Brad, look at this." She picked up a framed photograph from the end table at her side.

It was a picture of Molly and Duncan Barnes, taken in Duncan's living room, immediately after the wedding ceremony. Duncan was leaning heavily on a twisted, Harry Lauder cane.

Brad raised his head and gaped at the gently smiling Molly. Her eyes were dreamy with memories.

"You were at our wedding, Brad. I remember you had to change shifts with someone in order to be there. Your sister Sophie took that picture. Duncan insisted on standing for the ceremony, though I wanted him to use his wheelchair. Marge made the wedding cake. Angel food, Duncan's favorite." She grinned and added, in a teasing voice, "You ate three pieces of that cake!"

Brad's stunned expression slowly changed to one of acceptance. "Time travel," he mused. "I'll be damned. Time travel."

Nora recovered from the shock of the revelation first. She turned to Molly. "What I really want to know is, is Celia Chambers coming back to *Tangled Lives*?"

Dead silence reigned for a moment, then the four burst into laughter. An hour later, Brad and Nora got up to leave. At the door, Jake placed a restraining hand on Brad's arm.

"Are you two free next Saturday afternoon?"

The couple exchanged glances. "Sure. What have you got in mind?"

"You're invited to our wedding. We'll probably have it here in Molly's—"

Molly gasped aloud. "What? What did you say?" Her heart began to thud against her ribs. "Jake Anderson—"

"Yes, my love?" Jake's expression was all innocence but his chocolate eyes danced.

"You...you...." Sputtering, Molly poked a stiff finger in his chest. "It didn't occur to you to *ask* me first?"

"Of course I thought of it, but I decided not to give you the chance to say no."

Molly gaped at the smiling, complacent face of the man she loved. He expected her to marry him? Just like that? Why the nerve of . . . . Wait a minute. *Marriage*?

She narrowed her eyes and fought back a face-lifting smile. "Are you giving me an order, Mr. Anderson?"

He crossed his arms. "Yeah, I am. So?"

Molly pretended to think it over. She sensed Jake's tightly coiled tension. His uncertainty pleased her woman's heart. Finally, she drawled "Well, so . . . all right then. *This* time. Just see that you don't make a habit of it."

Jake exhaled a shaky breath and reached for her. Molly drew a deep breath and reached for him. Their mouths fused. Neither heard Nora and Brad burst into laughter, close the door behind them and walk away.

"Stop fussing," Nora commanded. "You look absolutely beautiful."

Molly peered into the full-length mirror for the hundredth time. The pale gray silk suit matched her eyes perfectly. A deep rose cowl-neck blouse echoed Nora's simple A-line knit dress. Molly's elegant Italian leather shoes and tiny, whimsical hat continued the color theme, as did the single rose orchid delivered an hour earlier.

"I don't know," Molly murmured. "Maybe the blue dress we saw would have been better. Do you really think Jake will like this outfit?"

"I promise you he will," Nora repeated patiently. "You know darn well that man wouldn't care if you wore a potato sack to your wedding. Besides," she grinned wickedly, "I doubt you'll be wearing it for long."

Molly blushed. Jake did seem to have a magician's talent for making her clothes disappear. And she loved him for it.

She peered into the mirror again. Her hair hung in smooth waves, thick and glossy. Her eyes were brilliant with excitement. The delicate pink of her cheeks owed nothing to a beauty product.

The only jewelry she wore were the opal earrings her

grandmother had worn on her wedding day. Somehow, the continuity assured her that her mother knew and approved of the son-in-law she would gain that day. Molly smiled at her matron of honor and drew a deep breath.

"Lights, camera, action," she whispered.

"Break a leg," Nora said cheerfully, and opened the bedroom door. A handsome, smiling Brad extended his arm to Molly.

Nora slipped past them and paused at the entrance to the living room. At her appearance, the lilting strains of the Wedding March filled the apartment. The guests turned to watch, as Molly paused, framed in the doorway, her eyes blind to all but the love-filled gaze of the giant man waiting to take her hand. Smiling, she crossed the room to Jake's side.

She hadn't the slightest doubt that this marriage, this love, would last through time.

Discover a world of **fresh fiction** at Avid Press

The Lion's Shadow
by Marthe Arends

Suffragette Cassandra Whitney meets her match in the handsome, infuriating Griffin St. John as they struggle through a web of intrigue and danger.
ISBN 1-929613-05-9 $6.99 US/$8.99 Can

Since All is Passing
by Elizabeth Delisi

When Marie Kenning witnesses the kidnapping of a little girl, she embarks on a dangerous chase to save her.
ISBN 1-929613-24-5 $5.50 US/$7.50 Can

Time Lapse
by Jane Ann Tun

In an inadvertent trip twenty years into the past, Jake Anderson and Molly Malone are involved as suspects in a murder—a murder still unsolved when they return to their present time.

ISBN 1-929613-12-1 $5.99 US/$7.99 Can

Cappuccino in the Winter
by Valerie Rose

African-American Alayna Alexander will do anything to have a family—including marry a man she doesn't love. All is well until Khavon Brighton comes to help her catch a cyberthief.
ISBN 1-929613-08-3 $6.50 US/$8.50 Can

When the Lilacs Bloom
by Linda Colwell

Emily Langford must travel back in time to save the lives of star-crossed lovers Elinor and Nicholas Langford from the devious plots of Nicholas's mother.
ISBN 1-929613-09-1 $6.50 US/$8.50 Can

Dead Wrong
by Robert L. Iles

Sheriff Walker Whitlow must solve the murder of a beautiful young girl as he struggles to keep his job, his family, and his belief in himself.

ISBN 1-929613-15-6 $5.50 US/$7.50 Can

The Rhythm of Revenge
by Christine Spindler

D.I. Rick Terry sifts through a storm of suspicion when tap star Jessica Warner disappears. Devious secrets are revealed as Terry delves into the intimate lives of the dance troupe.

ISBN 1-929613-18-0 $5.99 US/$7.99 Can

Song of Innocence
by Margery Harkness Casares

From the moment she first sees Charles, Mignon San Marco knows he is her true love. Through the perils of the Napoleonic War, treachery, and other intrigues, they struggle to find their way together.

ISBN 1-929613-02-4 $6.50 US/$8.50 Can

Ask for these books at your local bookstore, or order them below

---

Mail to Avid Press, LLC 5470 Red Fox Drive Brighton MI 48114-9079, or fax to (503)210-6765

Please send me the books I have checked above.
☐ My check or money order (no CODs please) for $_____ is enclosed (please add $1.50 per order for postage and handling--Canadian residents add 7% GST). Make checks payable to Avid Press, LLC.
☐ Charge my VISA/MC
Acct#_____ExpDate_____.(please add postage and handling of $1.50 per order; Canadian residents add 7% GST).

For faster service visit our website at
http://www.avidpress.com
Name:_____ Telephone:_____
Address:_____
City, State, Zip_____ Email:_____

"Run!"

They ran. They had just crossed the back lawn and entered the woods when a shout sounded behind them. Molly looked over her shoulder and saw policemen come round the side of the house and break into a run. Desperation fueled her feet.

Branches slapped at their faces and clutched at their clothing. Jake's long legs scissored slightly ahead of her as he used the carry-all bag to push aside the largest branches. Mac's cries had ceased.

Gasping for breath, she forced her legs to keep moving. What if they couldn't . . . . No, she wouldn't think of that. They had to find the way home. A quick glance over her shoulder revealed a welcome sight. The two policeman had dropped behind. She realized they had no reason to fear their suspects would get away. The woods were small and their prey was on foot.

When they burst into the small clearing, the light was almost gone. Molly led Jake around the edge of the rock until they were facing the direction from which she had arrived two years before. The scene looked normal, ordinary. Nothing at all hinted at the presence of some weird passageway through time. She lifted her face to Jake's.

"Ready?" he whispered. Behind them the sounds of cursing and stumbling feet drew closer.

"Yes." Her grip tightened on Jake's hand.

He leaned forward and pressed a quick, hard kiss on her mouth. Then, hand in hand, they walked across the flat boulder to the other side.

"I enjoyed TIME LAPSE enormously. The plot keeps the reader in suspense until the final page. This well-crafted, innovative romance is a keeper."

--Elizabeth Symes, author of KISS ME GOODNIGHT